tell me a Story

By
ANGELO THOMAS CRAPANZANO

Copyright 2024 by Angelo Thomas Crapanzano

All rights reserved. This book or any portion thereof may not be reproduced or used in any manner whatsoever without the express written permission of the publisher except for the use of brief quotation in a book review.

ISBN 978-1-965679-47-0 (Paperback)
ISBN 978-1-965679-48-7 (Ebook)

Inquiries and Book Orders should be addressed to:

Leavitt Peak Press
17901 Pioneer Blvd Ste L #298, Artesia, California 90701
Phone #: 2092191548

Dedication

I dedicate these stories to Colton and Ashley.

Contents

Story Number One 1
Story Number Two...27
Story Number Three 62
Story Number Four..86
Story Number Five...95
Story Number Six...105
Story Number Seven 115
Story Number Eight...135
Story Number Nine 165
Story Number Ten..186
Story Number Eleven 214

Story Number One

An Unexpected Event

Andy was just coming in from a surgery that he had performed. He sat at his desk and was checking his computer. A few minutes later there was a knock on his office door.

"Come on in," said Andy. "It was Betty, Andy's surgical assistant. She had just finished cleaning the surgical room after she had assisted Andy with the surgery.

"Doc, I have to talk with you," said Betty

"Betty," said Andy. "I didn't notice that it was you. Is our patient having a problem?"

"No," said Betty. "I just have to talk with you on a personal thing."

"Do you have a personal problem?" asked Andy.

"I didn't want to tell you until after the surgery was over and the patient was in good shape," said Betty hesitating to tell Andy her problem.

"What is your problem?" asked Andy.

"Well you know that my husband is suffering from a heart attack," said Betty. "You said that from damage that was done he may never recover."

"No," said Andy, "I said that he may never completely recover because of his age. I told you that he may live to be one hundred years old."

"The point is that he is now retired and has little energy to do anything around the house."

"So," said Andy, "I don't understand what you're trying to say"

"I am trying to tell you that I am leaving the company," said Betty with a soft and sorrowful tone. "We have a small apartment in South Carolina that my family has given me. I would like to spend the rest of my life together with my loving husband."

"Oh Betty," said Andy. "I hate to see you go. You have been such a help to me. I don't know what I will do without you."

"I have already talked to the hospital manager, Vivian," said Betty. "She sent me down to the employment office and I talked with Linda. She is putting out a request for a surgery assistant."

"I wonder how long that would take?" asked Andy.

"Linda said that it should not take long because there is not a great demand for such a nurse."

"Well as I said before, I hate to see you go," said Andy, "However I wish you all the happiness in the world. God bless you."

"Thank you," said Betty, "And may God keep you healthy and happy."

"Good bye Betty," said Andy.

"Good bye Andy," said Betty and left. Andy was in an unhappy state. What was he going to do now? He had two surgeries tomorrow. He could postpone one but the other needed surgery as soon as possible. She had cancer that was spreading rapidly.

"Hi Andrew," said Vivian. "We have to talk."

"We surely do," said Andy

"I know that you must be in a sad condition right now," said Vivian, "maybe I can help."

"Please do," said Andy.

"There is a nurse who I think is very intelligent," said Vivian. "She is the best nurse we have in the hospital. You will have to guide her but she is the best we have."

"That is the best we have," said Andy. "That doesn't sound promising to me."

"Talk with her," said Vivian. "What can you lose? She will surprise you."

tell me a Story

"All right," said Andy. "I need someone that doesn't have to stop to think of her next move."

"I'll call her and sent her to you," said Vivian.

"I can hardly wait," said Andy. It was about an hour later that a young lady knocked on his door.

"Hi Doctor Borio," said the young lady. "My name is Martha Keen. Vivian said that you wanted to talk with me."

"Yes," said Andy, "come on in and have a seat."

"What is this all about?" asked Martha.

"My assistant just quit on me," started Andy. "We are looking to find a replacement. Until we hire one I need some help."

"Why have you asked for me?" asked Martha. "I have no experience in surgery assistance."

"This is only for a short time," said Andy. "I will give you a short training. I will fake a surgery and have you help. I will tell you what to do and since I had trained you ahead of time you should remember what to do and do it."

"This whole thing scares me," said Martha. "I don't want a bad reputation in the Hospital. Right now I have a good reputation as a nurse."

"I promise you," said Andy, "That no one will know of your action here unless it is very good. I don't want to look bad either. So let's keep the next few days a secret. Are you available right now?" asked Andy.

"I'm all yours," said Martha. "Where do we go from here?"

"Let's go do a fake surgery," said Andy. He then took Martha to his surgical room. He set up several pillows to look like a patient. He was surprised to see Martha take out a pad and pencil. "You are going to write down what you are to do," asked Andy being very surprised that she was that alert to start a new job.

"You said that the next surgery is tomorrow," said Martha. "I will have to go home and study all night. We will have a patient's life at stack."

"Good thinking," said Andy. He then started to explain the complete procedure. He first showed Martha what they had to connect to the patient before starting the surgery. Andy had one device

3

to hook up to the patient and Martha was expected to hook the other device at the same time before they started the surgery. He showed her the device Martha had to have ready for him when he had a certain device in his hand. He showed her what she had to do when he needed her to do it. It took over an hour before they felt that they had all that they could do. Andy showed her all the equipment she might have to use. Mike was again surprised at Martha's quick action. Martha took out her cell phone and took a picture of all the devices that were in the surgery room and wrote down the name of each devise.

"You may not have to use all of the devices or hand them to me," said Andy, "but I do have to warn you that I will not know what I need until I open the body and see what I would have to do."

"I will do my best," said Martha. "You call out what you need and I will get it for you. The actual thing I will do, as my part in the surgery, at the same time you are doing what you need to do, I have already memorized. I will be ready in the morning.

"Well that is the requirement as a surgical assistant," said Andy. "What do you think? Do you feel you can handle it?"

I think it is easier than I originally thought," said Martha. "However, it is very important that you provide the signal when you need my help."

"I could do it in my sleep," said Andy.

"There is another problem I have," said Martha. "Since I don't have a college degree for this job, isn't it illegal for me to do it?"

"Don't worry about it," said Andy. "I won't tell if you don't tell."

"Ok then," said Martha, "see you in the morning."

"Take care," said Andy as Martha left.

The next morning came too soon for Martha. She even went to bed at nine thirty so that she got enough rest to be wide awake at the hospital. She got to Andy's office at eight.

"Hi Doc," said Martha as she entered his office.

"Hi Martha," said Andy. "By the way when we are alone you can call me Andy."

"I'm sorry," said Martha. "I have too much respect for you to call you by your first name. Do you mind if I just call you Doc?"

"That is so nice," said Andy. "Call me what pleases you."

"If you are ready," said Martha "I will go and get the patient."

"Don't forget to give her the shot as soon as you get there," said Andy. "We want her asleep as soon as possible."

"I have done this one hundred times in my mind since yesterday," said Martha as she left. About three minutes later, Martha was wheeling the patient into the surgery room. Andy was not there yet. Martha went through all the surgery room making sure she knew where all the equipment was. She also located the units that were her job to hook up to the patient. After feeling save she hooked up the patient just as Andy walked in. Andy then turned on all the equipment that Martha had hooked up and a few that he was going to use. After uncovering the patient Martha handed Andy the knife he would need. After Andy cut open the woman's chest Martha held it open and inserting the equipment that would keep it open. The rest of the morning went slowly. Andy removed the tumor and cleaned the inside to make sure there as nothing left that could turn to cancer. Andy was sure he had it all and that it had not spread all over her body. When Andy was over he started to sew the flesh together. Martha was about two inched in front of Andy holding the flesh together while Andy sewed it together. Andy was surprised, sine this was not one of the jobs Martha was told to do.

"Take her now to the recovery room and watch her carefully," directed Andy. "Make sure she is recovering properly. After you see that she is doing well you can take her into the hospital room where you got her. I have other patients to see," said Andy, "But I will visit once in a while when I can."

"This is back like I was doing before you got Me." said Martha. "I will call you if there any problem."

"By the way," said Andy. "You did a great job. I hope you are ready for the next surgery this afternoon. It will be a lot easier."

"I can't wait until this is all over and I could go back to my old job," said Martha. "Have you heard of any surgical assistant that could come and take over?"

"I have checked but they have not found anyone that could fit in that position. I will see you at one this afternoon."

The day went by slowly. The patient that Martha had helped woke up and seemed very healthy. At twelve noon Martha was ready to go to lunch with her old work mates but decided that at one o'clock she would be in the surgery room. She decided she couldn't go into the surgery room with a full stomach. The surgery was so much simpler than the one she helped in the morning. Martha was glad it was over. She however did get the satisfied feeling of helping someone. When it was over she took the patient to the recovery room until she woke up. Martha then took her back to her hospital room.

"How are you feeling Jane?" asked Martha. "The surgery went well. We removed the tumor and thank God it was not cancerous."

"Thank you for helping the doctor," said Jane. "How soon can I go home?" Martha didn't get a chance to answer when she was interrupted by Jane's family that came running in.

"I will check on you later," said Martha as she left. She headed to the second floor where she had patients that she knew before she was called to help Andy. She never got there when she got a call to go to Doctor Brio's office.

"Hi boss," said Martha when she entered Andy's office. "What do you have in mind now?"

"We just got a guy in the emergence that had a heart attack. Ex-rays showed that he has a couple of blocked arteries. We have to open them or he will die. So get ready for another surgery."

"I'm ready now," said Martha." All I need is the mask and robe."

"Here he comes," said Andy when he saw the body being directed to the surgery room. Martha remembered all that she was supposed to do. The surgery went well and they soon moved him to the recovery room.Before they left Martha turned to Andy.

"Boss," said Martha trying to be funny. "Do you mind if I come back. I want to check all the surgery equipment you have here. I want to get more familiar with them. I don't know if you noticed but I hesitated when you asked for the suction device."

"I noticed," said Andy. "You come back any time you want," said Andy. "It is your surgery room as well as mine." Martha checked all the cupboards and shelves where devices are stored. When she was to leave Andy walked in.

"Did you see my watch anywhere?" asked Andy. "I seemed to have misplaced it somewhere."

"No," said Martha. "However, since you are here can you tell me why you have that cupboard on the end locked?"

"I have personal special equipment there," said Andy.

"So why do you have it locked," asked Martha.

"Can you promise that you will forget what I tell you?"

"As you know I am a Born-Again Christian," said Martha. "So I promise in God's name that I will forget what you tell me. Besides I may have to help you use them some day."

"You are right," said Andy. "You never know when things you don't expect come up. Bye the way, I am a born-Again Christian also. I am surprised to hear that you are one. There are not very many of us."

"And we are getting less and less every day," said Martha, "however are you trying to change the subject?"

"A few weeks ago I heard about some experimental devices that were being sold. One was a heart replacement device, and the other was a breathing device. If the heart of a patient stopped and the regular procedures could not restart it, the patient was declared dead. This device can replace the heart and pump all the blood through the body, until the patient can be brought back to life. The other device pumps air into the lungs and sucked out the exhale air. The hospital leaders said that it was too expensive and would only perhaps save one patient a year. I keep them locked for two reasons. First they look so much like the devices we now use that I was afraid that they would get mixed up with the other. Secondly I want to keep them from the Hospital management. I Bought them because I thought I could use them, and since they look like the normal ones that no one would know, that I was using other than the normal. I want to save a life where the body was still alive."

"I would like to be a part of you saving a life," said Martha. "I will keep an eye for a patient that is declared dead but has a warm body that is still alive. I will get it to you." While Martha was still there, Andy got a phone call. It was the Employment office.

"All right," said Andy on the phone, "send her up." Andy then turned to Martha, "that was the employment department. They are sending up an applicant for the job of Surgical Assistant. Why don't you go out and check all of my patients on the third floor and then go back to the second floor to your old job."

"I hope you get a good one," said Martha. "Let me know how you make out." Martha then left. Andy felt funny. He was going to miss her. I will call you if I don't hire her," said Andy. It was about ten minutes later when a young lady showed up at the office door. Andy was shocked when he saw her. She was so beautiful with a nice body.

"Hi," said the lady. Looking like she had seen an angel. Mike had not noticed because he was so taken by her looks but also found that the sound of her voice brought butterfly's to his stomach

"Hi," said Andy not knowing what he said. He was at a mental incoherence.

"Doctor, surgeon," said the lady with a mind as disturbed as Andy's was.

"Can I help you," said Andy getting back some of his mind.

"I am Monica," said the lady. "I'm here."

"Come on in," said Andy still not knowing what to say. "Have a seat." Monica came in and sat across from Andy. Andy had forgotten that he needed an assistant. He was completely confused by Monica's voice and appearance. Andy wondered if it was love at first sight. It couldn't be her beautiful looks because Andy sees beautiful girls on TV all the time. They don't have the same effect on him as Monica is doing. Also this girl's voice has a strange effect on him. "How are you," said Andy not knowing what else to say.

"I'm fine," said Monica.

"What are you looking for?" said Andy getting back a little of his mind.

"I am," started Monica. Because of her mental problem, she delayed her answer because she did not remember why she was there. Then she added, "I am looking for a job."

"What kind of a job are you looking for in a hospital?" asked Andy. "Are you a secretary?"

"No," answered Monica. She then stopped to think. She made a strong effort to get her mind back. She couldn't let the handsome young man distract her from what she wanted. "I want a job with Doctor, I don't remember his name, but he is a surgical doctor." Andy stopped from answering questions for a few minute. He remembered that the Employment Office said they would send a person to fill his needs. However Monica was nowhere close to what he expected to see.

"Are you a surgeon's assistant?" asked Andy trying to get that possibility out of the way.

"Yes," said Monica.

"How long," asked Andy, "have you done that job?"

"Look" said Monica getting tired of getting question from this handsome young man. "Can you direct me to the right office?" she then opened her puce and took out a small pad. "I need to see doctor Brio."

"I can't believe that you are the woman that the Employment Department sent here to fill the job." said Andy, "I'm sorry I am doctor Brio. I expected an older woman with many years' experience showing on her face."

"I am also very surprised," said Monica. "I expected an older man showing years of experience on his face. Then seeing Andy smile she smiled too.

"Please answer my question," said Andy. "Tell me of all your experience, where you worked before, and why you left."

"Sounds like reasonable questions," said Monica, "I have been a surgeon's assistance for six years; I worked for a company in Chicago, named City Central Hospital. It was a very small hospital. It caught on fire and closed. I therefore lost my job."

"Well let me take you around and show you all that you will be working with. Let's start with the Surgery Room," said Andy. At the surgery room Monica looked at all the equipment.

"My lord," said Monica. "I have never seen anything like this."

"Is there a problem?" asked Andy.

"I have never seen such a wonderful case of equipment, said Monica. They look like you bought them yesterday. They are all of the most modern type.

"Glad you like them," said Andy.

"I see you have the last cupboard locked," said Monica. "What are you hiding in there?"

"They are special equipment that I think I will need to do, what I hope to do, in the future," said Andy.

"Well open up and let me see them." said Monica.

"Do you have to see them now?" said Andy. "We have so many other things to review now."

"If I am to work here," said Monica, "I have to have knowledge of all the equipment that you will use."

"I have a long story to tell you about them," said Andy. "Do you want to hear it now?" Andy then gave her the key to the cupboard. She opened the cupboard and pulled out the two large devices.

"These look like the standard heart Monitor and the Oxygen supplier," said Monica. "Did you get them mixed up?"

"That's interesting," said Andy. "They used the heart monitor system and just improved what it did, and did the same with the Oxygen supplier. I though they look alike. I didn't consider that they were the same basic devices."

"What do they do now that was not done before?" asked Monica.

"Well the heart monitor not only monitors the heart it also replaces the heart. It pumps the blood though the whole body like the actual heard would do. The other device pumps oxygen into the lungs but also draws out the exhale."

"Wow," said Monica. "I can't wait to use this equipment. It would be such a wonderful feeling to know that you brought back some one's life."

"Well you know all that you need to know," said Andy. "Let me take you through the rest of the Hospital, mainly the third floor which is my area of operation. Andy took her through the third floor area. He took her into some of the recent patients and introduced her to them and the area nurses. About an hour later they returned to Andy's office.

"I like the job," said Monica. "Am I hired?"

"You have my approval," said Andy. He then started to think of the strange feeling he had when he was near her. He hoped that it would go away soon. It affected his stomach and mental stability. He hoped that he wasn't falling in love with her. Even during the last hour he was with her he did the best not to look at her. He kept his eyes on what he was showing her.

Monica went back to the Employment office. She went into the office and got the attention of Laura the office manager.

"I just got back from visiting Doctor Borio," said Monica. "I like the job and the doctor said that he approved of me. So what else do I have to do to get hired?"

"I will have to call doctor Borio first," said Laura. She then got the phone and called Andy.

"Doctor Borio?" asked Laura, to the person who answered the phone. "I have Monica Rowland here. She would like to be hired as your assistant. Do you want her as your assistant?"

"Yes," said Andy. "I would at least give her a try. Make sure that we can let her go if she doesn't work out. I however, feel that she has a ninety present chance of working out."

"Thank you doctor," said Laura and hung up. Then turning to Monica she directed Monica. "Read this agreement and sign it if you agree. Today is Friday. You can start Monday morning at eight O'clock."

Monday morning at eight O'clock Monica was at Andy's office front door.

"Hi Monica," said Andy. "I'm so happy that you are here. We have a surgery at one this afternoon. Why don't you go and get acquainted with my patients."

"What are their names and what room are they in?" asked Monica.

"The one that is to have surgery is Ann. She is in room 312. The name of the others is listed on the front of the bed. The other two are in rooms 313 and 314." Monica then went first to the two that didn't need surgery. She introduced herself and checked their health condition. Lastly she went to Ann's room.

"Hi Annie," said Monica. "I am the doctor's assistant. My name is Monica. I would like to check all you Vidal signs to see that you are ready for surgery. After checking her over she told her that she was ready.

"Do you think that this surgery is going to be difficult?" asked Ann.

"No," said Monica. " I guess it is normal to worry. I promise you that you will not have any problem. This is one of the most common surgeries there is. Blockage of the blood arteries is the most common human problem. I promise in God's name that tomorrow you will feel back to normal."

After spending time with the patient Monica went down to the cafeteria for lunch. She wanted a light lunch. She wasn't looking forward for the surgery. Not because of the surgery, but because the strange feeling she always had when she was near Andy. She looked up to him like he was an angel. She didn't think it was his talent but something about him that gave her butterflies in her stomach. He was extremely handsome and that added to her problem. After lunch she went to Andy's office.

"Shall I bring Annie to the surgical room?" asked Monica when she saw Andy.

"It's a little early," said Andy. "Go ahead and get her. Let's get it over with." Andy started to worry again about his feelings for Monica. He was worried that his feeling for her affected his mind. With her across from the surgical table was he able to do a good job.

Was his mind going to wonder thinking about her? Then he wondered; was he falling in love with Monica? He had never been in love so he wasn't sure of how it should feel. He approached the surgical table with high concerns. He had to try and never look up to see Monica. When he entered the surgical room he noticed that Monica had a very large mask on. He never thought of that. He could not see her face. He decided that he would think that it was Martha that was helping him.

"Doc," said Monica, "shouldn't you be wearing a mask?"

"Dear Lord," said Andy. "I am so used to it I thought that I had it on." He then found his mask and put it on. The surgery went well. Andy tried not to look at Monica. However he was surprised at how well she performed. She was in there so much that Andy felt like he had four hands. When he was through with the surgery and sewed that cut he told Monica to move the patient to the recovery room and keep her eyes on Annie." Andy then left before Monica took off her mask. When Andy left he looked back and decided that he was madly in love with Monica, he decided that he had to tell her. He decided to hold off for a while.

Andy hardly got out of the surgery room when he got a phone call.

"Hello," said Andy. "Who is this?"

"Hi doc," said Martha, "this is Martha. The Reason I called is because we just go a young man who had a heart attack. His heart is missing every other peat. I would like to send him up to you. He may die on the way up. I think you may want to take care of him."

"Thank you so much," said Andy, "Please send him up to the surgery room. I'm surprised that you have that authority. Keep looking. See you soon." Andy then called Monica "Monica," said Andy, "Please report to the surgery room."

"I'm on my way," answered Monica. Two minutes later, Monica arrived with her mask and surgery clothes on. "I'm ready, what's up?"

"We have an emergency," said Andy. "A young man had a heart attack. He is still alive but his heart is missing every other beat. Obviously he has blocked arteries."

"Did they do ex-rays?" asked Monica.

"No," said Andy. "They felt, like I do, that there is no time. When I open him up we will see. If it is another problem we will fix it." The surgery went well.

"I'll take it from here," said Monica. "I hope that is enough for today." Monica got her wish. There was not another surgery until the next week on Friday. After the surgery on Friday, Andy made a fast decision. He had realized that he was deeply in love with Monica, so before she could move the patient to the recovery room he stopped her.

"Monica," said Andy, "we have to talk."

"Is there a problem?" asked Monica.

"No," said Andy. "I just want to tell you that I am very attracted to you and I want to ask you for a date."

"Oh Andy," said Monica using his first name for the first time, "didn't you see my employment paper? You were sent a copy."

"I trusted you," said Andy so I just put it away."

"I am happily married," said Monica. "I have been married to Paul for three years now. We are very happy. I love Paul very much."

"I'm so happy for you," said Andy, far from the truth. "I am glad that you have a happy life. I am jealous of him. We will just be good friends."

"Yes," said Monica. "I would like that."

"Tell me about your husband," said Andy. "What does he do?"

"He is a corporate attorney," said Monica. "He used to travels all over the country. However the job he got in Cleveland is more local so we could spend more time together. We rented an apartment half way in between. It takes us both about thirty minutes to get home." After Andy left, Monica asked herself what it was that that gave her a problem. She loved her husband very much but she had stronger feeling for Andy then she had for her husband. But she had to get over it. First she was a Born-Again-Christian. She could never leave her husband. The Bible says that once you are married you become one flesh with your mate and what God has put together let no man put asunder. She just had to live with it. It was one of the tests by God she told herself. She then took the patient to the recovery room.

Andy felt like he had a broken heart. However, he would have to live with it. He will try not to look at her. He will continue thinking that the one helping him on a surgery was Martha. Two week went by, and they only had one surgery during that time. However they had several with server problems, but they all could and were cured with drugs. It was a month since their last surgery when Monica at eight O'clock on Monday morning stopped at Andy's office.

"Hi Andy," said Monica. "Is there anything special this morning? Before he could answer Andy's phone rang.

"Hello," said Andy. "This is Doctor Borio"

"This is Martha. I have a special patient. He arrived dead just minutes ago. He died in the ambulance on the way here. His body is still warm. He was in a very terrible auto accident. I am sending him to you. Do your magic on him."

"Will they let you do this?" asked Andy. "Are you going to get in trouble?"

"You don't tell I won't tell. My supervisors don't know that he died. Fix him so that I don't get in trouble."

"Send him to me quickly," said Andy.

"Monica," said Andy "get ready for the special surgery. This fellow has been dead for about a half hour. Let's bring him back to life." The man was quickly sent to Andy's surgery room. His heart was not beating and he was not breading. His body had begun to cool down. Andy connected the heart unit and Monica connected the oxygen unit. Andy soon opened the man's chest. Inside he found a piece of metal that had just pushed against his heart. The heart was not damaged but could not beat because the metal strip was pressing against it. Andy quickly removed the metal strip. However, his heart would not beat. It was stopped from the sudden and hard hit that it got from the accident. Andy then turned on the substitute heart. The blood started to move through the entire body. In the meantime the body had cooled down quite a bit. Andy then applied some Mupirocin Ointment to help the sore portion of the heart. He then checked the rest of the body and repaired any other part of the body that had been damaged. Soon he closed him up and Monica and Andy tried to take him to the recovery room. The recovery room was taken up by one of the other victims of the accident. They kept him in the surgery room. About an hour later they brought him to the hospital room that had been prepared for him. The heart monitor showed that the heart was not moving. His lungs were also inactive.

"Well," said Andy. "Now comes the hard part. We have to wait to see if the body will heal itself. We are giving it oxygen; got his blood to flow and soon we will have to feed it through one of the veins. Later that day Andy checked the patient. Everything was the same. The next day Andy went in to check on the patient. Monica was there

"Hi Monica," said Andy. "Is there any change in our patient?" Monica found out that his name was Mark. She found this out by finding that one of the other persons in the car was on the second floor being treated from a broken leg and arm. She had been all day asking about her husband.

"I found out that his wife is on the second floor," said Monica, "with a broken arm and leg. She is frantic to hear about her husband. No one down there will tell her anything. Her name is Adele Melsey, his name is Mark."

"We will have to tell her something," said Andy, "before she wakes up the management." However it was too late. Vivian the hospital manager came to see what was going on.

"What are you doing having a dead man," said Vivian, "hanged up with equipment we may need somewhere else."

"I notice that the body is still alive," said Andy. "The body temperature is rising. As for equipment, there is a complete other set in my surgery room."

"I will give you two more days," said Vivian, and left. The next day when Andy went in to see Mark, Monica was there.

"How is he doing?" asked Andy.

"The only thing I noticed was that his body is getting warmer. I took his body temperature and it is eighty five. His heart however shows no sign of moving."

"That is good news," said Andy. "Stay with him. If he gets worse we have to know, so that we can see if we could help him"

tell me a Story

"If you don't mind I would like to go to the second floor and talk to his wife," said Monica. "She must be wild with worrying about her husband."

"Good Idea," said Andy. "I should be the one to go, but I just don't have time now. Go ahead, but don't stay to long." Monica left immediately and was soon on the second floor. She went directly to the room listed as Adele Melsey's room.

"Hello Adele," said Monica. "My name is Monica. I am your husband's nurse."

"How is he?" yelled out Adele. "I am so worried about him."

"He is recovering on the third floor. He is still unconscious. He was stabbed by a mettle auto part. The doctor removed the part from his side and fixed up his wound. He is in the first stage of recovery."

"How soon can I see him?" asked Adele.

"He has a couple of days before we will let him wake up," said Monica. "As soon as he wakes up I will see that you two get together."

"Thank you so much," said Adele. "I will not rest until I see him."

"You better rest because you will need energy when you are with him," said Monica.

"Will you keep in touch," asked Adele, "to tell me how fast he is recovering?"

"Yes I will see you perhaps tomorrow," said Monica. "Look, I have to go and watch over Mark and other patients. Take care." Monica then left and reported back to Andy. Back on the third floor she first went in and checked on Mark. His temperature was a little higher. That was good news to Monica.

The next day Monica went directly to Mark's room. Just as she was about to check on his temperature Vivian walked in.

"You still have that dead body in here?" she asked.

"What dead body?" asked Monica now getting very upset with her "Look at his heart," instructed Monica. "It shows that he is recovering." She said that hoping that Vivian would not look and if she did she didn't know what to look for. Monica pretended to look and was completely shocked. Marks heart had starting to very slowly beat. It missed ever other beat. However it was fantastic news.

"Well let's see if it is still beating tomorrow," said Vivian and left. Monica very excited called Andy.

"What's up," said Andy upon answering his phone.

"Our strange patient Mark's heart is showing a slight movement," said Monica.

"I will be right there," said Andy. Five minutes later, Andy showed up.

"Let's see if he can handle some heart function by himself. Andy then lowered the substitute heart function by 25%. The heart was till beating slowly as before. He also noticed that his breast was slowly moving. He then lowered the oxygen device. He was still as before."

"I can't wait until you remove all the equipment," said Monica. "I will celebrate our success."

"I will lower it another 25% tomorrow and see how he can handle that."

The next day the heart was beating at almost the normal rate. Andy lowered the equipment performance down to 25%. The heart kept at the same pace. It still missed about every third beat.

"It looks very good," said Andy. "Tomorrow we will remove all the equipment and stop giving him the sleep drug shot. Let's see if we can wake him up. The next day came sooner than they expected. Monica got there first. She went up to the patient and looked at his heart rate. Just then Vivian walked by.

"Are you still playing with that dead body?" she asked.

"Are you trying to be funny," said Monica. "His heart is almost back to normal."

"Don't pay any attention to her," said Andy as he walked in. As he walked up to mark he heard a slight moaning. "Mark," said Andy to him. "Mark, how do you feel?" Mark with his eyes still closed Spock softly. "Adele, where are you?" He then opened his eyes and started to wake up. "Where am I?" Monica was so happy and excited when she heard Mark talking that she lost control and threw herself into Andy's arms hugging him.

"Oh Andy, we were successful in bring a body back to life" Andy was so taken by the feeling of her body next to him that he almost passed out from the fantastic loving feeling he got. Andy kissed her on the cheek and as she pulled away he kissed her on the corner of her mouth. Monica pulled away and hesitated from speaking, and looking at Andy with a strange look on her face. "I am going to get his wife," said Monica and left. About ten minutes later Monica showed up with Adele in a wheel chair. When Adele got up to the bed she got up enough to throw herself on Mark.

"Mark honey," said Adele. "How are you? I have been so sick worrying about you."

"I'm OK said Mark. "I was worried about you. How are you?"

"I have a broken leg and a broken arm," said Adele. "That is great. I thought I was going to have a broken heart.

"Me two," said Mark. Andy looked around for Monica. She was gone. Andy stayed long enough to see that they were both OK and he left so that they could be together. He went back to his office hoping that Monica was there. She was not. He then went checking on his other patients. It so happened that at the last patient when he walked into the room he saw that Monica was there.

"Hi Monica," said Andy, "looks like we have the same patients we worry about.

"It's your turn now," said Monica and left the room.

"That wasn't too friendly," said Andy. "I wonder what is bothering her."

"I don't know," said the patient. "She was very pleasant with me. She told me that she was praying for me. I would guess with her personality she was praying for everyone."

"I think you are right," said Andy. "I get the feeling that she has covered you real well."

"I could not ask for more," said the patient. Andy spent a few more minutes with her and then he left. He went back to his office. He didn't see Monica the rest of the day. The next day Monica showed up at Andy's office at eight in the morning.

"What are the plans for today?" asked Monica.

"Well good Morning," said Andy. "How are you today?"

"I'm fine," said Monica. "If you don't need me I have some patients I know in the second floor," said Monica very business-like. "Call me if you need me."

"Wait," said Andy. "Is there anything I did that has you angry with me?"

"No," said Monica. "I just want to keep our relationship business-like. Remember we agreed on this."

"We also agreed on us being friendly with each other," said Andy.

"I am being friendly," said Monica. "However, I have a very serious personal problem that disturbs me very much. "Let me settle that and we will see what I am like after that."

"Well we have surgery planned for two this afternoon," said Andy. "Please be there."

"I will always do my job," said Monica. "I promise." She then left for the second floor where she became her sweet caring person. That afternoon Monica was there ready to help Andy. The surgery went well. Monica did her job as well as she always did, however every word she spoke was very business-like. Andy was very unhappy. All he could think of was how thrilled he felt when Monica and he were in each other's arms. The kiss he gave her thrilled his body all the way to his toe-nails. However Andy decided to wait for her to get over whatever problem she had. He decided to go along with her as long as she did a good job. After talking to Martha, Andy was sure that they would get more dead patients to bring back to life. That week went by slowly. Andy had not seen Monica more than once a day when she reported in.

The next two week went by quickly. They had several patients but no surgeries. It was on Tuesday the third week that Andy got a call from Martha.

"Hi Andy," said Martha. "I am sending you a woman that has stopped breathing and her heart has stopped beating. It has been about a half hour since she was declared dead. I am sending her to you. See what you think. Her body is still warm."

"Send her," said Andy. Five minutes later the body arrived. He notified Monica. She was ready as she usually was. They quickly attached her to the equipment and Andy did not hesitate to open her up. Three arteries were blocked and most important was that the main artery was opened and the blood was spilling out. Andy fixed that problem first. He took some of her blood and handed it to Monica.

"I know what to do," said Monica. "I will see if the blood bank has some of this type of blood.

"I can see that almost immediately the heart stopped," said Andy, "so that it didn't pump out a lot of blood."

"I will get about a pint," said Monica.

"I think that will be more than enough," said Andy. Monica found that the blood bank had the right type of blood for the current patient. Monica brought it back to the surgery room. Andy quickly added it to the patient. After cleaning up the insides Andy closed her up. Monica was just like before a great help. When they were done Monica took the patient to the recovery room. She stayed long enough to make sure that the patient was recovering as usual for that kind of surgery. Monica left for about three hours. When she got back it looked like Andy had completely depended on Monica. Monica checked her over carefully and when satisfied that she was doing fine, she brought her to her regular hospital room to her waiting family. The next two weeks were the same. Andy only saw Monica once a day. He also found out that she took several days' vacation. It was almost a month later that Andy got a call from Martha.

"Hi Andy," said Martha. "I have a patient that needs immediate attention. She has been dead for about forty-five minutes. What do you say?"

"Bring her up immediately," said Andy.

"On my way," said Martha. Andy then called Monica. She didn't answer her phone. He then called the department she originally worked for. She had not been there. Andy then called Vivian the hospital manager.

"Hi Vivian," said Andy. "I have an emergency surgery and I need Monica, but I can't reach her. Do you know if she took a days' vacation?"

"I'm sorry," said Vivian. "I should have called you yesterday. Monica has quit her job here. She left yesterday afternoon." Andy was devastated. He never felt this bad in his whole life. He felt like sitting down and crying. He did feel some tears in his eyes. However his high sense of responsibility made him call Martha.

"Martha," said Andy hardly getting his words out. "Monica has left the company. You have to get up here immediately if you want to save this patient."

"You start hooking her up and I am on my way," said Martha." Andy was so upset that he wasn't thinking well. He opened the woman's chest and found that she had been hit on her left side from the accident and a rib had pushed her heart to one side. From that point on Andy needed help from Martha. When she noticed that Andy hesitated she would hand him the tool he needed, then she would make a remark to awake him.

"I hope that you have cleaned the insides," said Martha. "We would not like to have her get sick instead of recovering." From statement like that Andy preformed the task he was reminded of. The surgery went well. Martha then took the patient to the recovery room. She had no family waiting for her so Martha stayed with her till she came to. She wanted to make sure all went well. Fortunately she woke up and all indications were that her surgery had been completely successful. Andy left Martha to do all the tasks required from then on. Andy disappeared and Martha didn't know where. Andy went back to Vivian's office. Vivian saw Andy coming and spoke first.

"How did your surgery go?" she asked. He had been dead more than any other that you have worked on."

"All indications are that she will recover," said Andy. "The reason I came hereis because I want you to help me find Monica. She is the best assistant I have ever had. I am willing to give part of my salary to have her come back. I also want to know why she quite so suddenly. Was if something I did or said?"

"I have no idea," said Vivian. "She didn't stop to inform me of the reason she quit. She looked like she was having problems and ready to cry. The way she spoke and the look on her face gave her away. But she would not tell me. She said it was a personal thing. I felt that you had strong feeling for her. Did you break her heart?"

"No" said Andy. "She is breaking my heart."

"I do have a couple of phone numbers in her file. I will happily give them to you."

"I have to find her," said Andy. Vivian pulled out Monica's file and wrote down the phone number and the name of the person it belonged to.

"This is all that I can give you," said Vivian. "Please be careful, I don't want to lose both of you." Andy left and went back to his office. There he called the first number. It was listed for Mariana Hover. A woman answered the phone.

"Hell," said the woman.

"Hello," said Andy. "I am looking for Monica."

"I'm sorry," said Mariana. "Monica doesn't live here anymore. She lives in Cleveland Ohio."

"Thank you," said Andy and hung up. He was sure he had the Cleveland number. Monica had mentioned that her husband had a job there. Andy then called the other number. It was listed under Paul Roland.

"Hello," said a male voice.

"Good morning," said Andy. "I would like to speak with Monica.

"I'm sorry," said the man. "Monica is not home."

"This is Ben," said Andy. I am a fellow that works at University hospital. I am very curious as to why Monica left University Hospital so quickly."

"Who are you?" asked Paul. "Are you the doctor that worked with Monica?"

"No I am just a friend," said Andy. "My job is to clean up the hospital room after a patient leaves. Since I have more spare time, the nurses here asked me to find out why Monica left so abruptly."

"She had a personal problem with one of the men that work there. That is all that she would tell me."

"Thank you so much for your time," perhaps I could call her later."

"You will be wasting your time. If she doesn't find a job here in an Ohio Hospital, we are moving back home. Sorry I have to leave now. Have a good day." He then hung up. Andy spent a lot of time that day and the rest of the month trying to reach someone who knows were Monica was. He failed on all accounts. He went on the rest of the month always thinking of Monica. Andy and Martha get a few more dead patients that they saved. The weeks went by like they were days. Soon the year was over. Andy and Martha started to make a valuable reputation. By the end of the second year the newspapers and magazines listed Andy and Martha's successes. By the beginning of the third year Andy and Martha had saved twenty one lives. On August 23, Andy became a thirty year old doctor. On his birthday he walked into his office and he was met by a dozen co-workers who were throwing a surprise birthday party for Andy.

"Happy birthday," said all of them all at the same time.

"What are you guys up to," said Andy with large smile on his face. They had not seen him smile for three years now. By this time they all knew about Andy's heart break. They were hoping that this party would help a little. However, it didn't help that much. As hard as Andy had tried to forget Monica he was still madly in love with her. He just couldn't get over her. He tried to replace her with other woman but no one gave him the same feelings. After they had Andy blow out the candles, Andy walked to the end of the room, He was so happy that his friends were giving him a birthday party, however he still missed Monica. Martha walked up to Andy and gave him a cup of coffee. At that time the room was filled with loud conversations. Everyone was discussing something that happened to them when suddenly the room got filled with silence. Andy and Martha were wondering what happened. They noticed that everyone was looking at the door way. They looked at the door way.

"Dear Lord," said Andy and looked like he was going to fall. Martha held him up.

"I would never have guessed that she would come to your birthday," said Martha.

"Monica," said Andy lightly sort of in a whisper. Monica saw Andy and walked up to him.

"Andy dear," said Monica. "We have to talk."

"I don't think there is anything to talk about," said Andy starting to recover.

"I came to tell you why I left when I did," said Monica. "If you don't want to know I can leave right now. I'm sorry Andy," she said backing off her statement. "Please come and talk with me. Where can we go and be alone?" Andy was not prepared for this but he wanted to be with Monica ever if it was for a minute. He decided he would ask stupid question just to keep her there. "Let's go into the play room just behind you." They then both left the entertainment room and went into the empty room next door.

"I want to tell you why I left the way I did," started Monica. "I am a Born-again Christian and I love Paul very much. However I was so in love with you that I felt I was walking against the Lord and I was kind of cheating on Paul. At first I thought I could live with it and just ignore it. However, after we hugged and you kissed me, all my heart felt like I was cheating on Paul and the Lord. After that I knew that I couldn't handle it. I felt if I got lost that in time I would think it was a bad dream. That was not true. I still loved you with all my heart. However, I promised myself and Paul that I would be a loving wife to Paul until death do we part."

"Well that doesn't explain what you are doing here," said Andy.

"Didn't you hear my last sentence, until Death Do We Part? Paul was killed in an auto accident two years ago. It took me two years to get over Paul. I thought my mind was cheating on him. My pastor convinced me that it was all God's plan and not my fault. God was testing me, and according to the Pastor I'm now free to continue my life as I dreamed it could be. So I am free, does that interest you? Have you gotten over me?"

"Are you kidding me," said Andy. "I am ten times more in love with you than you are with me," said Andy. "I thought and was willing to go through life secretly being in love with you. Apparently you could not."

"That is right" said Monica, "so what are you going to do about it?"

"Is it legal to get engaged without a ring?" asked Andy.

"It is with me," said Monica.

"Then Monica Rowland, will you marry me?"

"Yes," said Monica, "a million times yes.

"Tomorrow I will get you a ring," said Andy. "Let us not tell the people in the other room until I get you a ring."

"Whatever you say boss," said Monica with a loving smile on her face.

"Let's go in and enjoy my birthday party," said Andy. "I see they have some dance music. Let's dance. I want my arms around you." They went in danced the next three songs. Then they walked to the end of the room to rest. Martha walked up to them

"Well it is so nice to see that you to made up," said Martha. "I guess you two will soon get married."

"As soon as I get a wedding ring," said Andy.

"So Monica, are you going to take the assistant job back?" asked Martha.

"No way," said Monica, "the job is all yours. I am going to be a stay at home wife. I am going to spend the rest of my life taking care of my husband and our home. I will keep the house clean and homey. I will cook a very special dinner for Andy every night. But mostly I will be a stay at home mother raising my children.

What do you say Andy?"

"I agree one hundred percent with all of my heart."

The End

Story Number Two

Nine Months in Sicily.

Important Information:
From the time that Andy, his mother and sister reached Naples, and the full nine months, the language that was spoken was Sicilian. No English was spoken. However to let the reader know what was going on the language was translated into English.

Andy spent all morning packing his suitcase with the clothes he wanted to have in Sicily. Andy with his mother and sister were going to move to Sicily. Andy's father was going to stay behind to sell the house they had and make sure his kids got along in Sicily. Andy was twelve years old. He was born two months after his mother and father landed in the USA. Andy had a hard time in the USA. He went to kindergarten not knowing how to speak English. He slowly learned but not at the level of the other children his age. All the children his age looked down on him. He was a foreigner to them. After world war One, Joseph, Andy's father came to the USA to be with his sister who was with her husband Uncle Joe. Uncle Joe came to America before World War One started. Uncle Joe foresaw the possibility of world war and so came to America. He barely escaped being drafted. Andy's father however didn't make it. He got drafted and spent the war as an Italian solder. He finally came to America after the war was over. He went back to Sicily got married and came back to America where he got a job. Unfortunately the company he worked for closed and Joseph decided to return to Sicily and go back to being the farmer he was as a teenager. He made arrangements for his family to go to Sicily. Fortunately he had inherited a large farm and a beautiful house where the family could live.

When Andy finished packing he realized he had two days to say goodbye to Pat who he felt was his girlfriend. She lived next door. Both families where deep Christians and trusted their children to always do right. They agreed that during the summer after school let out for the summer, they could go to the movie together, which was only down the street from them. Andy remembered the last time they went to the movies. The movie they went to see was canceled and a new romantic movie was shown instead. During the movie the main characters kissed very often. Pat reacted to that.

"What are they getting from touching their lips like that?" she had asked.

"I don't know," Andy remembered that he had responded. "I think that it is some kind of friendly jester. "Why don't we try it and see what it does." Andy remembered doing it several times to find out why the actors where doing it. Andy remembered that in reality he had enjoyed it hearty. Andy then went out to find Pat. He found her in her father's car. He got in next to her.

"Hi Patty," said Andy. "What are you doing sitting here by yourself?"

"I just wanted to have a little time to rest." said Patty. "I hear that you are moving to Sicily. I guess after Sunday I will not see you again."

"I will move there until I'm old enough to come back. I'm an American citizen. I was born here. I will come back as soon as I can. I want to come back to be with you.

"Why me?" said Patty. "I'm not in your family."

"Don't you know that I care very much for you? In my heart you are my girlfriend."

"Don't be silly," said Patty. "We are just friends. We are neighbors, noting more."

"Are you saying that you are not in love with me?" asked Andy. "I admit that I am in love with you and I promise that as soon as I can I will come back to you."

"We are only friends and always will be," said Patty.

"Are you saying this because you believe that I will never come back," said Andy.

"It doesn't matter to me if you come back or not," said Patty with stern look on her face.

"Well," said Andy with anger in his voice. I guess then this is goodbye." That said he left the car and went home. He didn't feel the broken heart until that evening when the anger subsided.

Monday came quickly. Early in the morning they said goodbye to Joseph and took the train to New York. In New York they got two rooms for the night. The ship to Italy didn't leave until Wednesday morning; however they were allowed to enter the ship Tuesday morning. They entered the ship early on Tuesday. They got settle for the long trip. The trip took eight days. Andy enjoyed most of the trip. He sent most of the time on deck and the game room. It was seven days later when they got to the rough waters of the Strait Of Gibraltar that Andy got sick from the swaying of the ship. He ran out on the deck and leaning over the railing he threw up his lunch. The rest of the day until the ship got through the Strait Andy laid in his bed. Andy's mother was slightly affected so she stayed in her room. Andy's sister was not affected at all. Finally they go to Naples. As they walked through town to get the small ship to Palermo, Andy yelled out

"Mom," said Andy. "Look at that man. He is peeing on the outside of the building.

"That is the way it is here in Italy," said his mother. "The little board on the side keeps you from seeing the actual urination."

"I hope it isn't this way were we are going," said Andy.

"I'm sure they have bathrooms in Barrafranca," said his mother.

"I surly hope it is so," said Andy. "If they don't I will walk back to America." From there they got a small ship that took them to Palermo Sicily. There they were met by Uncle Sal.

"Hello," said Sal grabbing and hugging Andy's mother. "It is so nice to see you in person instead of pictures. Welcome to Sicily."

"Hello Sal," said Marianna, Andy's mother. "It is so nice to see you." She then pointed to Andy. "This is my son Andy, I don't know if you have seen pictures of him."

"Hello Andy," said Sal. "It is so good to meet you."

"And this is my little daughter Stella," said Andy's mother. "She is my baby girl."

"Hi Stella," said Sal. Stella hugged her mother's legs.

"She is a little bashful," said her mother. "Give her some time and she will be friendly."

"Come on and get into my car," said Sal, "It is a long drive." It was four hours later when they got the house that Joseph owned in Barrafranca. There were several people there to greet them.

"Hi everyone," said Marianna as she got out of the car. Three of the women hugged her one at a time.

"It is so good to see you," said one of the women. Then turning to Andy, "Andy," said one of the women. "I am your mother's mother. I am your grandma Rosina.

"Hi grandma," said Andy.

"And I am you mother's father," said the man standing beside his grandma. I am your grandfather Arfansio. Everyone calls me Fred."

"Hi grandpa," said Andy.

"And Andy," said his mother, "this is my sister your Aunt Trina.'"

"Hello Aunt Trina," said Andy.

"And this is my sister," said Andy's grandfather "She is your aunt Stellina.

"Hello Aunt Stellina.

"Please call me Aunt Stella," said Stellina. "This young lady next to me is my daughter Catherina. She is about your age."

"Hi Kathie," said Andy. "Aren't there any boys in your families,' asked Andy being very surprised.

"They are all at work," said grandma. "This is spring which is planting season. They are all out on the farm planting this year's crops. Unfortunately it can't be put off."

"For a couple of months you have me and your grandfather and perhaps Cathy will keep you busy. We can play cards or Cathy can show you around town."

"It will only be a couple of months and my brother will be available. He is already very excited to meet you. He doesn't have very many friends his age to play with. Until then you and I can play together."

"I'm sure it is all going to be very exciting," said Andy. He felt that Cathy looked like she will be a lot of fun to be with.

"We will be good friends," said Cathy. "I will see that you don't get board until the boys' become available."

"Grandma," said Andy. "Can I go up and see the house. This is our house that we are standing outside of isn't it?"

"Yes," said grandma. "The front door is open. You go ahead. We will follow you in a little while." Andy quickly ran to the front door. He went in and he found that there was a little step and a door on both sides of the small hall on top of the steps. Andy decided he would try the right hand door first. As he walked in he noticed that it was a great kitchen. At one end of the kitchen was a door. He went to the door and found that it went into a large porch that had on celling. He noticed that at the other end of the kitchen was a door way that led like a living room. Andy then went to the other end of the kitchen which it led to a staircase. Andy went down the stairs to what looked like a family room and the other was like a plain room, almost like another family room. There he found a little hall way that led to a stair case. He went up the stair case and it ended up in what looked like a little hallway which had doorways to four bedrooms. At the other end of the hallway was another set of stairs. Andy went up the stairs and was surprised at where he was. It was a completely open area. Except for the area where the stairs were, the area was completely open to the outside. There were no windows. The open area's had a little railing to keep anyone from falling off the roof. There were four columns on each of the other three sides which held a roof about ten feet above the open area. In the center of the area were four columns that held the roof in the center. Andy went and looked out the open area on his right. He looked down and viewed a beautiful farm land. On the next mountain he saw a city right on top of the mountain. Later on he found out that the city was Mazzarino. That was on the east side of the building. Andy next walked over to the next opening which faced the north. Andy noticed some smoke in the sky. A closer look he saw a volcano with smoke coming out of the top. Later he found out that it was the Mount Etna volcano. Next he went to the opening on the left. He leaned on the railing and looked down. It was the front of the house.

"Hi Mom and everyone," yelled Andy to the people on the ground below. "This is such a beautiful view. I can't believe we are going to live here. See you downstairs." That said he found the stairs that took him down to the kitchen. It was about noon so he felt they would soon come to the kitchen. To wait for them Andy went out to the outside porch that was like a build in patio. It was only about ten minutes later that his grandparents and his mother came to the kitchen. He was surprised that his Sister Stella was with them. It was time for her afternoon nap. Grandma made a quick and tasty lunch and after lunch they all decided to get some rest. Andy's mom showed Andy which bedroom was his. Andy already knew because he saw his suitcase in the room when he was investigation all the rooms.

"I think you are as tired as I am," said Andy's mother. "It has been a long day."

"I will try to take a small nap," said Andy. "He didn't feel that tired. He went to bed and fell asleep as soon as he covered himself with the blanket. Andy woke up and found that he had to go to the bathroom. He had not seen a bath room during his investigation. He thought that he had only been asleep for a few minutes, He looked at his watch. He was shocked it was six PM. He heard noise downstairs; it must be grandma cooking dinner. He quickly went down to the kitchen. There he found his mother,

"Mom, I have to go to the bathroom, but I didn't see one when I was checking the house. "What do I do?"

"Follow me," said his mother. She took him to the family room. "See this door. That is the door to the bathroom. You have one upstairs off the bedroom hall. There you will find a small tub for your bath; you will also find a toilet. After you use it you have to flush it with the long hose that you take your shower with. You turn it on and flush the toilet. Andy quickly went inside and closed the door. When Andy was finished he went out to the kitchen

"I can't believe it but I am very hungry," said Andy. "However I feel like I just ate.

"You have been asleep for about five hours," said his mother. "I decided to let you sleep. Yesterday and actually the last week have been very hard days. You needed the rest." After dinner they sat down in the Family room. Grandma and Grandpa wanted to know about the lives of Andy's mother and about his life. Andy's mom took up most of the evening. She explained what life was like in America. She explained the job that her husband had. It was about nine thirty when they turned to Andy. Andy had almost fallen asleep listening to his mother's answers to stupid questions. They also asked Andy what he thought were dumb questions. He realized that they had no idea what life was like in an area that didn't have farming as the main thing in a person's life. At a quarter to ten Andy asked to be excused and went to bed.

The next morning Andy got up about eight o'clock. He went to the bathroom got dressed and went down to the kitchen.

"Good morning sleepy head," said his grandma. "I'll have breakfast ready in about ten minutes. Sit down, Grandpa already ate and went out to do his duty. Your mother already ate and is in the family room reading a paper she found in the entrance way."

"Good morning grandma," said Andy. "I didn't have much to do, so I just lay in bed for a while."

"I have here two scrambled eggs," said Grandma. "I don't know if you have this in America."

"We had scrambled eggs about twice a week," said Andy. He then sat down and had a nice breakfast. After he finished he got up to go to his bedroom and get a book he had brought from America to keep himself busy in case things go boring. He was hardly out of the room when the doorbell rang.

"Will you see who that is?" asked Grandma.

"Yes," said Andy. "I will get it" When he opened the front door he was surprised.

"Hi Andy," said Cathy.

"Hi Cathy," said Andy, "What are you doing so early in the day?"

"It is early to you but not to us working people," said Cathy.

"Come on in," said Andy. "I'm glad to see you."

"I usually spent most of the day in summer helping my mother," said Cathy. "This morning I have most of the morning free. I had a list of places to take you. I was going to start by taking you down town. However, I changed my mind. I think we should find a nice place to sit and get to know each other first."

"Sounds good to me," said Andy. Let's go the upstairs porch. It should be shady this morning since the sun is coming up from the other direction. There we have a couch and a couple of chairs. The weather is fine right now so being outside is the best place to be."

"That is great," said Cathy, "Lead the way." Andy took her to the porch that was just outside of the family room. There thy both sat on the couch. It was shady and the temperature was just comfortable.

"Now," started Cathy. "I know that farming is not the main job in America.

"No," said Andy. "I don't even know where there is a farm near where we lived. I'm sure that there is one somewhere in the country."

"What was the thing you were planning to do for a life time," asked Cathy?"

"I am only twelve," said Andy. "I didn't have my mind make up. However there were several things I was considering."

"Just name each one," said Cathy, "and tell me what motivated you to consider that as a possible job?"

"Well the first is the engineering. I was walking down our street to the corner where I buy stuff for my mother and I heard a radio playing some music. I was in wonderment. How did they get music and voices through the air without a wire? Most communication devices like the telephones were connected by wire. I thought I would be an engineering to find out how it was done."

"That sounds logical," said Cathy. "In America, I think, it wouldn't be too hard. So what was your next thought?"

"Next I thought I would be an Artist," said Andy. "I always liked to draw on paper. I loved to go to the museum and see the painting on the wall. I final was given equipment to paint a picture on canvas. I noticed that most pictures of Noah, shows Noah's family getting into Noah's ark, I painted a picture of Noah's family getting out of the ark after the flood waters receded."

"That was intelligent thinking," said Cathy. "Where is the painting now?"

"I gave it to my Aunt Nicolina and Uncle Joe. They have it hanging in their Living room."

"I would love to see it," said Cathy. "Do you have a picture of it?"

"I think I may," said Andy. "I have to look in my suitcase."

"So now," said Cathy, "What is your third consideration for a life time job?" asked Cathy.

"My third consideration is being a carpenter," said Andy. "I enjoyed working with a family friend who had a carpenters shop. I helped him one summer after school let out. I helped him make a casket for a little girl who unexpectedly died.

I learned how to use all the carpenters' tools. I enjoyed looking at the results."

"Is there anything else that you considered a possibility?" asked Cathy.

"Yes," said Andy. "It is the one I love the most. I would like to become an author. When asked to write a short paper on a subject picked from a list the teacher provided, I always ended up with an "A" grade. I have a gift of writing. However, either as an Author or as an Artist, I would need a second job until I was accepted as an Artist or Author. If I have to stay here in Barrafranca, I would want to be a repair man or a sales man at one of your city stores. I will never be a farmer."

"Thank you so much," said Cathy. "I have learned so much about you. Of course I will learn more as we spent time together."

"Well that was about me," said Andy. "Now let's hear about you. What are your thought about your future?"

"I have not given it much thought," said Cathy. "I just assume that I will marry a farmer and raise a couple of children. To be anything else I would have to leave Sicily and go to school in Italy or another nation."

"Well Cathy," said Andy. "I have already learned a lot about you. I can tell by your questions and statement you made about my thoughts of the future. You are way above the standard intelligence. You are out of place here in Sicily. So, consider if you decide not to live as a farmer's wife, what would you like to be?"

"Why thank you very much," said Cathy. "I never considered myself above anyone else in this city. I have to think about what you asked."

"Come on now, Cathy. I would guess that you have done very well in school. I bet you got a lot of high grads."

"I got very high grads," said Cathy, "but I worked very hard to get them."

"What would you like to be," said Andy.

"Well let me think about it for a moment," said Cathy. "Anyway, talking about above average intelligence, I never met anyone that is more intelligent then you, even much older boys. However, trying to answer your question I am thinking of who I heard about that I admire. That will give me an Idea of what I would like to be. My first thought is a teacher. I think teaching children is a very important job for the future of this country. My second thought would be a nurse or even better a doctor."

"What if you wanted to stay near your family here you could find some kind of a job here in Barrafranca," said Andy. "I don't believe you would be happy just as a farmer's wife."

"You have given me so much to think about," said Cathy. "Now let's talk about what we are going to do until the boys finish their spring planting."

"I have a couple of things I brought with me to keep me busy. I could share them with you."

"What do you have?" asked Cathy.

"Well I brought two books," said Andy. "They are novels. I also brought a kit. I don't remember what it is. We will see later."

"Listen Andy," said Cathy. "It is getting close to noon. I have to go home to help my mother. She has a job she says she needs help in doing." As they left the porch they came down through the kitchen.

"Hi you guys," said grandma. "I was just coming up to get you."

"I am going home grandma," said Cathy, My mother needs me."

"You can go home after you have eaten lunch here with us," said Grandma." I cooked for three. If you don't want to eat with us then you can take your lunch home."

"All right grandma," said Cathy knowing that grandma was kidding her. She sat down and had lunch with them. It was a great lunch. Grandma made scrambled eggs. Andy's mother came down and ate with them. During the meal they had some small talk. Grandma asked Cathy about the health of her parents. After they all finished Cathy said goodbye and left. Andy went upstairs to his bed room and took out one of the books he brought with him. He read it and sometime in the afternoon while reading he took his afternoon nap. When he finished the first two chapters he felt tired of reading so he went downstairs to spend time with his grandmother. Andy sat and talked with his grandmother while she cooked dinner. She wanted to know a little about America. Andy told her what he felt she would understand. Soon Grandpa came home. After saying hello to each other they sat down for dinner. Andy's mother joyed them. Grandpa told them what he had accomplished that day. After they finished eating the doorbell rang. Grandpa got up and answered the door. A few minutes later grandpa showed up with a young man.

"Andy," said grandpa, "this is your mother's brother Salvatore. He is your uncle."

"Hi Uncle Salvatore," said Andy. "It is so nice to meet you. My mother has talked so much about you."

"Please call me Toto, like everyone does. I also don't want to hear the title uncle. I am about your age."

"Whatever you say Toto," said Andy. "You are still my mother's brother which holds a special place in my heart." Before they could say more the doorbell rang again. Several family members showed up. Andy suddenly realized that this was the picture of the next few months or more. He would see Cathy in the morning, and sometimes in the afternoon. After dinner there would be many visitors. Andy also noticed that most of the visitors were older people. Toto was the only male person his age that would show up in the evening. The younger men were too tired from the day's work and they were not interests in visitors from another country anyway. That was their parent's thing. The next morning Cathy showed up after breakfast.

"What do you have in mind for today?" asked Cathy.

"I would like to relax this morning," said Andy. "Then if you are available I would like to build my airship and we can fly it this afternoon."

"I am available," said Cathy, "and sounds like fun. But what do you want to do this morning?"

"Would you like to play cards this morning?" asked Andy.

"Can we play Uno?" asked Cathy.

"I love Uno," said Andy. Andy then got his cards. When Cathy saw the cards she looked confused.

"These cards are different from the card I am used to. I think that the pictures inside are all different. I have to study them if I am to play with them."

"I will help you," said Andy. "I'm sure that they are the same accept the pictures they use." Then Andy took each section and they discussed what of the Italian card it would represent. They played the game and even when Andy explained what she didn't understand she played feeling unsure. Strange as it may seem, she won half of the games they played. At about noon they put away the cards and went down and had lunch. After lunch Andy took out his aircraft package and began to glue the parts together. It took about an hour before the plane was complete. Cathy thought it looked like the real airplane.

"Let's go to the upstairs porch," said Andy. "We can fly it from there. We will have a better view from here."

"Where you go I go," said Cathy. When they got up there Andy started the aircraft engine and let it fly out toward the olive orchard. He then using his controller and brought it back so it flew by Cathy, just under her jaw. She looked delighted. Andy then flew the ship in circles out over the road down below. Andy made the ship make several flipping moves. They watched the ship fly for over an hour with many interesting moves. Suddenly the ship, heading back toward them, suddenly stopped running and nosed dived into the side of the building. Andy and Cathy quickly headed down stairs. They found the ship on the road. It had a broken propeller and a broken wing.

"I can glue the parts back where they belong," said Andy, "but I think that the aircraft battery went bad."

"Do you have a backup battery?" asked Cathy.

"I don't think so," said Andy. "I never thought of it. Can we buy one here in the city?"

"Well," said Cathy, "I was about to make a suggestion. It is only around two o'clock. Let me take you on a tour through the city. There perhaps we could find a store that carried batteries."

"Sounds like a good suggestion. Let me remove the battery so I can show it to a sales man." It only took about a minute to remove the battery and place the ship inside. They then were on the road to downtown Barrafranca. The road which Andy's house was built on was a main road that was on the edge of the city. On the western side was the farmland and on the east side was the city. The city was built on the top of a mountain for protection purpose. All the farm land was away from the city.

"Look on the Westside of the road," said Cathy. "What you see down there is the apple orchard. On the east side will be the city. Right now there is not much to see since we are still on the outside of the city. Soon you will see side roads with houses."

"How far do we have to go to see the city's down town streets?" asked Andy.

"We have plenty of time to get there," said Cathy. "For now enjoy what you will soon see."

"What am I going to see?" said Andy.

"You are going to see the residential neighborhood," said Cathy. "Look there on your right. See that road leading away from the highway. The buildings you see are homes to some of the people."

"I see that they are higher than the road we are walking on," said Andy.

"If you look carefully you will see a small road up there that is parallel to this road," said Cathy. "They don't want the local people on the main highway." After walking a mile or so Cathy stopped. "See that road just ahead," said Cathy. Look down the street and see the third house. It is where your Aunt Stellina lives."

"It looks like one large building," said Andy. "Does Aunt Stellina live in an apartment?"

"No," said Cathy, "These are all private homes built next to each other. They save a lot of money when they built their house sharing the side walls and the rear wall with their neighbors. The richer people build on the end where they have to pay for the complete wall on one side. All the houses are separated with a garage where most of the people keep their horses. If you were a late builder and the street was not completed you build your house using your neighbor's wall and you pay him half of the cost your neighbor paid for the wall."

"Sounds like a smart idea," said Andy. "I hope they all get along with each other."

"What I started to say is that the third house, which is past the third garage door, is you Aunt Stella's home. She has an older son who takes care of her. She can't walk." They walked down the road until they go to the next side street.

"Who do you know that lives on this street?" asked Andy.

"I know the complete family," said Cathy. "That is my house. I promised my mother that I would bring you there when we were nearby. After we see the main streets down town I would like to bring you there."

"I would love to do that," said Andy. "I would love to see the inside of one of those homes."

"After that, if there is enough time," said Cathy, "we will stop at your aunt Stellina house. She has begged us to bring you there."

"Well if we don't have time today we can go tomorrow," said Andy. It was a few minutes later that they got to the end of the road.

"That large building in front of you is the school building," said Cathy. "That is where you will be going this fall." On the right

Andy could see a street full of stores like there was in his home town in America.

"Wow," said Andy. "I feel like I'm home in America." However, he soon found out that there were only about five stored on each side of the street. They walked down the street looking seriously in each Store. As they walked down the street the first thing they ran into was a restaurant. Next was a hardware store. They went in and asked if they had batteries. Andy showed the sales man the battery he had.

"I'm sorry," said the sales man. "We have batteries but not that kind. All the batteries we have are the round kind. I'm so sorry."

"Do you know where we could find a battery like this?" asked Andy.

"I'm sorry I don't know of any place," said the salesman. The next store was the Drug Store. Gino went in and asked them. He was told that they didn't carry batteries. The next store was A General store. It had a little of everything except batteries. The last store on that side of the street was a grocery Store. They didn't have batteries either. They crossed the street and went to the first store on that side. It was an office building. It had an Attorney's office and a real estate office. The next building was a Police Station. They were sure that there would not be a store that carried batters on that side of the street. However Andy wanted to see them all. The next building was a clothing shop. The next building was a Furniture store and the last building was a doctor's office.

"Well that is it," said Cathy. "You may have to go to a big city like Palermo or Syracuse. When the boys are free they will like to take you to famous places. You may get the battery there."

"Where do we go next?" asked Andy.

"Let's go to my house," said Cathy. "My mother will like to see you. She said that she would be home this afternoon.

"Good," said Andy. "I would like to see her too." Cathy led Andy down the inner road to the side road where she lived.

"Hi Aunt Trina," said Andy as they walked into the house. "How are you today?"

"Hi you guys," said Trina, "So glad that you have showed up. I need to talk with you."

"What's on your mind Aunty?" asked Andy.

"Cathy and I discussed you situation," said Aunt Trina. "We realized that you suddenly showed up in a strange land among strange people. You must have felt out of place. So I suggested to Cathy that you, being her first cousin, should get to know someone well so that you feel like you are in an accepted area."

"Well Cathy sure has done that," said Andy. "She taken me to the down town area and we have discussed our past and future lives. We know each other well."

"The reason that I brought it up is that I need her very badly," said Trina. "I don't run a farm as I'm sure you know, but I run a fruit Orchard. The Peaches are almost ready to pick. The wild animals are already starting to show up. The other fruit trees will not be ready until later in the summer. Right now I only have my son Nicole to help me. I need Cathy very much"

"We have already discussed this," said Andy. "We are waiting until the farmer boys are available. The problem is that I not only don't have anyone I know that I could spend time with, but that I am also in a house and land where I don't know what to do. I am bored just thinking of it. If it wasn't for Cathy I would have been bored to death. However, I understand your problem. I would be very thankful if I could see Cathy at least an hour once a week. It would give me something to look forward to. When the boys are available I'm sure they are all looking forward to spending time with me. Then I will be the one that will be unavailable." Trina smiled and they went into small talk for about another hour.

"I think that we better go now," said Cathy. "We have only one other place to visit this afternoon and one tomorrow and then I will have done all that I could do for Andy."

"I didn't know that you had a brother," said Andy.

"I'm sorry," said Cathy. "The subject just didn't come up." They then said goodbye and Cathy took Andy to another house in the next side road. It was the house of Nicolina. She was the wife of Andy's father's father who passed away several years ago and left his wife alone. Nicolina got a stroke and was left unable to walk and take care of herself. Fortunately she had a son Thomas that took care of their farm and his mother.

"Hi Aunt Nicolina," said Andy when the door was opened. "I came to say hello. I know that you can't travel."

"Hello," said the woman sitting in a wheel chair. She had trouble getting out of the way once she opened the door. "You must be Andy. I was hoping to see Marianna, your mother. Will she come to see me?"

"I'm sure she will," said Andy. "Cathy and I happen to be in the neighborhood so we came first."

"Hi Aunty," said Cathy. "I am just showing Andy around the city. How are you?"

"Hi Cathy," said Nicolina. "You guys please call me Aunt Nicky. As for how am I, I guess I should thank the lord for my life. The doctor thought I was going to die the day after my stroke. God kept me here to be company to my son."

"Thank God," said Andy, "and God bless you."

"Thank you Andy," said Auntie Nicky. "You are very kind. Before they could say another word a young man came into the house.

"Hello," said the young man in a very jolly voice. "You must be Andy."

"And you must be Tomas," said Andy.

"So good to see you," said Tommy. "Please call me Tommy. Hello Cathy," said Tommy then turning to Cathy. "It is so nice of you to take care of our cousin."

"I know what he must have felt in a new area not knowing anyone," said Cathy. "He now knows me."

"Well if you are willing I want to spend time with and get to know you Andy," said Tommy. "When are you available?"

"I'm available all the time," said Andy, being impressed with the Jolly mood that Tommy had. "When will you be available? I know of the work you have to do."

"How about this Monday, where would you like to go?" said Tommy, "What would you like to see that you have not seen yet?"

"I understand that my father has a farm here in this area," said Andy. "I have not seen any farm let alone the one that I will probably be working on helping my father."

"Then be ready Monday morning," said Tommy. "I will be your Gide until you feel at home."

"I understand that the farm is pretty far away," said Andy. "How are we going to get there? Do you have a car?"

"No," said Tommy. "We will go on horseback. You do ride a horse don't you?"

"I rode one a couple of years ago," said Andy. "I don't know if grandpa will let me use one of his horses. I will ask him and if his answer is yes just come over I will be ready. If it is no I'll let you know."

"Great," said Tommy. "See you Monday."

"We had better leave," said Cathy. "I have to go help my mother."

"It is so nice seeing you both," said Aunt Nicolina. "Whenever you get some time please come again." They said goodbye left.

"I was going to take you to see your uncle Toto," said Cathy. "But it is getting late so let's go home. Your grandma will have dinner ready soon." When they got outside Cathy turned to Andy.

"Just to make things clear, I would like to discuss our relationship," said Cathy. "We are cousins. I have a great respect for you. I even have developed a love for you, but it is a brotherly kind of love. It is not a romantic kind of love."

"I know what you mean," said Andy. "I love you too like my big sister."

"Why like a big sister?" asked Cathy.

"Well Stella is my baby sister and you are like my older sister," said Andy. They both had a little laugh.

"I'm glad we understand each other," said Cathy. "I think that we should meet at least once a week. You may not have time when the boys get time off. You could see how Tommy acted."

"Yes," said Andy "Is he always so jolly and happy?"

"If you are free next week I'll take you to see your uncle Toto," said Cathy. They soon got to Andy's house and Cathy said goodbye and left for her home. Cathy was right Granma was cooking dinner.

Andy's mother got home just minutes after Andy She had been visiting someone.

The next couple of days went by smoothly. Soon it was Sunday. Andy's mother had informed her parents that they were no longer Catholic. She asked them to ask around to see if there was a protestant church in the city somewhere. So far they had not heard of one. That Sunday they went to the local Catholic Church. That action was better than no Church they thought. However when they walked down the local Catholic church they changed their minds. As they walked down the church isle they noticed that at the head of the center stage was a statue of the Virgin Mary. A statue of St Joseph was on the right wall and a statue of Jesus was hanging on the left wall. They then realized that the church worship the Virgin Mary more than Jesus. After church, talking to Grandpa, Andy learned that they had only two holidays a year worshiping Jesus, but they had four that worship Virgin Mary. Three of them they carried the statue of Mary down the main street. That was the last time Andy and his mother went to the Catholic Church.

Monday morning Andy's grandfather put a saddle on the meekest one of his horses and got everything ready for Andy to go with Tommy. Tommy showed up at nine.

"Good morning everyone," said Tommy as he showed up just outside where Andy was waiting with his grandfather.

"Good morning," said Andy. "I thought you were coming at eight."

"I know," said Tom. "I thought it over. At nine all the road will be clear. To many farm workers will be on the road from six to eight. Let's go we have all day. They said goodbye to grandpa and left. On the road Andy enjoyed the horseback ride.

"You know," said Andy. "It has been a couple of years since I rode a horse. Near, where I lived in America, there was a person who owned a large wooded area. He decided instead of pulling out the trees and making the land a farm land he would create a horse riding company. He charges a small fee and the person then rode a horse through the small forest. He has a path made that took you around the complete wooded area. It was a lot of fun."

"Well we will travel in a lot of different areas," said Tom. "I'll take you all over the country area here in Sicily."

"I am enjoying just a ride around here. Let's first go see my father's farm land." After going down the road on the outside of the city they turn left down a small road off of the main road and headed south.

"Enjoy looking at all the different farms. There are many different things they are growing. Just a head is a fruit orchard." After they rode for a while they came to a section of the road that had a large stone wall on the right side of the road.

"What is that wall doing out here?" asked Andy.

"If you look closely you can see that it is hiding a fruit orchid that I told you about. Look, you can see some branches that have peaches on them."

"That makes me hungry," said Andy. "There is nothing that tastes better than a fresh picked fruit."

"If you want one lets pick a couple. You are making me hungry also."

"How can you pick one?" asked Andy "Do you have a ladder nearby?"

"No," said Tom. "I can stand on the horse and pick a couple. When he got to the side of the wall just under the branches with the fruit, he got up, to Gino's surprise, on his horse and picked two pears. One he threw down to Andy. After picking the second fruit he heard the sound of a rifle shooting at him. He could hear the bullets traveling through the leaves. "Run for your life," said Tom as he got down on his horse and left at a full gallop. Andy's horse followed Tom's horse. The full gallop made Andy feel like he was going to fall off the horse. But he held tightly to the saddle and didn't fall. After about five minutes that seemed like an hour Tom brought the horses back to a normal trot.

"Wow," said Andy. "That was close. Do you think that he will look for us especially when we return to go home?"

"No," said Tom. "He was just scaring us to stay away from his Orchid." After going about fifteen minutes they came to a place where you can look into the land and see a small hut.

"What is that small building back into the woods?" asked Gino.

"That is where we are going," said Tom. "That is your father's cabin." When they go there Tom got off his horse and walked over to a pile of rocks. He found the rock he was looking for and found the cabin key under it. "Come let's look inside." Andy got off his horse and they both went inside. Gino was surprised at all the tools they found inside.

"One of these days I'll be using one of these," said Andy. "I hope you and my other cousins will teach me how to use them and be a good farmer." After a look at the land and surrounding land they decided to go home. When they got to Andy's house, Andy got off his horse.

"Thank you so much," said Andy. "I really enjoyed the day."

"I enjoyed it two," said Tom. "If you like we can go on a horse ride at least once a week"

"I would love that," said Andy. "Is that a promise?"

"Before you go inside and since we are here alone I would like to discuss something with you. They say that you should never discus religion, but I think that is the worst thing to do. One should help each other in the truth."

"What are you talking about?" asked Andy.

"I understand that you and your mother are not Catholic," said Tom.

"What makes you say that?" asked Gino.

"I want to help you," said Tom, "the story gets around in a small town. I understand that you stopped going to the Catholic Church."

"So why are you bring this up?" asked Andy being surprised that he wanted to discuss Andy's' believes.

"I know how you feel. The Catholic Church as departed to far from the Bible," said Tom. "I know of a friend I went to school with that had a bad thing with one of the Priests and talked about starting a new church that centered everything on the bible. Would you like me to look him up and find out what he has done?"

"Yes I think that would be great," said Andy. "I and my mother have been wondering if there was a Baptist church in the area. In America we went to a Baptist church."

"Good," said Tom. "I'll see what I can do. Actually I would like to do it for myself also." Tom then left and Andy unsaddled the horse and brought in to the stable. He then went upstairs and found that Grandma and his mother were cooking dinner. Andy felt that the day was perfect.

Tom kept his promise. Once a week he and Andy would take a horse ride around the country. Andy enjoyed the rides. In the meantime Sal was discussing with Andy's mother about taking an automobile ride to some exciting place. He had mentioned to Andy's mother that he had visited the Greek Ruins down southern Sicily. They were playing around for a date.

"I am available any time." said Andy. "It's up to you guys."

"I have Thursday available," said Sal, "are you available Marianna?"

"I will make myself available," said Marianna Andy's mother.

"OK then," said Sal, "Be ready Thursday morning at about eight o'clock."

"We will be ready," said Andy's mother. Monday Andy spent the day with Cathy. Tuesday Andy went horseback riding around the country side. Wednesday Andy stayed home and relaxed. He found his camera and along with three film units, he was ready to take picture all day. Each unit took twenty pictures. Sal arrived at five minutes past eight. Cathy decided to go with them to Andy's delight. Andy sat in front with Sal and Marianna, Andy's mother and Cathy sat in the rear seat. Soon they were on the road. Sal turned left on the side road away from downtown. It leads to the bigger highway. They drove about fifteen minutes. Sal told them to look out the window. There they saw a beautiful landscape that was surrounded with small mountains. Andy quickly took pictures of it. "What is that beautiful green plants just below the mountain," asked Andy's mother.

"I think they are only some wild bushes," said Sal.

"Look at the City out there," said Andy taking a picture of it.

"That is the city of Mazzarino," said Sal. "It is the city you can see from your house."

"We can see it much closer from here," said Cathy.

"We will not go there but at the next turn we will be a lot closer," said Sal. Just as Sal say he drove right outside of the city. Soon they passed it.

"What a beautiful sight," said Andy, "that mountain on our left is so beautiful."

"It is mountain Gricuzzo. If you look just in front it says Mt. Gricuzzo. They don't want to spell out the hole word mountain so the mark it Mt."

"It is a little bigger than the other ones we have seen."

"They are small in comparison to some other mountains in Sicily." said Sal. "The next time I take you out I will show you one."

"I see a sigh on your side that says Butera," said Andy.

"Yes," said Sal "It is a little city we are going through it soon." As they drove through it, Andy spoke his opinion.

"It is smaller than Barrafranca, isn't it?" soon they came up to a split in the road. Sal took the one on the left. It brought them to Mt. Nicola. Sal then followed a road called Gattano around the mountain and came to a door way by a brick wall. Sal drove up to the wall. He got out and bought ticket needed to get inside the area.

"You guy go inside," said Sal. "I will park the car and follow you inside."

He handed the tickets to Andy and drove off. Andy and the other two went inside. The tickets were marked, Greek Ruins. Inside the first thing they saw were four columns that looked like they used to be the columns of a city that fell down and was ruined by time. "There was a road along the side of the ruins. The three walked down the pathway past the one they were looking at and noticed another one. It looked like it was a small castle.

"It looks like it was a wonderful castle," said Cathy.

""I wonder what it really was," said Andy.

"It probably was an office building for the leaders of the area at the time it belonged to Greece Big shots," said Andy's mother. Andy did not hesitate in taking pictures of what they saw.

"How about you two stand in front of the building so I can take a picture," said Andy. The girls did as Andy asked. Andy took a picture. He then decided that he would take a picture of his mom and Cathy at every new place they went.

"Let's go inside and see how it is inside," said Cathy.

"Good Idea," said Andy's mother. "I always wondered what these building were inside."

"You will probably never know," said Andy. "I would guess that the inside as it is now is nowhere near what it was when in action." As they entered the building they found that what they saw outside was misleading. Inside the found that it was absolutely empty. It was only a large open area. Most of the roof was missing. After a minute they left and went to the next building.

"This looks more like an office building,' said Andy's mother. "I have seen one that looks very similar in America. They walked down to the next building. This looked more like a place that housed soldiers. As they kept on walking the structures from there on looked more like storage and small living quarters. They had walked about three miles and the path was still in front of them. They walked past the odd structures and finely came to a clearing.

"What is that thing on the ground about in the middle of the area," said Cathy.

"It looks like some kind of structure that fell over," said Andy.

"Let's go over there and look at it up close," said Andy's mother. All three stepped up on the land and approached the object. It was about twelve feet long.

"Look at his," said Cathy who approached the object from the left side. It is a giant man's head." As Andy walked around the object he recognized it.

"It is a giant statue that has deteriorated and fallen over," said Andy. It looks like it is a thousand years old." After walking around the statue they were about to returned to the path when they ran into Sal.

"Where have you been?" asked Andy. "We missed you. You could have explained some of the things we saw."

"I have been here three times," said Sal, "but I don't know anything about the structures except it was built several hundred years ago when Greece owned Sicily."

"Where did you go?" asked Andy's mother.

"I got the car and drove around the area to this end of the ruins," said Sal. The area is about three miles long. Did you want to walk back? I got the car out front just a few feet from here. Are you all ready to go home?"

"It is after twelve," said Andy's mother. "Shouldn't we stop somewhere for lunch, or do you want to wait until we get home?"

"It will take about an hour to get home," said Sal. "We are not in a hurry to get home anyway. What were you going to do home? Let's stop on the way home."

"You are the driver," said Andy. They walked to the car. Sal was right. It was right around the corner. They get into the car and drove on the road home. They stopped at the first little city they came to. It was the city of Butera. They had a quick lunch. Andy's mother paid for it and they headed for home. Andy still enjoyed the way home. He took many pictures from the window. On the way home he was viewing the opposite side that he did when they came south. When they got home Andy turned to Sal.

"Were can I find a place to buy more film?" asked Andy, "and have the pictures I took to day develop?"

"I think you have to check out the Drug Store," said Sal. "I think they have a lab in the back of the store. I think they also carry film." The next day Andy went down town and went directly to the Drug store. Sal was right they accepted the film to develop and also sold Andy two new film packages. Andy then went happily home.

The next few weeks were the same. He would see Cathy and visit his Aunts. Tommy would take him on a horseback ride. He would even spend some time with Toto. The days went by sweetly. One day when he got home from walking with Cathy he heard Sal talking with his mother.

"I think that July will be the good time. We need it to be hot outside."

"Why does it need to be hot outside?" asked Andy as he walked into room.

"Because where we will be going will be very cold."

"Sal is planning to take us along the east side of Sicily. It will be very cold up mount Etna."

"Why are we going up Mount Etna?" asked Andy.

"That is where you will see the volcano," said Sal.

"Wow," said Andy. "I want to go with you on that trip. Am I invited?"

"It probably will be a two day trip. We will visit the city of Catania. I think you and your mother will be they only ones that will go with me."

"When can we go?" asked Andy

"I will make arrangement and get us three rooms in a hotel in Catania going and coming back. I think July five will be a good time. Is that OK with you Marianna?"

"I guess it will be OK but I'm not sure I want to go up Mount Etna," said Andy's mother. "I don't like heights."

"All set then," said Sal. "I will let you know when I have everything ready."

The next weeks were the same as before. Nothing new was added. Soon it was July. Andy couldn't believe that he had been in Sicily for over five months. He was getting used to being there except he missed his father. When will dad come here he kept on asking himself. Soon it was July. Sal had reported that everything was ready. Soon it was July five. Sal was at their door at eight in the morning. Andy and his mother had packed a small suitcase each with what they would need on the trip. Soon they were on their way. The first city they came to was Piazza Armerina. It was a little larger than Barrafranca.

"It looks like it is a little more modern that Barrafranca," said Andy

"It has more business than Barrafranca. Not as much farming," said Sal.

"Because of that they probably have more money," said Andy. From there they drove around Mt. Nicola on to the clearer highway. At about ten thirty they reached the city of Ramacca.

"It looks like we got back to Barrafranca," said Andy.

"It's a big farming community," said Sal.

"How about you mom?" said Andy. "You have not said a word since we left our house."

"I am just sitting here enjoying every minutes of the trip. Just the beauty of the land keeps me busy." Soon they got on the super highway. At about twelve thirty they arrived at Catania. Catania was a large city. It is about the same size as Palermo. For unknown reasons it was very congested. People and horses fill the streets. Sal let us off in front of the hotel and then parked the car on the next side street. There were no other cars in sight. They decided to eat dinner there at the hotel. The food ended up to be excellent. The next morning they walked to the car. Sal got out his map.

"I thought you have been her before," said Andy

"I have been, but look at this map. They have roads and wide path surrounding the city and all over." After looking at the map and the street signs Sal headed for the street that headed for Gravina. After they went through Gravina he headed for Micolosi. After they drove through Micolosi, they drove up the road that headed up the side of the mountain. It looked dark due to the dark material on the sides of the road.

"What are all these black rocks?" asked Andy trying to take pictures of it all.

"They are the overflow of the volcano," said Sal. "I have no idea why they are black. However, I have been here when the volcano was erupting. It overflowed most of what you see. They have to spend a month clearing out a road to the top of the volcano. You are lucky that it is not erupting. It is only smoking. You will be able to go up there and look down the volcano opening." They stopped at a restaurant that was half way up the mountain. There were a few spots for cars to park. There also was a bus parked there that came from Catania.

"It looks like this is the highest we can go with our car,' said Sal. "We will have to take the Cable Cars."

"You guy go," said Andy's mother. "I will go into the restaurant and have soft drink."

"Come on mom," said Andy, "this is the chance of a life time."

"I just don't want to up that high," said Andy's mother. "I can watch it from here." After a few more attempts to change her mind, Sal and Andy got on a Cable Car. It was a very joyful ride. Andy took some pictures on the way up. When they go to the top they were led to a small cabin that was a foot away from the Cable Car exit door. It was still too far away. It was freezing outside. Inside the cabin they rented them heavy coats. Andy and Sal then walked up the rest of the mountain to the edge of the volcano opening. Andy looked down and saw what looked like bubbling mud. The smoke got into his eyes and he had to pull away.

"This is fantastic," said Andy "I never dreamt that I would look down a volcano."

"The volcano erupts about once or twice a year," said Sal. "It throws out a ton of black stones from this little hole."

"It does look like a small hole to pour out all that stuff.

"There is probably a lot of force behind the eruption," said Sal.

"On the other hand," said Andy. "Our interpretation of what we see could be distorted."

"Why would say that?" asked Sal.

"Because," said Andy. "Look at the other side of the opening. Do you see the people on the other edge of the opening? They are about the size of a mosquito."

"My goodness," said Sal. "You are right. With all the area around us our sight is distorted."

"Yes," said Andy. "I have seen this before. One year my father took me to the Hawaii Island. We took a helicopter ride over a mountain with a river below between the two mountains. When we looked across to the other mountain on the other side of the river it seemed like it was only a few feet wide. They I saw another helicopter going the other way on the other side and it looked like fly."

"I know what you mean," said Sal. "They walked around the surface of the volcano. Andy took several pictures in all directions.

"You know Andy," said Sal. "I would like to stay up here longer but I think I will lose my hair. My head is already frozen. We had better leave."

"I know." said Andy. "I have lost feeling in my hands and face. Let's get out of here. They were soon in the Cable Car on the way back to the restaurant

"I can use a hot cup of coffee," said Sal. They found Andy's mother.

"Well mom," said Andy. "You have missed a great experience. I looked down the mouth of the volcano. I saw bubbling volcano mud"

"That is fine," said Andy's mother. "You can tell me all about it." Andy did just that. He explained it minute to minute. About a half hour later Sal made a suggested.

"I think we should leave here, "said Sal. "I would like to spend what we have left of the afternoon to visit the stores in Catania." Without question they left. A few minutes they drove into Catania.

"Look you guys," said Andy's mother. "You guys go do what you want. I would like to go to the hotel restaurant and have some coffee until dinner time. I will meet you there."

"Don't you want to just walk around," said Andy, "looking at what they have here?"

"I'm tired," said Andy's mother. "If I feel strong I'll go myself." Sal and Andy then left. They walked down what looked like the main street. Andy started to think about the batteries he needed. Whenever they passed a store that Andy though might carry batteries, he stopped to check. No one he talked to had the type Andy need. Around dinner time they walked back to the hotel and met Andy's mother. They all had a fantastic dinner. After a couple of cups of coffee they all went to bed. The next morning they all met at the hotel restaurant and had breakfast together. After breakfast they gathered their suitcases and headed for home. They stopped at a restaurant in city Ramacca. After a small lunch, they headed for home. Andy's mother was happy get home and spent time with her parents. The next day Andy went down town to the Drug Store. He had his pictures developed and bought two new film packages. He was ready for his next trip.

The next two week, Andy spent time with Cathy and a couple of days with Toto. He loved both of them. It was in the beginning of the third week when Tommy approached Andy.

"Well Andy," said Tommy. "Are you ready for your next horseback trip?"

"What do you have in mind?" asked Andy.

"I'm thinking of taking a nice trip before school starts," said Tommy. "I know of a place that you will remember for a long time."

"What is it?" said Andy, "and where is it?"

"It is north of here," said Tommy. "It is a special sight from Mt. Cannarella. It is very close to the city of Enna."

"Enna," said Andy. "I heard grandpa talking about it. It has some business that grandpa is interested in. He said that it is pretty far away. Are you going rent a car?"

"No," said Tommy. "I have been there several times by horseback. Some of the times I had to come home after it got dark. Are you afraid of the dark?"

"No," said Andy. "When do you want to go?"

"How does next Wednesday sound to you?" asked Tommy. "I have off on that day. Don't forget to take your camera"

"I also have that day off," said Andy with a large laughter. Tommy knew that Andy was being funny. He knew that Andy had every day off. Andy mentioned the trip to his mother. She was very hesitant about approving of it. It was too far away. Grandpa answered Andy's mother.

"It isn't that far," said Grandpa. "Let him go. It is a little more than a week after that he will have to go school."

"All right," said Andy's mother. "I will be worried until you get back."

Wednesday came sooner that Andy's mother wanted. She started to worry ahead of time. At eight on Wednesday morning, Tommy and

Andy left for Andy's last trip that year. The scenery was very similar from the other trips Andy had taken. His camera was active the whole trip. However the trip took them around mountains. First they rode around Mt. Lassini. After they returned north, they had to drive around Mt. Polino. Next they had to drive around Mt. Geraca. Finally they got to Mt. Cannarella. There they drove around it going up to the top. The top was pretty flat. Tommy led his horse to a horse stand where he tied his horse. Andy followed his actions.

"We are on the top," said Andy. "What is the big deal?"

"Look at the other end. Can you can see a fence at the mountain open area. The fence will keep you from falling down the mountain. That is where we are going."

"I can't ever guess what we are going to do there," said Andy. When they got there Andy's jaw fell to his chest. The mountain side went straight down from there. Looking down the other side of the fence you could see the complete city of Enna. It was like looking down on the city from an aircraft ten miles high. The view was so clear that you could see horses like little bugs traveling down the roads. Wow," said Andy. "I was not expected to travel this long. Traveling around those mountains has made this a much longer trip." Andy then looked at his watch. "Because of going around those mountain is why it took us so long. It took us about six and a half hours to get here. I think it would have taken us about two and a half hours to get here if it was a straight road. I'm not complaining mind you. I think this trip has given me the best pictures."

"Are you sorry you came?" asked Sal.

"No" said Andy. "I would like to come again someday. I am just sorry that the country hasn't found a way around the mountains. By the way, can we go down and visit Enna?"

"I'm sorry we can't do it this trip," said Sal. "That would be a two day trip. One day for the trip and one day to visit. You have the rest of your life to see Enna." It was about two thirty and they were hungry. Sal went to his saddle and brought out a package. It contained four chicken Breasts sandwiches and some cookies for desert. They ate quickly. After the lunch they sat down on the ground and viewed the city through the openings through the fence. It was such a trill to look down on the whole city. At four thirty they decided to go home. They got home around ten in the evening. Andy's mother waited up for them and offered them some left over dinner. The next day Andy went down town to have his pictures developed.

The next two weeks went as most of the weeks went. He saw Cathy at least once a week and also Toto and Tommy. Soon it was September fourth. Andy had to register in the school building. He knew the way so he went by himself. When he got there he was directed to Mr. Doloni.

"Good morning," said Mr. Doloni. "I take it you are Antonio Luici. "I understand that you want to register as a student in this school. What was your last grade in your American School?"

"I finished the seventh grade and am to start the eighth grade," said Andy. "We only go to the ninth grad here in this location. "You would have to go to one of the large cities to go higher."

"I have already considered that," said Andy. "I have two years to solve that problem."

"The only thing I am worried about," said Mr. Doloni, "is, how well is the education you have already had."

"All the information I have obtained," said Andy, "tells me that the education an American gets is superior to that obtained in other country. I hope it's not true here. I hope you are better then what I already had."

"Well we can get you a trial period. If you fail the eighth grade, we will have to lower you to the seventh or even the sixed grad depending on how you do this year."

"I promise to make you proud of me," said Andy. "I will work very hard." Mr. Doloni gave Andy a sheet of paper with all he needed to know to get to class including the room number and the teacher's name.

"You can start this Monday," said Mr. Doloni. "Have a good day." Andy left feeling satisfied that he was going to get the education that he wanted.

Soon it was Monday. Andy walked down the school and entered the class room he had on the sheet of paper Mr. Doloni gave him. Soon the class room was full. When the clock reached Eight a man walked into the class room.

"Students, for all that do not know me, I am your teacher Mr. Lurbano. This semester we are going to continue our study of math, Italian reading and writing, and good literature, and good farming technics last of all we will study history. These will be covered Monday, Wednesday and Friday. Tuesday and Thursday will be covered by Mr. Masono. He will cover Chemistry, Law and what other subjects he will come up with. Each day we will cover math from eight to nine. At nine to ten we will study reading and writing. You will be told of an action or subject and then you will write a report on that action or subject. From ten to eleven you will have a study hall time. From eleven to twelve we will study new farming technics and equipment's. At twelve you will go to lunch. At one to two you will study history. At two you will go home." Mr. Lurbano began his teaching. Andy felt inferior to the rest in the class. After all he was a former and new nothing about farming or the other subjects that will come up. Andy under estimated himself. However from that moment on he was going to work very hard on all the subjects. He was going to prove that he was as good as the other kids in the school. The first thing he decided to do is make friends with other students. The other students in the class did look down on Andy. However it was not the way Andy suspected. They were afraid that he was going to make them look bad. After all he was an American with a lot of education. While the teacher was talking about mathematical division, Andy decided to say hello to the boy in the desk next to him. Andy put his hand out to shake hands with him when suddenly he felt pain in his hand; the teacher had struck Andy's hand with a ruler.

"When I am teaching you are to listen and not do anything else." Andy was shocked. Then thinking it over he remembered that in America there was a law against teacher spanking students, Here there apparently there wasn't that kind of law. He now became a constant listener. He wasn't going to miss a word. This was going to make thing tougher for Andy. He was out to out shine the other students to prove that he was equal but the students were afraid that he would make them look bad. The next month thing seemed to go on smoothly but quietly. None of the other students talked to Andy. Andy thought it was because they looked down on him. That made him work harder. Whenever the teacher asked a question Andy would be the first to raise his hand and give a good answer. This went on until early November. One day the teacher called a student by name to answer a question. He couldn't answer, Andy raised his hand but the teacher knew that Andy had the answer, that's why he decided to call student by name for each question. The teacher ignored Andy's hand and called another student. He couldn't answer the question either. Andy raised his hand but was again ignored. He called two other students and neither had an answer. Then the teacher yelled out. "Does anyone have an answer?" Andy was the only one who raised his hand.

"Yes Andy," said the teacher. "What do you think is the answer? Andy gave a brief statement as to what the answer was and why. He was right. The teacher then changed the subject, Andy felt proud. He had answered when the two who were asked could not. He felt that he had proven that he was one of them. Unfortunately the two felt angry because Andy had made them look bad.

After the class was dismissed Andy headed home feeling satisfied with that day. As he walked down the road home he felt a little pain in his shoulder and leg. He also noticed small rock rolling past him. He looked around and saw the two class mates throwing rocks at him. Defending himself he grabbed two of the rocks and threw them at the one in front. The second rock hit him in the forehead. He fell to the round. The other fellow laid down over him protecting him. Andy then determined that from now on he was going to walk on the upper path instead of the road. When he got home he was surprised on all the turmoil that was going on in the house.

"What is going on?" Andy asked his mother as she approached him.

"Go and pack your suitcase with all your belongings. Sal is on his way to pick us up."

"What is going on?" asked Andy.

"I just got a letter from your father. Because Germany and Italy are have problems it is believed that they are preparing for a war between each other. It's a matter of hours when they will start the war. Your dad thinks we will be safer in America. He has sent up tickets and got approval for us to go home. The ship leaves tomorrow. They believe it will be the last ship that will go to America. Andy then went up to his bedroom and packed his suitcase. It only took five minutes. He left the model airplane on the living room shelf. He got down stairs just in time. Sal had just arrived. He grabbed all the suitcases and placed them in the car trunk.

"We have to hurry," said Sal. "Not only do you have to get to Palermo but I have to pick up some business men not too far from there. After a quick hug with every one they started to get into the car. Just as Andy was getting in the front seat, Cathy showed up. Andy and Cathy hugged and said goodbye. Soon they were on the way to Palermo. Four hours later Sal left them off at the Palermo pier. Sal hugged all, said goodbye, and left. Andy's mother paid for a ticket on a small boat to Naples. They got to Naples at about nine o'clock. Fortunately they were allowed on board. They were all set to go home.

It took eight days for the ship to get to New York. At New York Andy's father met them at the pier. They hugged each other for five minutes,

"Oh Marianna, "I missed you so much," said Joseph Andy's father. After little romantic sayings, they got into the car. On the way home Andy thought that he was back to his normal day. He felt like he had been on a trip like this just a couple of days ago. Every were they went in the past Andy's mom would sit up front with dad and Andy would sit in the rear with his sister. That happened about twice a week. It always started on Sunday on the way to Church. This started Andy to wonder if the great and fantastic days in Sicily were a wonderful dream. However he thought, the pictures in his camera will answer that question.

The end

Story Number Three

A Tangled Web

Dale was at Giant Eagle to pick up a drug he needed. While there he noticed that it was six o'clock. He decided to go to the Red Lobster for dinner. He loved their fish dinners. When he got there and was seated, he heard a voice calling his name.

"Hello doctor Urbo," said the voice. Dale turned around and saw the speaker.

"Hello there Doctor Loden," said Dale. "It's so good to see you. Come and join me for dinner."

"I will be glade to," said Doctor Loden. "Please call me Mark."

"Ok Mark," said Dale. "And you can call me Dale."

"What are you doing in this part of town?" asked Dale.

"I came looking for you," said Mark. "I thought I would eat first and then look for you."

"What can I do for you?" asked Dale.

"I find that you no longer work at the Universal Hospital," said Mark. "I also hear that you are doing some kind of research. What happened?"

"After my wife passed away I quit my job. The sorrow I felt made me think unwisely. I thought if I couldn't save my wife I couldn't save anyone."

"I understand that you were doing some kind of research," said Mark.

"Not really," said Dale. "I was looking into what caused my wife and parents to die."

"Are you interested in doing some research?" asked Mark. "When I was looking for you on line I found a Lieutenant Urbo," said Mark. "Do you have a brother who is a policeman?"

"No," said Dale. "It is a long story."

"I have all day," said Mark.

"Well OK," said Dale. "You asked for it. When I was a student in college studding to be a Doctor, we had a very big problem. There was a gang of men who robbed and caused a bad problem in the neighborhood. My parents' house was robbed and my mother was badly beaten. Since it was my parents and my neighborhood I helped the police catch the thieves. It so happened that I was the one that found and collected most of the evidence that found them guilty. When we caught and the court placed them all in jail the head of the city police department called me in. He wanted to talk with me. I went to his office. When I got to his office he asked me to come in and have a seat. I walked in and sat opposite the Chief.

"Hi," I said to the chief. "What can I do for you?" He told me that he was very impressed at the help I gave them. He said that I had a very special gift in finding the important little things. He said that I knew how to find the things that turned out in being important evidence. He asked me if I ever considered on being a police officer. I told him that I had not. He asked me to think it over that he was willing to give me a job as Lt. Dale Urbo. I then went to a police academy for two years and became a police officer. I still have the honor of being a police officer. Then my mother, father and Uncle Fred all came down with a disease that slowly worked down their bodies until they died. The medical society couldn't find out what it was and was not able to save them. That is when I decided to go back to school and become a doctor. I wanted to save other lives. When my wife died I was ready to quite everything. But I found out what killed my wife and so I have been doing a research to find out what killed my parents."

"Are you interested in doing some research with me?" asked Mark.

"What are you talking about?" asked Dale.

"I have a little emergency unit that takes in small problems," said Mark. "Most of the problems we sent to the local hospital. I do have three rooms for patients that we care for. In the main area I do research."

"What are you researching?" said Dale.

"I am wondering if the body has an age control unit somewhere hidden in the human body. Think about it. The child was born and slowly grows up. Each year it develops a new body. Slowly the whole body is replaced with an older body. Somehow the body has age control as it replaces sections with newer and older parts until the child has reached in its twenties. There the body parts are replaced with the same aged parts. From there on, the body starts to replace itself with older body parts. Is there a unit in each body that controls the replacement parts depending on age?"

"Sounds like an interesting theory," said Dale.

"How would you like to join me in this effort? There is not much pay. I will do this with donation funds."

"I have not gotten over my wife's death," said Dale. "However I was thinking of going back to the hospital. I think I could save people there."

"Why don't you wait a little while and work with me. If a short time passes with us not having some success, than you can go back to work in the hospital."

"All right," said Dale. "I'm not in a hurry and God knows I don't need any income."

"Not too far from my emergency building is a small building called Food for the Hungry. It helps people who have lost everything. I hope to find at least one who is willing to be my subject. I will give them a home and feed them until they are able to take care of themselves."

"I know that area," said Dale. "It is too small to have any success."

"I am expanding the area," said Mark. "I am making most of the area the Emergency department. It will accept small injury problems and sent the ones with more serious injury problems to the Hospital.

I am adding a small section to the building and will use it for the experimental department. It should be complete by this weekend."

"You will not need me for some time," said Dale. "You have to finish the area, get yourself special equipment and then find someone who is willing to be an experimental object."

"Your right," said Mark. "Do you need something to do in the meantime?" said Mark.

"I was thinking of going back to the Universal Hospital," said Dale.

"If you need something to do you can just work in my emergency department," said Mark. "Rita, who runs it now, is very good but she sends most of the patients to the hospital. She is only a nurse. She can take care of cuts on a hand and a broken bone but noting more serious."

"That sounds like an interesting job while you get things wound up at your experimental Department. I feel like you are going to have problem getting someone to volunteer."

"I think Rita would like some help," said Dale. "You can start Monday. I will keep you up to date on my experiment progress." After they finished there meal, they said goodbye and left.

Monday came sooner than Dale hoped for. That morning he entered the Emergency Department and met Rita.

"Hi Rita," said Dale. "I am Doctor Dale Urbo. I have been sent to help you. I'm sorry if I am taking away some of your work."

"No I'm so glad to see you. I need a lot of help," said Rita. "I send most of my patient to the hospital. Now the ones I can't help maybe you can help. I find it very sad that I can't help them all."

"About how many of the patients that you get do you send to the hospital?" asked Dale.

"I am a nurse," said Rita. "I can only handle small injuries. I take care of less the ten present. I hope that with you here we can take care of more than double that."

"I hope so to," said Dale. "I take it that the door across from yours leads to the other office. Is it mine?"

"It is yours as long as you want it," said Rita.

"I'm going into that office," said Dale. "Send me any patient that you don't think you can help. It was only a few minutes when a patient came into the room.

"My name is Ruth Menden, said a middle aged woman. "The woman out there, told me to come I here."

"Come on in," said Dale. "What is your problem?"

"I have very severe pain in my right arm. The nurse out front took a picture of it and found nothing."

"I understand," said Dale. "Do you remember how you hurt it?"

"No," said Ruth. "I got up this morning with the pain."

"What part of your arm huts the most. Can you point it out to me?"

"No, it huts all over," said Ruth. Dale then gently ran is finger down her arm. At a point Ruth yelled out.

"Ouch," said Ruth "That part hurts the most now that you put pressure on that spot."

"It is just above the elbow," said Dale. I think that somehow, in bed, you twisted your elbow." Dale the grabbed her arm and twisted it side way before Ruth could respond. Suddenly Ruth got a funny look on her face.

"Wow," said Ruth. "The pain is gone."

"It may be a little sore for a while "said Dale, "but it should be back to normal by tomorrow"

"Thank you so much, doc," said Ruth.

"Have a great day," said Dale. Ruth understood that to mean she should leave. And so she said goodbye and left.

Dale had four more patients that day that Rita couldn't handle, that Dale did. They only sent one patient to the Hospital. This went on for several weeks. Every once in a while when he had a minute he checked in with Doctor Loden. He was only reading books on the subject he was interested in. One day he checked in and he had an old man on the bed.

"Hi," said Dale. "I see you have a volunteer. Have you found anything?"

"No," said Mark. "I just got him yesterday. Give me a few days to see what I can find. How are you doing at the emergency room?""

"All is going well." said Dale, "The number of patients we receive daily has increase about five times since I joined them. I don't know how but the fact that we have taken care of most of our patient has somehow gotten out. We have become an emergency Center. I suggest that we buy the empty building next door and connected it to our building and create a truly Emergency Center."

"I think you are right," said Mark. "I will see to it right away. Also I have a relative that has just graduated from medical school. I would like you to accept him and help him join our company."

"That is great," said Dale. "We really could use some help." Mark then immediately started the process of expanding the company. Dale was surprised to see men working on expanding the current building. It took less than a month when the new entrance had a large sigh, Emergency Center. Dale had no problem training Sam the new young doctor. He was very competent. One day Sam went into Dale's office

"Doctor Urbo," said Sam, "do you have a minute to discuss something?"

"Of course," said Dale, "come on in. what do you have in mind?"

"The number of patient is getting out of hand," said Sam. "I wonder if you could use another doctor."

"Who do you have in mind?" asked Dale.

"I graduated with a friend," said Sam. "He got better grades than I did. He is still looking for a job."

"Sounds great," said Dale, "Bring him in."

The next day, Dale went into the hall way that led to Doctor Loden's office. It was empty. Dale then walked down the hall to the test room where Mark was doing his testing on the old man.

"Hi Mark," said Dale. Have you gotten any success?"

"No," said Mark "I think he is too old. I don't think that his body is replacing any of his cells."

"So what is your next move?" asked Dale

"I think there is another woman who I am talking to that may volunteer. She has no house, no family, or friends that could help her. She is twenty years younger than the old man I have. She needs help."

"What are you going to do with the old man?" said Dale.

"I have to take care of him," said Mark. "That was the deal. I have given him one of the medical rooms with a TV and I will see that he gets fed."

"Sounds like a lot of work," said Dale. "When are you going back to being a Doctor?"

"I want to see if I can find anything with this woman, said Mark. "I may still have to find a younger person."

"Rita tells me that she is now more of a clerk than a nurse," said Dale. "She spends most of her day at the entrance desk getting required information on each patient, although she is not complaining. She likes the job. You know that this is now a fulltime business. You need to start running this business. I am going to pull out pretty soon. It is going to need a couple of new doctors."

"I know that what you are saying is true," said Mark. "It is going to need a manager. I just have a couple of little ideas to try and then I will close this department and start running the Emergency Center."

"All right," said Dale. "I will help running the place until you are ready."

"Thank you so much," said Mark. Dale then went back where he did both jobs. He tried to control the financial end and also when necessary take care of a patient. It was about two days later when there was an unusual excitement in the lobby. A Young lady was brought in and was handled as an emergence patient. She had been shot in the shoulder and stomach both where bleeding badly. Rita quickly transferred her into Sam's office. He took care of her wounds and closed the openings he make removing the bullets. He then placed her in a room and waited until she woke up from the drug that had put her to sleep. When she woke up, Sam spoke to her.

Hi," said Sam. "How do you feel?"

"I feel pain all over my body," said the woman.

"You will soon feel better," said Sam. "What is your name and who can I call of your family?"

"I don't have any family," the woman said. "I was originally coming here to volunteer for doctor Loden's Research. "Can you move me into his Lab?"

"Perhaps," said Sam. "But I must know your name."

"My name is Laura Benson. Please take me into Doctor Loden's lab."

"Just wait a while," said Sam. "Let me talk to the manager." Sam then went into Dale's office.

"Doc," said Sam as he walked into Dale's office. "I have a young woman who was shot. I have taken care of her wounds but she wants to volunteer for Doctor Logan's research. Do you want to talk to her first?"

"No," said Dale. "Let me call doctor Loden first. We should both see her." Dale then called Doctor Loden.

"Mark," said Dale when Mark answered his phone. "I have a young woman who wants to be a volunteer to your research. However she has been shot and is in the recovery room."

"Have her moved into my lab. This is more serious than just a volunteer. I will meet you there." He then hung up .Dale then called Sam.

"Sam," said Dale when Sam answered his phone. "Please move the young lady to doctor Loden's lab."

"I will do that right now," said Sam and did as he said. He moved Laura into Doctor Laden's Research Lab. About ten minutes later Dale and Mark met in the Research Lab. Dale was shock when he saw her siting up on her bed. She was the most beautiful woman he had ever met. He felt something funny in his stomach. He was so taken he needed time to recover. He let Mark take over.

"Hi," said Mark when he got next to Laura's bed. "My name is Doctor Mark Loden. What is your name? And why do you want to volunteer to my research efforts"

"My name is Laura Benson. I fit all that you requite of a volunteer."

"You don't have any family here," asked Mark, "or in another city?"

"No, I have no family anywhere," said Laura.

"Do you have a home somewhere," asked Mark

"I have nothing anywhere," said Laura. "I don't have a family, don't have a home and don't have a car. I have nothing." Dale then intervened.

"I think you have to start from the beginning," said Dale. "My name is Dale Urbo. Where did you come from and how did you lose your family. Please be truthful." Laura seemed to be shock upon seeing Dale as Dale was on seeing her. She was taken by him also.

"I was in New York," said Laura. "I was going to the university there. I was studding to be a surgeon's assistant."

"What made you come here?" asked Dale. "It is too soon for the universities to close for the summer."

"My father called me," said Laura. "He said that he didn't feel well and someone killed my brother. My mother had passed away about three years ago. I came to be with my father to bury my brother."

"Was you brother really dead?" asked Dale. "So where is your dad now?"

"He was not home when I got there," said Laura. "I have not seen him since. The house exploded as I left it early this morning"

"Well you do have a parent," said Dale. "He is considered family."

"You are right," said Laura, "that is if he is still alive. I think someone is trying to kill my whole family. Someone shot me as I left the house. Since I was not killed in the house explosion they shot me."

"Well let's sit down and go over your family," said Dale. Dale pulled up a chair and stated the family research.

"Tell me," said Dale, "do you have any brothers or sisters?"

"Yes," said Laura, "I had a brother but he died a year ago in an auto accident."

"Did your father have any family?" asked Dale.

"Yes," said Laura, "He had a brother Frank and a sister-in-law, Cathy."

"Have you talked to them?" asked Dale.

"No," said Laura. "A truck went through a stop sign and hit their car on the driver's side and killed both of them."

"Did they have any children?" asked Dale.

"No," said Laura.

"I think I have enough to work on," said Dale. "You stay safely here and I will get back to you." Dale then went to the business that Laura's father Steven Benson had owned. He went into the main office.

"Hello" Dale said to the man in the office. "I am Lieutenant Dale Urbo of the Fairlawn police department. "I would like to ask you questions on the previous owner of this business."

"I'm sorry but I don't know much about him. I bought this threw an agency." Dale got all the information he could get about the agency and went there.

"Hi" said Dale to the girl on the front desk. "May I talk to the person who sold Steve Benson's business?" He was led to an office and was introduced to the sales man.

"What can I do for you," said the salesman. "I am Lt. Dale Urbo. I would like all the information you have on the sale of the Steve Benson business."

"I can't tell you much," said the salesman. "Mr. Benson brought his own byer. All I can tell you is that he sold it for two million six hundred dollars. We deposited into the PNC bank."

"Thank you very much," said Dale and left for the local PNC bank. At the bank Dale was let to the Money market Manager.

"Hi" said Dale. "I am Lt. Dale Urbo. I would like a copy of all the information you have on Mr. Benson's deposits."

"I am Jim Manson. " I will give you a copy of all I have on him. Why do you wanting this information?"

"I need it to figure out what happened to Mr. Benson. He has been missing for three days."

"Well here is a copy of his deposits here at this bank. He just deposited one million six hundred dollars. This other document is what he had already deposited here. His total is four million eight hundred sixty five dollars. I also have a copy of his will so that I would have an idea as to who could come for the money should something happen to him. Do you want a copy?"

"Yes please," said Dale. "That document my help me also." Then Mr. Manson printed a copy of all he had and Dale thanked him and left. He went directly the emergency center. When he walked into the area that was keeping Laura he was surprised to see paper dollars all over the floor.

"What's going on here?" said Dale.

"Your friend at the police station brought what they could find in the completely burned Benson house." said Mark. "One of the plastic packages was melted enough to make it hard to open. We finally snapped it open and the money flew out of it."

"Did they find anything important?" said Dale.

"Yes" said Mark. "They found his wallet with money and all of his credentials in it. It had his driver's license and all his credit card."

"That tells us that he did not leave on his accord," said Dale.

"How about you," said Mark? "What have you found?"

"I have checked various places," said Dale. "I have found that Steve Benson has sold his house and placed the money at the PNC bank. He now has four million eight hundred dollars in the PNC bank. "Laura almost fell over. Lucky there was a chair where she suddenly sat in.

"That gives us a very good idea what this is all about," said Mark.

"I am now going to follow up on Steve's Brother Frank," said Dale.

"The latest information that we got was that he and his wife were killed."

"I will follow up and find out who did it," said Dale. Just as he was ready to leave, one of the police officers walked in.

I'm sorry to bring this information in but I think they found Steve Benson's body in the lake. I have a picture of him. Please check it to make sure it is Mr. Benson we found."

"Let me look," said Mark. "I have seen a picture of him before."One look at the picture and he responded. "That is him alright." At that remark Laura broke out crying loudly. She almost fell out of the chair. Dale caught her before she fell.

"I'm sorry sweet heart," said Dale. "I promise you I will find out who did this to you. I promise."

"Thank you," said Laura hardly getting it out of her mouth. "Please put me in bed. I need to rest and be alone." Dale put his arm around her and helped get her up.

"Bye the way," said Dale. "I checked his bank and found he had four million eight hundred in his account. I also got a copy of his Will." He has left Laura one million. He has left one million to his favorite charity and left the rest to be equally divided to the rest of the family." Dale then left for his follow up of Steve's brother Frank. He arrived at the house hopping that one of their families would be there. It was locked and closed. Dale was ready to leave when he saw one of the neighbors.

"Hello," said the lady next door. "If you are looking for the Benson you will not find them. They have been killed."

"I know," said Dale. "I am Lt. Dale Urbo. I was wondering if they had some kind of a family that would take over their home."

"I'm sorry," said the woman. "They had no children and the only other relative they had was his brother Steve Benson. We have been trying to contact him but have been unsuccessful. Perhaps you can contact him."

"Do you know if his wife had any relatives?" asked Dale.

"I don't think so," said the woman. "She was from Germany."

"Thank you," said Dale and left. He went straight to the police office that he hoped still had the truck that killed the Bensons. He brought with him the equipment he needed to get some finger prints if there were any.

"Hello," said Dale to the officer at the front desk. I am Lt. Dale Urbo. I am investigation the death of the Bensons. I believe it was murder. The officer led Dale to the truck.

"It is not repairable," said the officer. "I also think it was cleared of any finger prints."

"Thank you," said Dale, "there is always a place they forget to clear. By the way, do you have the name of the person who originally rented the truck?"

"Yes," said the officer. "I will get it for you." He left and came back about five minutes later. "The person who rented the truck was Dan Smith. He came back the next day and reported that the truck had been stolen."

"Thank you," said Dale and went to the truck. Dale checked the rear view mirror. As he suspected he found two different finger prints.

"How are you doing?" asked the officer.

"Great," said Dale. "I found two different finger prints. It is normal for a driver to adjust the rear view mirror when first driving a car or truck. They always forget that they did it."

"I will have to remember that," said the officer.

"Don't let it out," said Dale. "We don't want anyone to realize that as a possibility. I have arrested several criminals by their finger prints on the rear view mirror."

"That is good to know," said the office.

"You have a good day and thanks for letting me in to check on the truck." Dale then left and headed for the lab. At the lab, using his special equipment he made a clearer picture of both finger prints. He then He then gave them to the lab assistant.

"Please," said Dale, "Can you see if you can find the owner of these finger prints," said Dale to the assistant.

"I will do my best," said the young man. Dale then left and went to the Emergency center. There he went in the special room where Laura was held.

"Hi Laura," said Dale. "How are you holding up?"

"I don't feel so good," said Laura. "I am without family. Have you found someone?"

"I have gone through most of you father's side your family," said Dale. "I may have found one but he may be the bad guy. I'm working full time. I am now going to check all of your mother's side of your family. I hope to find a good member of your family. However, it might not be the best time to tell you," said Dale, "I want you to know that I am very attracted to you. You will never be alone. I will be your family if we don't find anyone else."

"Oh how sweet," said Laura. "That does make me feel better."

"I ordered a dinner for myself and I understand that you have ordered yours."

"Yes I did," said Laura. "In fact it should be on its way up." She had just finished talking when her dinner and Dale's dinner was brought up to them. "Perfect planning," said Dale. "Let's eat and spend time together."

"I would like that," said Laura, "Most of the time I eat alone. Doc and the others go home and eat with their family." After Dale said a prayer they both started to eat. "What are your plans on finding my good family and the bad one if the killing is being done by a family member? I hope it is an outsider for another reason besides the money."

"I promise I will find out for you," said Dale, "even if it takes most of my life."

"What are your next efforts?" asked Laura.

"I spent the last days following your father family. Tomorrow I will start following your mother's family," said Dale. "I understand that her maiden name was Mary Brew and her married name is Mary Mador. I have found that her husband is Joseph. I will find out all I can on that name and their offspring's and hopefully will find the culprit." Laura smiled and looked much happier. They pasted the rest of the evening having small talk of their past lives. Dale promised to see her tomorrow and left for his home.

The next morning Dale checked every option he had. He made several phone calls and spent a lot of time on his computer. Before he went to the Benson house he stopped at the police office. The young lab assistant, Raymond walked up to Dale.

"Good morning Lt. Urbo," said the young man. "I got the information you wanted." He then handed him a sheet of paper.

"Why thank you very much," said Dale. "That was quick."

"It was easy because both men had a police record," said the lab assistant. "These two men, Dan Smith and Peter Mador," said Dale, "are possibly two men I am looking for. They may have murdered three persons, perhaps others that I don't know about. I will have to talk to them both soon." Dale then left to go to the house of Laura's Aunt Mary Mador, Laura's mother's sister. Dale walked up to the house and rang the doorbell. A woman answered the door.

"How can I help you?" said the woman.

"I am trying to get information on the couple that owned this house not too long ago. Do you know what happened to them? Are you related to them?"

"No," said the woman. "We are renting the house from their son."

"This is a very nice house," said Dale. "Why doesn't he live here?"

"We asked him the same question. He said he needed the money. We did go to his apartment and we were surprised that his apartment was smaller than our bathroom."

"Do you know what happened to his parents?"

"I think that both the original owners died of cancer. Mary, the wife died three years ago and her husband Joe last year. I am told that they only had one son, Peter." Dale then decided he had to talk with Dan first. Dale believed he lied about the rental of the truck. After thinking about it, Dale was not sure that he had enough evidence to convince Dan to confess his part in the schemes of Peter. He decided to go and spy on Peter. He felt he needed more information on peter's activity. He got permission to investigate peter's living quarters. As he was looking to park he saw what he thought was Peter. He stepped on his gas petal and went down the street and parked where he could see peter. Dale figured that Peter headed for his car that was parked right in front of his apartment. Dale was shock to see Peter walk right past his car and walk to the curve. A couple of minutes later, Dale saw a large truck carrying about four large lawn equipment tools. He recognized a lawn grass cutter. Dale waited a while and after they left he drove to the apartment building. Dale decided to check the car before he got permission from the manager to check Peter's apartment. He used his equipment that soon opened the door. Dale was looking to open the trunk where he felt was the most logical place to have the weapon. However since he was in the car he checked the glove compartment. To his amazement he found a pistol. He quickly closed the car and got into his car a drove to the police lab. There he met Raymond.

"Hi Ray," said Dale. "I have an important job for you. I found a pistol in my suspect's car. Will you check to see if it is the gun that shot Mr. Benson? I believe you have the bullet that was gotten out of Mr. Benson."

"I will take care of it right away," said Raymond. It was about fifteen minutes later that Ray came into the room where Dale was waiting.

"What did you find?" asked Dale.

"You were right said Ray. "The bullets match. It is the gun that shot Mr. Benson." Dale left, feeling he had all that he needed.

Early the next morning Dale went to Dan's house. He wanted to catch him before he left for his job. He was lucky; Dan was just finishing his breakfast.

"Hello Lt. Urbo," said Dan. What are you doing here this early?"

"I wanted to catch you before you left for work," said Dale. "I will only take a few minutes."

"Well come in," said Dan. "What is the reason you are here?"

"I need to talk to you before I arrest you friend Peter."

"What do I have to do," said Dan, "with any of his problems?"

"It depends on your decision today," said Dale. "I know that you lied about your thing with the truck. So listen, you can join me in agreeing that you were caught in a position you had no choice. I will do my best to get you off the best I can. Or we can forget it and I will arrest you as a partner of Peter. You then can be charged with conspiring to murder. So what do you think?"

"You are right," said Dan. "We worked together and I was aware that he had killed a fellow worker that gave him trouble. You probably don't even know of that crime. Anyway he asked me to rent the truck for him. He said that he had a problem with the company with a past rental and that they would not rent to him. I had no choice. I had no idea that he was going to kill someone with the truck. Although I admit I expected evil."

"So I take it that you will admit your relationship with him," said Dale. "I will do whatever I can to clear you of murder."

"I'm all yours," said Dan.

"Very good," said Dale. "See you in court." Dale then left to arrest Peter.

Dale, after the arrest, went to his office to review all that he had. He had the murder weapon with Peter's fingerprints on it and the finger prints of the truck used in the murder. Dale then reviewed who Peter was. He found that Peter was the son of Sal Mador the brother of Joe Mador the husband of Mary Brew Mador. Mary was the sister of Stella Brew Benson, Laura's mother. Two days later, Dale set up a private meeting with Peter in the police Investigation room.

"Peter," said Dale when he walked into the investigation private room. "I would like to talk with you before the court hearing next Wednesday.

"We have nothing to talk about," said Peter. "I have no relatives or good friends; I have nothing that I own except the house I inherited from my father when he passed away. I had to rent it to get enough money to pay the money owned on it and the taxes. I have nothing except a big dept."

"Peter," said Dale. "I want to see if there is some way I could help you, so tell me do you believe in God?"

"No" said Peter, "I think it is a way for the government to control the people."

"Do you think that a strong wind in a desert blew sand together and created man.?"

"I never tough of where man came from," admitted Peter. "What does that have to do with me?"

"We were all designed by God who gave us complete freedom. Unfortunately we turned our back on God."

"I never thought about that," said Peter. "Teaching me about God should have been my parent's job."

"Your right" said Dale, "I think before you meet him, it will be my job. Anyway, God designed us and loved us very much," said Dale. "He loves us so much that he gave his only son to die for our sins. What I am suggesting is that you accept his son Jesus as your savior and accept him with all your heart. I can't tell you that you will not be put to death for murder but I can guaranty that God will give you more time then you expect. He loves you. You are one of his children. Trust me. You will see a big difference in the result of your trial, if you accept Jesus as your savior. Even if they take your life you will go to heaven. It is all your choice."

"Thank you so much for caring," said Peter. "I will think about all you have told me. Thank you so much."

"I also recommend that you tell then your whole life story. Telling the truth always helps. They may feel a little sorry for you. OK then, see you at the trial Wednesday." Dale then left and went to visit with Laura.

"Hi Laura," said Dale when he entered her room. "How are you doing?"

"I am a little nervous as to what you have found," said Laura.

"I have all the evidence I need for the trial. Your distant relative Peter Mador is in jail. I just come from talking with him. I hope I got him to accept Jesus as his savior and that he will tell his whole story at the court house. Anyway it is almost over. After the trial is over we will have to file the inheritance documents for you to inherit your father's money. Anyway let's change the subject. We will just have to wait."

"I know," said Laura. "I wonder if I could survive the waiting time."

"I will help you think of something else," said Dale.

"What else do I have to think about?" asked Laura.

"I will keep you busy thinking about us," said Dale.

"What about us" said Laura, with a very romantic smile on her face?"

"You know how I feel about you," said Dale. "I will not let you get away."

"Are you interested in my money?" asked Laura with that smile on her face.

"If that is all you see," said dale getting angry. You will not see me after the trial. You go get your money yourself." Laura seeing that her statement got

Dale angry, she responded quickly.

"I'm sorry," said Laura. "I was only teasing you. I would give up all the money just to be with you."

"I hope you care for me as much as I care for you," said Dale. "Besides I have almost as much money as you will have after you inherit your father's money."

"I'm sorry," said Laura. "I was only trying to be funny. Let's change the subject."

"Alright", said Dale. "Let's talk about you. You are now safe and don't need our protection. What is your next move?"

"First, after I can afford it, I will want a place to live. I will have to decide with your help if I will rent or buy a house."

"A future outcome will help make that decision," said Dale. "That is a future decision."

"Then I have to decide if I should go back to college," said Laura. "I want to be a nurse."

"You know," said Dale. "All that we are thinking about is in the future. I have a plan that might over ride all the others. With my plan you don't need to buy a house and you can go back to school without any problem. Let's forget that for now. We have the murder and you are safe to go anywhere. Let's go out and celebrate our success."

"Lead the way," said Laura. Dale did all that. All the days till the trial they spent together celebrating the joy they had being together.

On Wednesday, the day of the trial, Dale went to the courthouse. He had no Idea how long the trial would last. He had no part in the trial. He was there as an observer. However he had notified Peter's lawyer and the accusing lawyer that he was available if need. Dan was called up first.

"Will you tell us who you are and tell us how you are related with the case against Peter Mador?" instructed the accusing attorney. Dan started from the beginning just as he had with Dale.

"My name is Dan Smith. I worked with Peter. I heard that he had killed one of his partners at work. So from the first time I met him I was afraid of him. I tried to stay away from him; however I couldn't turn him down when he asked me to rent a truck. He said that he had a bad reputation with company. I did not know that he was going to kill someone with the truck although I must admit that I knew that he was going to do something evil. He then asked me to go to the renter and tell them that someone had stolen the truck. This was just around when he ran into the Bensons." Dan gave all that he had given Dale. He didn't leave out anything that he knew about Peter and his time with him. "I guess that is all that I was involved with," ended Dan. "Do you want anything more?"

"No," said the judge. "Thank you for giving us the information of your relationship with Peter. Who is next?"

"I think that Peter would like to speak next" said his layer.

"OK," said the judge. "Bring him up here." Peter then was led into the chair next to the judge.

"I'm not sure how to explain my mental condition several months ago when all of this started," began Peter. "My mind was angry with everything and everyone. I had nothing except the house my father left me. I had to rent it to pay for the large mortgage he had on it. I also had a large dept. from a bad investment my father made. I had nothing but a dept. and people coming after me for payments of my father depts. I think I went crazy. When I remembered that my Uncle Steve had money I decided I was going to get some of it. However I remembered that he had a son and a daughter and a brother and his wife I figured that when he passed away they would get it all and I would get nothing. So I decide to reduce the number of inheritors. I killed four people in my stupidity. I felt that I deserved the money more than they did. I tried to kill Uncle Steve and his daughter Laura by blowing up the house. However neither one was there. After I settled down the thought suddenly came into my mind. What have I done, I suddenly realized that I had done a terrible thing. I remembered that I was created my God. I then decided to accept Jesus as my savior. I know that I have to pay most likely with my life. But that is OK if Jesus forgives me. He would take me to a place in heaven. So I figure I am better off if I confessed my sins to you and to God. I trust that God will give me the strength to live with the earthly punishment. That is all I have to say."

"Thank you very much," said the Judge, "does anyone have any questions?" No one answered. "We have his finger prints on the Truck and on the murder weapon. We also have his confession. Therefore I think the trial is over. Except for the lawyers the rest may go home. Dale was one of the first to leave. He went directly to give the results to Mark and of course to Laura.

"Hi" Laura," said Dale when he got there.

"How did everything go?" asked Laura.

"Well the trial is over," said Dale. "Dan and Peter were found guilty. So they will not be around to bother you. What the punishment to Dan and Peter is not known yet. It will be available in a couple of days."

"So I am free from danger from them, thank God," said Laura with a happy look on her face. "Where do we go from here?"

"I think now is the time to talk about you and me. You know that I am very attracted to you. I was thinking of getting down on my knee and asking you the question I have had on my mind for a long time. But First what are you thinking about your next step?"

"I would like to finish college," said Laura. "I have always dreamt of being a surgical assistant. However, I feel the same about you. I don't know what to do. What do you think?"

"Thinking about it," said Dale. "I feel that you should go back to college. Our relationship can wait. Your being at least a nurse, makes us having more life in common. I would love to spend the rest of my life with a nurse. Maybe we could work in the same hospital or medical organization like the Emergency Center. "Sound great" said Laura. "I feel so good now that we both agree on our future. I will call them tomorrow. The next class will start this September. That is two months away. I hope I will get the money before then."

"If you don't get it," said Dale, "I will lend you from my savings. If my plan works out it will be your money also." Laura smiled one of her jolly happy smile.

"I guess we have taken care of everything," said Laura.

"Not at all," said Dale. "I have never kissed you." He barely finished when Laura threw herself into his arms. Quickly their lips found each other. Dale was shock. He never dreamt how fantastic it would feel. Her skin was so soft and a thrilling line from her lips filled his heart. The thought of how she felt about his kiss never entered his mind. He didn't have room in his brain's fantastic excitement. However he suddenly was awaked by the fact that Laura almost fell out of his arms. He suddenly realized the she felt the same way by the kiss that he did. He held her keeping her from falling. When their lips parted she proclaimed,

"Dale,' she softly said. "I love you so very much."

"I love you too," Dale heard himself saying. It took a few minutes to recover.

"I never dreamt that I could feel this way about anyone," said Laura.

"I know, me too," said Dale. "My mind is so excited that I can't think straight," said Dale.

"I know," said Laura. "What do we do from here on?"

"I think we will have to live as boyfriend and girlfriend," said Dale until you graduate from college."

From that day on they spent every day they could together. They spent a lot of time alone when they could. They were very careful that they as Born-Again Christians didn't exceed the Christian limits as lovers. Slowly, the time went by and soon Laura had to go to college. The last day before she left was more romantic than the first time they kissed.

The next month went by slowly. They talked over the phone several times during the week. Dale was very careful that he didn't keep her from her home work.

Dale went back to the University Hospital as the surgical doctor. It was the day before the thanksgiving holiday that Dale decided to spend the holiday's home relaxing and taking a day to rest. He had just finished breakfast when the doorbell rang. He was thinking of calling Laura about ten. He also, because of the time difference was going to call his parent, who in lived in California, later. He was worried that a guest would keep him from calling. He went to the door. He was shocked at what he saw.

"Laura sweet heart," said Dale, "What are you doing here? Are you not going to get in trouble at the University?"

"I have been working very hard to do what I have to do to satisfy by heart."

"What are you talking about?" said Dale.

"At the end of this semester I am going to quit Ohio State and am going to finish my education at Cleveland State University here in Ohio."

"That's great," said Dale, "then I could see you more often."

"Not often enough," said Laura. "At the university a young friend that I was in classes with was married and went home every night. I think you said that you wanted to marry me after I graduated. Why can't we get married and I can live at you home as your wife."

"I will have a hard time letting you do your homework," said Dale.

"We will work it out," said Laura. "I just can't go on without you in my daily life."

"Just wait here for a minutes," said Dale. "I have something to take care of." He left and came back a few minutes later. "When do you want to get married?"

"I will have time off during the Christmas Holiday," said Laura. "I have the week before Christmas off. I think that would be a wonderful time to get married" Dale then went down on his knee and pulled out an engagement ring.

"Laura Benson," said Dale, "will you marry me?" He hardly finished when she threw herself into arms.

"Yes," she said and then their lips touched and not another word was said. After dinner Laura headed back to Ohio State University. Dale and his mother, who came up from California to help him, set up the wedding. They spent a lot of time and money getting everything ready. It was very difficult since it was the week before Christmas, but money can buy anything. However, they set up a fantastic wedding. They invited all the friends they had. They invited Rita, Mark, Sam and two young doctors who worked at the Emergency Center. Dale invited two doctors and three nurses that worked with him at the University Hospital. Altogether there were about twenty people at the wedding. The time finally came. Every one met at the West hill Baptist Church. Dale's father, who came there on the last day, walked Laura to the church alters. The pastor after a small speech married them. After the service, they all went to the hotel that had a large room for the wedding. After the dinner, the large band started to play. Dale and Laura started to dance first. After the first song the rest of the people started to dance. At that moment, no one in all of the country was as happy as Dale and Laura.

The End

Story Number Four

The little dream that came true

Tom was a Detective for the Fairlawn Police station. When there was no crime to investigate he was a regular police man. They had more police then they needed so Tom had some time off on slow days. Tom originally was a farmer's boy. He loved farming. However his father sent him to college to be someone better. Tom's mother died when he first started college. His father getting very sick three years later sold the farm thinking that Tom would never want to get it and be a farmer. His father died a week after he graduated and left him a sum of money. Today was a very slow day so Tom decided to take a drive through the country. He felt that he loved the farming business. Since he didn't have a chance to be a farmer he can at least drive by and view it. He was only about forty miles from the city while he was looking at a house that was in the middle of a farm that Tom heard a large explosion. He looked and the house that he was looking at showed that it was on fire. Tom found the drive way to the house and went to see if there was any one there that was hurt. When he got there he saw a woman in front of the house lying on the front steps. He rushed to her. He was shocked on how she made him feel. She was so beautiful. He found that she was out cold. He checked her heart and it was beating. However, she was not breathing. He was ready to give her air through the mouth when he saw she was beginning to bread. He held her and waited to see what would happen next. After a while she awoke. She looked around a felt Tom's hands on her chest. She then wondered if she had died and was brought back to life.

"Did I die?" she asked.

"No, I was ready if you needed help. You will be alright," said Tom. "I see that you are alive and where not killed with the blast because you were about to leave the house."

"Yes I came out to hang my clothes on the cloths line." Tom then picked her up and laid her on a soft spot on the lawn.

"Just relax and give yourself a chance to recover," said Tom. "Are you hurting any place?" We have to be sure you don't have any broken bones. How do you feel? Do you want me to take you to the hospital?"

"Let's wait a while," said the woman. "I don't feel any pain anywhere except my head. That must be the place I was struck."

"We can't wait too long," said Tom. "We have to make sure you are alright." Ten minutes later the woman sat up.

"Help me get up so I can walk." Tom helped her on her feet. Tom wondered if she was close to dying. She was now too active to have been near to death. Tom decided he misunderstood the situation. He was not a doctor. However, he felt he was ready to do the right thing.

"Thank you for your help," said the woman. "Who are you and what are you doing here?"

"I was driving by and saw that the house was on fire. I stopped to see if anyone needed help," said Tom. "I am Detective Tom Dundie. I am a member of the Fairlawn police department. Who are you?"

"My name is Mia Sater. I was going to college to be a nurse. My dad died before I could finish. My mother died three years ago. All my father left me was the farm that was my mother's family. I don't have anything else."

"So where are you going to live?" asked Tom.

"I see that the fire in the house is out," said Mia. "I think someone put a bomb in my kitchen through the kitchen door way."

"You can't stay here for several reasons. First, someone is trying to kill you. The house has smoke and an open side and most of all you should not have come alone to live out in an open area."

"I have nowhere else to go," said Mia. "I don't have the money to rent or even stay at a hotel. I have no choice."

"There is no way I am going to leave you here alone," said Tom. "Do you have any other relatives in the area?"

"The only relative I have in his world is my brother Brian. He does not want to be a farmer and wanted to go to college to be a financial adviser. But since dad passed away neither one of us has any cash to live on. I have no Idea where Brian is."

"Then you are coming home with me," said Tom.

"Who are you living with?" asked Mia.

"I live alone," said Tom. "My parents have both passed away. They left me their house."

"There is no way that I am going to live with a single man," said Mia.

"You have nothing to worry about," said Tom. "You need not have to worry because; I am a Born-Again-Christian. God and Jesus are my first love. I would never do anything to offend them."

"I can't believe it," said Mia. "I now believe that God sent you down the road to help me. He is still watching over me. You see, I am also a Born-Again-Christian. There not many of us here in America anymore. So God must have sent you."

"I'm surprised also," said Tom. "I have met only a few truly Christian people in my life time."

"Well I will go with you," said Mia. "But first let's go inside and see if I can salvage something. Especially let's get the cloths that can be salvaged." They went inside and were surprised how much damage was done. The heat had caused small flames to damage many items. There was even one in her bedroom and a lot of the cloths were damaged. Mia found a suitcase and collected as much clothes that were salvageable. Mia got some paper work that she got out of one of the drawers. They left at eleven thirty. Mia looked back as they left. She felt bad leaving it. They got to Tom's house and Tom brought Mia to one of the bed rooms. He picked the one that was down the hall from his bed room. It was about an hour later that Mia came down to the kitchen. Tom had lunch ready. After lunch they sat there to discuss their situation.

"So what are you thought on what we do next," asked Mia.

"I don't really know," said Tom, "but the thoughts that circulate my mind are that I want to be a farmer and that God brought us together for a reason. I think it has to do in doing something at your farm."

"I think so to," said Mia. "I was raised on a farm, not this one but one in southern Ohio. If you noticed at the other end of the farm is the fruit orchard. There is a small cabinet there and a road that allowed a truck to move the fruit. I think there are about six different fruit there. I have a booklet that I just got from one of the draws that had the name and phone number of Mexican orchard. I suspect that great grandfather bought fruit there that will not grow here.

"Let me check the farm thoroughly. I have a friend that has a plane. He could fly me over the farm so I can take a picture of it," said Tom, "but first let's decide how I will fit the picture."

"You can buy half of the farm so that we could become partners and so I could have some money to upgrade the place," said Mia. "It is probably too soon to talk about this but I am very attracted to you. However, I think for now we should be partners."

"Sounds like a good plan," said Tom. "To balance our feelings I am attracted to you also more than I have ever been attracted to anyone. However why don't you go take an afternoon nap. I will go get a picture of the farm. Tom then called his friend and make plans to fly over the farm. Later that afternoon Tom came back home. He had taken a picture of the farm and had it enlarged to the size of a newspaper. Mia heard Tom come in and came down to meet him.

"Wow," she said when she saw the picture, "that is fantastic. However we have a problem. I have called all the stores and business that could buy our fruit or vegetable that we grow on our farm but they are not interested in any contracts. She said she would check all the other producers when she needed anything.

"That makes sense," said Tom, "they want to buy where they could get the best price."

"Where does that leave us," asked Mia?

"I hate to say this but it means that we have to sell everything ourselves. Let me check this farm picture and let me think about it and we can discuss this tomorrow morning." Mia then went back to her room.

The next morning after breakfast Tom and Mia sat together looking at the picture of the Farm.

"I hate to say this," said Tom, "but we have to open a grocery store."

"I trust you," said Mia. "Please go on and describe to me what you think we have to do."

"First of all look at the long narrow building near the road," said Tom. "I think this will make a great grocery store. We can limit it to two isles. One isle for all the fruit you can pick and one isle for the vegetables that we will grow as farmers.

"I'm surprised that you noticed the orchard that is part of the farm," said Mia. "It is way at the other end of the farm. I wondered if it was part of the farm. It has six different fruit trees. They are ready to be picked right now."

"Great we will build that part first," said Tom. "You notice that the doorways to the building are at each end. The one near the drive way we will make the entrance. In front of the building, to the street, is an area that is full of grass. We can make that the parking lot for the guests. At the other end of the building we will set two areas with the checkout registers. Up grating that building will be our largest job. Other than that we will get rid of the house that was on fire where I saved you. That property and the parking lot uses up one third of the farm. We will clear all that and add it to our farming land. We will build our house on the land that is on the other side of the drive way that is across from the grocery store entrance. I think all the farming equipment that we will need is stored in the building that is next to the fruit orchard. That's where we will do our seeding and growing our vegetables."

"That all sounds great," said Mia, "where will we get the money to do all this?"

"I have enough but can I spend it on someone else's farm," said Tom. "Let me find out the value of the farm and I will buy half of the farm."

"Perhaps this is too early to talk about this but the situation makes it necessary," said Mia. "What I am saying is that I am madly in love with you. I feel by the way you look at me and all that you are doing for me that you feel the same way about me."

"You are right," said Tom. "I am crazy about you. I want to spend the rest of my live with you. So let's finish the work we need to do and after we are finish and everything is working fine we needed to talk about our future together."

"All right," said Mia. "You go on and do what you think is necessary. I have several phone numbers about places we could get Fruit and Vegetables when we are out of growing season. I have several places to call and negotiate."

It took Tom over a week to get all the people he needed to up grad the building that was going to be the grocery store. He soon found two young ladies that were out of work who he investigated. They were hired to be the checkout clerks. He next had the land between the grocery store and the road dug out and cemented in as the parking lot. It was wide enough that cars could park on both sides of the lot. The inside of the store was finish in two weeks. He had fruit put in the store from their own farm and vegetables that Mia had purchased from foreign farms. It was only two month after they started that the grocery store was opened to the public. Both Tom and Mia were surprised at the amount of business they got. Things were starting to look good. Tom then removed the house that had been burned and all the parking area there and dug it up as farm land. The last thing he did was Build a home for Mia on the east side of the store across the drive way. Everything was fine except Tom and Mia were unhappy as store managers. They still wanted to be farmers. However, they had no time to do farming work. It was on one very busy day that a fellow came in the manager's office. He walked right up to Mia.

"Hi sis," said the gentleman. "How are you doing?"

"Hi Paul," said Mia. "What a fantastic surprise. What are you doing here?" do you still live in Arizona? I have been trying to contact you for years. I could never find you."

"I had a very special Job," said Paul. "I worked for a company that investigated other companies that were questionable. I moved too much that is why I quit. I got tired of traveling. "My wife almost divorced me. "She was tired of traveling also. She wants to get a real job. You remember Jane. Remember she graduated as a financial adviser. She didn't know if I could get to see you. We thought that you would be in the field. Let me go get her."

"Fine," said Mia. "I will get my husband." Mia found Tom at the back of the store. She explained the surprise she had seeing her brother. They both then went into the main office where they met Jane. They all hugged and enjoyed their company.

"So what are you going to do now?" asked Tom.

"We are going to look for a steady job that requires no traveling. We would love to live up here in Ohio."

"How would you like to work for us?" said Tom hopping to get someone to run the grocery store so that they could go back to running the farm.

"No thank you," said Paul. "I hate farming."

"I was thinking of getting someone to manage the store. Mia and I would like to do all the farming. We hate the store but it is the only choice we have to sell our products."

"You own the store," asked Paul. "I thought it was an independent store. Why do you own it?"

"We just built it," said Mia. "We have a large orchard with six different fruit and a large farm area where we plan on growing several types of vegetables. However we had a problem. We could find no organization or store that would sign a contract with us. We had no other choice but to sell it directly to the public. We also have a department that packages our product for the stores that want to buy our product for their stores."

"So what makes it hard to run along with doing the farming?" asked Jane.

"We remember that our product is available only a short time during the year. The rest of the time you have to buy products to fill the store from other countries."

"I see where that could take a lot of time and work," said Paul. "What job would I do?" asked Paul.

"You would be the store manager and Jane could be your assistant to help you with the store finances. "I want you also to understand that your income will grow with the store profit."

"Wow," said Jane. "Sounds like a very interesting responsibility. What do you think Paul?"

"I would like the challenge," said Paul. "I accept the job."

"Me too," said Jane. Tom then brought them all over the store area. Tom showed them the main office.

I want you to understand that the whole store management is yours. Mia and I will be doing the faming work only," said Tom.

"I understand," said Paul.

It took Paul and Jane a couple of days to settle down in the city. They had to rent a three bedroom apartment to live in. The next Monday they moved into the office and took over the store management. Jane took over the financial management. She soon found ways to improve the stores income. Paul started to contact fruit and vegetable producers in South America. It was about two weeks later that a young teen aged young man walked into the store office.

"How can I help you?" asked Jane who was in the office at that time.

"I understand that a woman named Mia Sater works here," said the young man. "I would like to talk with her." Jane got on the phone and contacted Mia.

"Hi Mia," said Jane. "There is a young man here to see you."

"Send him to my house by the front of the store." Mia then jumped into her car and went to her house. The young man was there waiting for her. Mia got out of the car and walked up to the young man.

"Are you Mia?" asked the young man.

"Yes," said Mia. "What can I do for you? Let's go and sit on the front porch." After they sat down the young man continued.

"My name is Sal Sater. I am a very distant cousin. "I just want to see you to apologize to you for my stupid action. I have not been myself since. I feel so guilty." "What are you talking about?" asked Mia.

"Well, I come from a very poor family," said Sal. "When my great, great, great grandfather passed, I was so hurt and disappointed. I was hoping that he would leave me something. He left everything to you and your brother. I got drunk and tried to blow up your house. I am so sorry."

"So why are you here?" asked Mia. "What do you want me to do?"

"I just wanted to apologize and let you know who did it and let you know that you are safe." Sal then got up to leave.

"Where do you live now?" asked Mia.

"I just lost my parent's house. I couldn't pay the tax since I lost my job. That was when I asked God to help me. I accepted Jesus as my savior, and I expect that God will take care of me. I am his son. I have confessed all my sins, and I trust that God will find me a job and a Place to live."

"I think God has already set out to help you," said Mia. "After all you are a relative. I would like to help you. Have you ever worked on a farm?"

"No, but I have worked peoples yards," said Sal.

"I need someone to go down the vegetable lanes and pull out all the weeds," said Mia.

"That will be a perfect job," said Sal. "This fall I plan on going back to college."

"You're hired," said Mia. It all worked fine.

It was about two years later that Tom and Mia were surprised at the results of their efforts. The grocery store was always full thanks to the good work of Paul. The income had more than doubled. It was during the slow farming time that year that Tom and Mia got married. Tom's parents came from California. There were more than twenty at the wedding. Tom and Mia were the happiest persons in the nation. They married the one they loved with all their hearts and did the farming they loved.

The end

Story Number Five

True Love Never Dies

Trudy got up late this morning and decided to go the hospital for breakfast. She was hoping to get acquainted with one of the other nurses in the hospital. She has worked there for only two weeks and has met a few but no one got close enough to become a personal friend yet. She thought maybe one was having breakfast so that she could join her and become a personal friend. When she got there she found no one she knew. A few minutes later Mark showed up.

"Trudy," said Mark. "Good morning. What are you doing here?"

"I got up late this morning so I came here for breakfast."

"Good to see you," said Mark. "I suspect since you are eating alone you are having the same problem I am having. We have no buddies here. I suppose it will take a little time to be accepted as a coworker." Mark ordered his breakfast and while eating a woman came up to the table.

"Good morning Trudy, said the woman. "Listen, I have a very sick patient, so please don't delay coming to my office. Who is this you are with?"

"Oh, I'm sorry," said Trudy. "Mark, this is Doctor Delane. She is my boss here in the hospital I'm her assistant. And Doc this is Mark Cory. We met in high school and we both went to collage together. We have known each other for a long time. Mark is a Medical assistant here."

"Nice to meet you Mark," said the Doctor. "Please, Trudy, come quickly." She then left.

"You had better go," said Mark. "How about meeting me here for lunch?"

"I'd love that," said Trudy. "I think we should do this every day and every lunch. I think we should have some fiends. It's lonely with only you as a friend."

"I agree with you," said Mark. "I will try hard to get someone interested in us." They met again for lunch the next day.

"Hi Mark," said Trudy, "Did you have anything interesting this far today?"

"Yes said Mark. "I met a very up grade young lady. She is married to one of the male nurses here in the hospital. She is very upbeat and seems like a very happy person. She was very friendly to me."

"Tell them that we are lonely and would like some friends," said Trudy. "See if they need some company. If they say yes invite them over to my house for dinner. I will cook them a fantastic decision making dinner."

"All right," said Mark. "We will see if they would like new friends." It was early that afternoon when Trudy was visiting one of her patient that Mark showed up at the room door.

"Can I speak to you for a minute," said Mark to Trudy. Trudy then walked out into the hall.

"What's up?" said Trudy.

"I ran into the couple that I talked to you about," said Mark. "I asked them if they would like to have dinner with me and my girlfriend. They said they would love to. By the way I told them that you were my girlfriend. I think that we should hold that from now on."

"They are coming tonight?" said Trudy. "I had better take off work early so I can get some shopping done. And yes, you are right. You are my boyfriend. I love you very much except not romantically, but like a brother."

"We don't need to explain that to them," said Mark.

"Right," said Trudy. "I'll see you tonight." She went back to her patient's room. That night the couple that Mark invited showed up five minutes after Mark showed up. When the doorbell rang, Mark answered the door.

"Hi Andy and Rose," said Mark. "Come on in and meet Trudy. Trudy had just walked in.

"Hello coworkers," said Trudy. "I'm Trudy."

"And these are Andy and Rose Calonti," said Mark.

"Come on in," said Trudy, "dinner is almost ready. Come on in and talk with Mark. He will tell you about what we are trying to create." They came into the dining room and they sat down waiting for Trudy to bring dinner.

"What Trudy was talking about," said Mark "is that we are trying to start a Medical club. The reason we would like to have one so that we could have some company. Trudy's family died in an auto accident and my family, when grandma died, they returned to France. So we have absolutely no family or friend. We have only been here two weeks."

"That is fantastic, said Andy, "God is so good. We are in the same situation. We have no relatives or friends in this area. We would love to join your club."

"Well, we are only four since you joined us. We have to find others who have the same problem we have. By the way, you mentioned that God is so good. Are you Christians?"

"We are born-again-Christians," said Andy.

"Wow," said Mark, "God is so good. We are Born-Again-Christians also. Soon Trudy served the food and they began to eat. Just as Trudy sat down the doorbell rang.

"I'll go see who it is," said Mark. A few minutes later Mark showed up with a couple.

"Hi sis," said the man that walked into the dining room with Mark. "Is it someone's birthday?"

"HI Ryan," said Trudy. "What are you doing here in Ohio?"

"I got a job as a teacher at the Akron University," said Ryan.

"Hi Trudy," said Jane braking into the conversation. Good to see you.

"So good to see you too," said Trudy. "Come in and have a dinner with us."

"No I'm sorry," said Ryan. "We have to go and find a place to live."

"Why, you can move in here with me," said Trudy. "Remember when mom and dad died they left the house to you and me. It is your house as well as mine. I live here all alone. I would love to have you two live with me."

"Are we disturbing a party of some kind?" said Ryan.

"We are trying to start a Medical Club," said Trudy. "Come and joined us. You both meet the requirement."

"I am not in any medical profession," said Ryan. "How would we fit in?"

"I think we are going to change the name. We have only been designing this club for a week. We are thinking to call it, the lonely Christian Club. We will probably change it several times before we are done. Come on in and join us."

"We are growing," said Mark. "We are now three families a total of six members."

"What is the goal of the club?" asked Andy.

"It is to bring people who have no relatives or friends in the area, who are also Born-Again-Christians. There are not too many of us." After some getting to know each other they decided to meet again every Friday. During the next week they did not add any one new. On Wednesday, the next week, Mark went to work and as he entered his floor he saw a beautiful woman sitting on one of the benches. Mark was so taken with her that he lost control and standing there he spoke.

"Hi" is all that he said.

"Hi" she said, looking as disturbed as he was. They both looked at each other but neither spoke a word for a few minutes. Then Mark getting control back spoke.

"Who are you," asked Mark, "and what are you doing here?"

"I'm Emily and I had a very bad chest pain. I'm here for a checkup."

"I am Mark and I'm a medical assistant. I'm sorry but I lost control." He then sat down beside her. I think I will only have one chance to explain it to you."

"Please explain," said Emily.

"I think I am attracted to you with a feeling that I have never felt before. You gave me butterflied in my stomach that I never felt before. I think it was something like love at first sight. I would like to get to know you better."

"I am thrilled to hear that," said Emily. "I felt the same way on the minute I laid eyes on you. I would love to get to know you better. Are you free this Friday?"

"I have a special project that I am working on," said Mark. "What do you have in mind?"

"I am a high school teacher," said Emily. "They are having a special Graduation party. I hate to go alone."

"I have a special project," said Mark. Mark then explained all that he and Trudy were trying to create.

"That is great," said Emily. "I also am alone here and I am also a Born-Again-Christian. I will fit in perfectly."

"Well I think your Friday requirement is greater than mine," said Mark. "So what time do you want me to pick you up?" After she gave him the information he gently hugged her and left.

Over the next two weeks Ryan noticed that Mark was always late for a meeting and that some days he got home after dinner. One day he turned to Trudy and asked her.

"What is Mark up too?" asked Ryan. "He has been coming home late several days of the week, and last week he missed the Club meeting."

"He is trying to get more people to join our club," said Trudy. She suspected something like Ryan did but she wanted happiness for Mark. She loved him very much but not romantically. She loved him more like a brother. However Ryan did not even suspect it. Ryan then decided to follow Mark when he left the house in the afternoon. He kept far enough so that Mark was not aware of it. Several days Mark went to some stores and one time to the hospital. Ryan was ready to give up but one day Mark drove to an apartment building. Sure enough a beautiful young lady came out and got into Marks car, and they drove off. Ryan followed them to see where they were going.

When he realized that they were going to the Corelli restaurant that had music and dancing, Ryan turned around and went home. The next Monday, early in the morning, Ryan drove to the apartment where Emily lives, and waited to see if she came out. He decided that if he had to wait all day that he would. He wanted to keep his sister from having a heart break. It was only seven o'clock that Emily came out of the apartment and walked to her car. He drove up to her and yelled out his window.

"Hi Miss, My name is Ryan Dale. Mark had sent me to pick you up."

"Where is he?" asked Emily. "He was to meet me here at seven."

"He is where I am supposed to take you. Please get into my car," said Ryan and I will explain everything to you on the way there. I have somewhere I need to go after I drop you of, so please hurry."

"Emily first looked into the car. She was not sure if she should go with him. However, after seeing his gentle smile she trusted him and entered his car. Ryan then took off.

"Who are you again," asked Emily?"

"Well has Mark told you about the club we are starting to create?" asked Ryan.

"Yes he was working with his old friend named Trudy and another couple who I don't remember their name."

"Well you know about Trudy," said Ryan, "well Trudy is my sister."

"So you think I am stealing her boyfriend," said Emily."

"Are you stealing her boyfriend?" asked Ryan.

"He told me that he loves her with all his heart, but not romantically. He loves her like a sister. I was worried about the same thing so I called her. She told me the same thing."

"Well a small test will not hurt," said Ryan.

"What small test?" asked Emily?

"Just have patience," said Ryan. They drove for about two hours. On the way they talked about their past lives. He told her about his life as a Collage Professor and she told him about her High School Teachers life. Ryan suddenly turned onto to a field and drove around the mountain about a mile away until he came to a small cottage off of the lake that was there.

"Where are we?" asked Emily.

"We are at a very nice place to be during our vacation from teaching," said Ryan. "We can relax and spend some time siting by the lake. The cabin is mine and the land all around it is mine."

"This is a very beautiful place," said Emily. "How long are we going to stay here?"

"As long as we have to," said Ryan. "I will come back and forth every day to see that you are alright. You will stay here enjoying the land until I find out what is going on."

"What is going on?" said Emily "is that you don't understand how Mark and I feel about each other. I love Mark with all of my heart, And Mark loves me with all of his heart. You will see. He will fight for me."

"Then you will not be here very long," said Ryan. Ryan then grabbed Emily's purse. He looked inside and removed her Cell Phone. "You will not need this"

"Is there a place near here?" said Emily, where I could get something to eat?

"Two days ago," said Ryan, "when I decided for you to disappear for a while I perched about two week of fantastic food. Most of it is in the freezer and the rest is in the refrigerator. I got the best of everything. Please enjoy your stay here. As for a restaurant or any other building the nearest is about a hundred miles away. So please do not try to walk any were. Trust me on that." Ryan then took her inside and showed her the food. They ate a very enjoyable breakfast. After breakfast they sat by the water front and discussed how nice and quite the place was. At about twelve Ryan decided he had better leave. He had two hours to drive home. He told her he would see her tomorrow and left. Ryan went back twice in the next weeks to see if Emily was OK. He was surprised that she was always very friendly. He asked her once about her feelings.

"I thought that you would be very angry with me," said Ryan.

"Why should I be angry," said Emily. "I'm in a nice summer camp. I get a free meal every day and it's always a fantastic meal."

It was about a week later that Ryan noticed the difference in Mark. Mark seemed so quit and unfriendly

"What is the problem with Mark?" Ryan asked Trudy.

"He is so sad because he lost his girlfriend," said Trudy. "He has not seen her in over a week and she doesn't answer her phone."

"I though her being missing would bring you and Mark together."

"Ryan dearest," said Trudy. "Are you losing your mind? I have told you several times that I love Mark with all my heart but not romantically. I love him like a brother. I was so happy that he met Emily."

"Where is he?" asked Ryan.

"He went in to bed," said Trudy. "He said he couldn't live without Emily.

"What an idiot I am," said Ryan running to Mark's bedroom. He found Mark in bed crying.

"Mark, get up," said Ryan. "We have somewhere to go right now."

"I am not going anywhere," said Mark.

"Don't you want to see Emily?" Mark jump out of bed immediately.

"Where is she?" said Mark. "Did you find her? Is she alright?

"She is taking her summer break," said Ryan. "That is where we are going. Let me call my wife." He got his phone and called his wife. "Jane, get ready for we are going to have a summer break this week. I'll pick you up in a few minutes." Jane knew what Ryan was up to. She knew that she could not argue with him. However she also wanted to spend some time at their cottage in central Ohio. She was sure to be ready. Mark jumped out of the bed and had his shirt and shoes on in a minute. They went and picked up Jane and two hours later they pulled into their summer camp. On the way Ryan explained what he had done and why. Mark forgave him. Emily was sitting by the lake and seeing the car got up and ran to the car. Mark jump out first and hugged Emily. After many romantic kisses Mark pulled his head back.

"I thought that I had lost you," said Mark. "After they all hugged they went inside and got chairs to sit by the lake all together.

"How long are we going to stay here," asked Emily?"

"We have to be back next Friday," said Ryan.

"We are having a Club ball with a band and dinner. We have to be there."

"We must come back here sometime later," said Emily."

The four of them enjoyed the next days with great joy. It was Friday afternoon that Mark got a phone call.

"Hello," said Mark. "Who is this?"

"This is Trudy," she answered. "Where have you been? I have been trying to contact you all week."

"I'm sorry," said Mark. "I left my phone in the bedroom. We are enjoying our vacation."

"Don't you remember," said Trudy. "This is Friday. We are having our first Ball today. Can you be here by five today?"

"We are leaving right now," said Mark. He then turned to the women. "Get ready, I forgot all about it. We are having the first Ball of our club. We have to be there. It starts at five. It is three now, so we will get there just in time." They all got ready as quickly as they could and soon were in the car on the way home. As luck would have it there was a very bad accident on the road home. A large truck with many supplies it cared spread all over the rood. There was no way they could get around it. There was a mountain on one side and a deep hill on the other side. They were held up for more than an hour. They got to the Ball at a quarter to seven. The band was playing good dance music and many people were dancing.

"You're late," said Trudy as she lifted up her hand and showed them her engagement ring. "Larry asked me to marry him. I said yes."

"Congratulation," said Mark, "we were held up by a large accident."

"Well you are here which is important. We now have about six couples. That is me and Larry, You and Emily, Ryan and Jane, Andy and Rose and two other couples that you will meet soon. There is so much love in this room that I think I will change out clubs name to, The Love Nest."

The End

Story Number Six

Unpredictable Life Occurrences

Antony was on the Tread Mill as usual his morning. However he had never felt this happy. First of all from the joy he felt last night when his family celebrated his eightieth Birthday. And secondly that he could still be on the Tread Mill. He so enjoyed spending time with his family and friends. His wife Annie was still asleep. She was pretty tired from last night's celebration. She was seventy four and was going to be seventy five in two months. She was as active as Antony was. However she liked to sleep in late every day. Usually Antony got up at seven and went and spent a half hour on the Tread Mill. He then would go down to his office and study the Bible for a half hour. At about nine he would go up and make breakfast for them both. They had a set plan. On Monday they had Mother's Oats, on Tuesday they had Waffles, on Wednesday they had scrambles ages, on Thursday they had Farina, On Friday they had Mother's Oats again and on Saturday they had Scramble eggs again. On Sunday they skipped breakfast. This day was Wednesday and at about nine Anthony went up to make some scrambled eggs. When the eggs were done he walk to the staircase and yelled up to his wife.

Annie sweetheart," he yelled. "Breakfast is ready."

"I'm coming," Annie yelled down. A few minutes later she came down.

"How do you feel this morning sweet heart?" said Antony. "I'm surprised you are up after the time we had yesterday." He then hugged her and kissed her.

"I'm fine," said Annie. "I see you have the eggs ready. How about a piece of your birthday cake as desert I don't see it out here."

"It is in on the table in the dining room," said Anthony, "I'll get it. There isn't that much left." They sat down and ate their breakfast. After they finish Anthony got up.

"Listen Tony," said Annie, "I have a ton of work to do. I have to clean up all that is left of yesterday and I have a lot to do upstairs. Why don't you got back to writing you novel?" "Can you use my help," asked Antony, "with any of the work that needs to be done?"

"I'll call you if I need your help," said Annie.

"All right," said Antony. He left and went into his office that was off the family room on the bottom floor.

On the week end they recovered and were back to normal. They went to Church on Sunday looking forward to Annie birthday a couple of months away.

The following two weeks went as they normally went. It was soon the fourth of July. The city had a very exciting feast on the fourth of July. They had all the city businesses join in a city parade. Antony and Annie used to drive to a business that closed on festival day. They parked in their parking lot. They each would take a folding chair down to the street and siting on the curb watched the parade march by. That was about five years ago. During the last five years they only watched the fireworks from their front porch. The city hall was on the next street west of Antony's house. Their parking lot was behind the houses across the street from Antony's house. That is where the fireworks are fired from. It was always after the parade was ended. It was always around ten o'clock. Antony and his family and friends sat on Antony's front porch. The fireworks were seen come up from behind the house across the street. That evening around five thirty, Dan showed up.

"Hi dad, hi mom," said Dan as he shock his dad's hand and hugged his mom. "What's for dinner?"

"We are having your favorite Pasta and fagiuolo." said Annie." It is ready, but we are waiting for your sister. Five minutes later Terry showed up.

"Hi mom, dad," said Terry. "I almost didn't come. I had a stomach ache. But just a few minutes ago I went to the bathroom and now I feel better. But I have to watch what I am eating. After they all ate they got some folding chair and went and sat in the front porch. It was still too early so they just sat there make small talk about their latest experiences in their lives. It was about five minutes to ten when a car pulled into the drive way. A man and a woman got out of the car and walked to the front porch.

"Hi Harry and Sara," said Anthony. "I wasn't sure you were coming. Welcome. Take a folding chair and joined us. Anthony then turned to his kids.

"Do you remember Harry and Sara?"

"Yes," said Dan. "They were our neighbors in Garfield Heights when we lived there. They all saluted each other and they sat down. They barely got talking about their current lives when the fire Works started. About ninety percent of the fireworks were well above the houses across the street. A few you can just hear them going off. It was extremely enjoyable. Soon it was midnight. The fireworks gave its last great explosive notice and ceased the fire Works. The six on the front porch discussed a few past experiences and then one by one said good bye and left. No one of the gests came into the house. They all walked to their car and left. Anthony and Annie were soon in bed happy to have enjoyed the holiday.

The next two weeks were very joyful days for Anthony and Annie. Their love for each other seemed to grow every day. It was on the fifteenth of the month of July that things changed. It was six in the morning one day while they were still in bed that Annie noticed that Antony was moaning and trying to sit up in bed.

"Tony honey, are you all right," she asked?"

"I can't," he started but couldn't finish "I'm dizzy." He continued having a very hard time to speak. "I can't breathe," he finally got out. With a big attempt to breathe he passed out. Annie reach for the phone with was on the table besides the bed. She dialed 119. She put on a dress and was putting on her shoes when the ambulance came. One of the larger men picked up Anthony and brought him to the rear of the ambulance. Annie closed the door and went up to the man driving the ambulance.

"Can I come with you?" she asked.

"Get in the front seat," said one of the two men that were with the ambulance. Annie got into the front seat. They soon were on their way.

"What is going on in the rear of the Ambulance?" asked Annie hearing some activity in the rear.

"Ralf is giving him oxygen," said the driver. "He is also giving him chest compressions to try and get his heart working. Ralf is a nurse. He will do his best to keep the man alive until we get to the hospital."

"What hospital are we going to?" asked Annie.

"We are going to Akron General," said the driver. "It seemed to Annie that the trip took all morning. They final reached the hospital and Annie was lead to the waiting room. A nurse came in and had Annie fill in a sheet with all the information on Antony. Mainly they wanted to know his name, his age, and his weight. There were a few other questions that were not as important. It was two hours later that another nurse walked in to the waiting room.

"Can you tell me how my husband is doing?" asked Annie. They are performing a dozen of tests on him. Currently I think he is in the x-ray room. They are going to check his whole chest."

"Thank you," said Annie feel relieved. She figured that he was still alive if they are doing all these tests on him. It was after twelve when a doctor walked into the Waiting room.

"Are you Mrs. Gusto?" asked the doctor.

"Yes said," Annie.

"I am Doctor Royston. I am in charge of helping your husband."

"Hello doctor," said Annie. "How is he doing?"

"He is recovering," said the doctor. "The problem he got was because the heart was pressed with water on each side. What I am saying is the area that the heart is in was full of water. This is a common problem. We are not sure why this happens. One theory is that the body has gathered to much salt. Somehow the salt causes water to get into the heart area and the lung area. Our main effort is to find why it gets into the heart and the lungs area. Your husband had water in his lungs also. We have sucked out the water from his heart area. We are not yet sure that the body will not fill it up again. We are also testing the other parts of his body. This problem can affect other areas of the body. We are doing a thorough check of his body. The problem we have is that we are not sure we have turned off what started it. We will let you know when we finish for today and put him in a private hospital room. When we do that we will let you go there and be with him. Until then be patient."

"Doctor," said Annie. "Is it OK for me to call my children and have them come here?"

"Yes but they will not probably be able to see him today. Tell them to try to plan a time after a couple of days so they can at least talk with him. Annie called her daughter Terry and related all that was happening. Terry came anyway just to keep her mother company. It was about four thirty in the afternoon when a nurse came and got Annie and Terry and took them to the private room Antony was brought to. They found Anthony in bed with about six things attached to him. At the end of each was a little monitor. Just as the nurse left the doctor came in

"Hi doc," said Annie. "What can you tell me about my husband and these devices that are attached to my husband?"

"I think he will recover a little at a time," said the doctor. "The things you see attached to him, are instruments to show us how he is doing. They are vital sign monitors. They show us his vital signs like his temperature, his heart rate, his blood pressure and other signs that tell us how his body is recovering. That one tells us how his heart is doing. That is the most important one." said the doctor as he pointed to one of the devices. You should watch them all and tell the nurse if any one goes down instead of up. As you can see all his vital signs are below average. We will have to watch them to make sure he doesn't go back to the way he was. We are keeping him under sedation. We will let him wake if the signs tomorrow are where we hope they will be." The doctor then left. A nurse did come in every fifteen minutes to check up on him. Annie found a soft chair to sit in. she planned on using it all night long. She had no plans on going home that evening. It was about seven when Terry decided to go home.

"Tell your brother to wait a couple of days before he comes to visit him. Give your dad some time to recover." A few minutes after she left, a nurse brought Annie a dinner. Annie didn't eat it all. It was about eleven o'clock that evening when Annie fell asleep. She woke up about eight o'clock in the morning. It was the sound of a nurse working in the room. The first things she checked where Antony's vital signs. She was exactingly happy to see that most looked like they had risen to near normal conditions. His temperature was normal, his blood pressure was one hundred ten over sixty and his hear seemed to be beating well.

"I see that my husband is much better," said Annie to the nurse who was writing down what she saw.

"When I show these vital sign numbers to the doctor he will order me to wake him up," said the nurse. She was gone about half an hour when she returned.

"Did the doctor O.K. to waking him up," asked Annie, wanting to speak with Antony so badly.

"Yes," said the nurse. "That is what I am doing right now." She put a needle on Antony's arm and injected him with a drug to wake him up. "It will take a few minutes for him to wake. Have patients." She then left. It was about ten minutes later when Antony woke up. He moaned for a minutes and then opened his eyes. Seeing Annie he began to speak.

"Where am I?" was his first question. "What am I doing here?"

"You had a heart attack," said Annie, happy to see that he was recovery.

"I remember," said Antony thinking back a little. "I was in bed and had a very dizzy feeling and found it hard to bread. What did they do? Did they fix my problem?" Annie then explained to Antony all that the doctor had told her.

"I have to stop eating salt?" asked Antony.

"Don't you understand," said Annie. "Salt gathers water and water was your problem."

"What else do I have to do?" asked Antony.

"Wait until the doctor comes to see you," said Annie. The rest of the morning they spent the time on small talk. At twelve o'clock a nurse brought Antony lunch. It was a bowl of Mother's oats and two toasted slices of bread. Antony said a prayer and started to eat.

"Wow," said Antony. "It feels like I am eating mud. Food doesn't taste good without salt. How long do I have to eat without salt?"

"We can ask the doctor when he comes this afternoon," said Annie. Antony ate the complete bowl of food. It was evident that he didn't like it. At about five that evening he was given dinner. The results were the same. Antony didn't like the taste of the food he had received. That afternoon the Doctor came to check on Antony.

"Doctor," said Antony as soon as the doctor walked in. "How long do I have to eat without salt?"

"You are just recovering," said the doctor. "We are more interested in what caused your problem and to watch that it doesn't return. If you can't eat the food without salt, put some spice in it like Paprika or better yet add some Dash. Dash is salt free. That will give your food some taste. Anyway you are aloud about six hundred mg. of salt per meal" the doctor did a complete exam of Antony and left. Anthony felt like he had completely recovered. The nurse did allow Anthony to walk to the bathroom. That evening and the next day went the same as the second day. On the third day Antony received company. First his son Dan came to visit him. About an hour later Ben his neighbor and his wife Donna came to visit him. Anthony was so happy to see his son and friends. It was a very joyful day. After they all left Annie turned to her husband.

"You know sweet heart," said Annie. "I think you are back to yourself. The doctors only want to keep you here to make sure your problem doesn't return. I don't know how long they want to keep you. What I am trying to say is that it is no longer necessary for me to stay here over night. First I need some rest and good food and secondly I have so much I left that need to be done at home. So if you don't mind I will go home at dinner time and I will come back tomorrow."

"I was going to recommend it at dinner time," said Antony. "I can see how tired you are. I felt bad seeing that you had to sleeping in that chair all night. Please honey, go home and come back tomorrow. Come after lunch."

"I'll come when I get some of the house work done." Soon it was dinner time. Annie kissed Antony and left for home. This went on for eight days. It was on the morning of the eight day that the doctor came into Antony's room.

"Hi Mr. Gusto," said the doctor. "How are you feeling today?"

"I am feeling great," said Antony. "How is your investigation of my present condition coming?"

"I think it is fine," said the doctor. "Are you ready to go home?"

"I have been ready for six days," said Antony. "But I understand that you wanted to make sure that my problem wasn't coming back."

"We are pretty sure that you are going to be fine," said the doctor. "However we have a couple of conditions that you have to follow. First you must keep you salt down as low as possible. Check your food before you eat it. Most foods have a lot of salt in it. It is put into the food to keep it from spoiling. You must keep your salt in each meal down below six hundred mgs per meal. Remember we went over this about five days ago. I think that your wife wrote it all down in her pad that she had in her purse." Just then Annie walked in.

"Hi doc, Tony," said Annie as she walked. What is going on?" The doctor went over everything again feeling that Annie will take care of her husband.

"There is one last thing," said the doctor as he got up to leave. "I recommend that you take a bottle of Synobot at every meal. It will give you strength and health. It has twenty seven vitamins and mineral in it. It will help you get back to normal. The doctor then said good bye and left. Annie helped Antony dress with the cloths she brought six days ago believing he would come home sooner. It was ten o'clock when they go home. Annie quickly ordered the Synobot. Then she started to make Antony his favorite lunch. For the next two days Antony's health slowly improved. When he started to take the Synobot drug he expected to improve faster. However, he began to get worse. What was worse he started to get heavy mucous in his throat. He found that he wasn't hungry and that when he ate he got heavy coughing. He would cough until he caught up a heavy mucous that looked like the white of an egg. It was a week later when he tried to get up in the morning that he couldn't get out of bed. His wife helped him but when he tried to walk he fell, fortunately the bed was there and he fell into the bed. Annie became worried so she called the doctor's office. She told the nurse the problem Antony was having. The doctor came on the phone.

"Hi" said the doctor. "I told you that it would take some time for your husband to get back to normal. It will take about a month for his problem to go away. Have patience." With that he hung up. She then went up to her husband.

"Honey sweet heart," said Annie. "I spoke to the doctor and he said it will take about a month for you to get back to normal."

"Yes," said Anthony, "If I live that long."

I'll pray for you," said Annie. "You have to pray also."

"I have prayed five times a day," said Antony. "I know that God has never let us down. I believe he has a good reason to let this happen to me. Perhaps he is testing me. I have not lost faith in him. I would love to go to heaven but I tell God that I don't want to leave you and the children." Three more days went by. Antony only got worse He could hardly eat. He was losing weight every day. Final he could hardly get out of bed. She got a little upset.

"Dear Lord," said Annie. "We don't just believe in you, we know you are there. Please don't test us anymore. You promised in the bible that you would never let us get sicker then we could handle. We are getting to that point." The next day she got a call from the nurse.

"HI Annie," said the nurse. I am calling to see how your husband is doing."

"He is at the point that he can't eat and is losing weight. The problem is that the mucous and the constant coughing have made him sicker."

"That doesn't sound like the problem he had. The mucous is caused by eating something that creates the mucous and blocks the throat. Is he eating anything he hasn't eaten before?"

"Not that I know of," said Annie. The only thing that he is eating is the Synobot the doctor told him he had to eat to get his health up. Evidently it isn't working.

"You know," said the nurse, "Sometimes the good things cause the opposite. There may be something it the drug that he is allergic to. I would suggest that you take him off of the Synobot for a couple of days and see if it makes a difference." Annie though that it was a good idea. She remembered that her husband was almost back to normal for two day and got bad when he started to take the drug. The next morning she took the drug away from Antony. She explained to him what she and the nurse had discussed.

"You know said Antony. "We should have thought of that. I was good until I started to take that drug. Let's stop taking it."

"Hope this is God's answer to our prayers," said Annie. "God has never let us down."

"We will see tomorrow if this is the answer," said Antony. "I think we should stick to soup and liquids for today"

"As you wish," said Annie. That night Antony went to bed early. The next morning he woke up feeling so much better. Every hour of that day Antony got closer to the normal being he used to be. After diner he felt that he was back to normal.

"Honey," said Antony. "I feel like I am back to what I was before I got sick. After you wash the dishes come on down to the family room and we will watch a movie." He then went down to the family room, sat on the couch and waited for Annie. After Annie cleaned up the kitchen she went down to the family room and sat next to Antony. She raped her arms around him and said,

"Tony honey, Welcome home."

The End

Story Number Seven

The Bad times can end in good times.

Tom sat in his home office considering what he should do next. Two months ago he had left collage with a Management Degree. He has tried for employment in New York. He loved New York. He was born there and has so far spent his life there. Just as he sat there he received a call. It was from the last business he visited for a job.

"Mr. Ladosi," said the man.

"Yes this is he," said Tom.

"I'm sorry to inform you," said the man on the phone, "that we do not have an opening for you. We considered you for an assistant management job but our manager said he didn't need an assistant. Sorry. Bye," he then hung up. Tom realized that his next consideration had to be out of state. He thought of his parents. They left six months ago to return to Italy where they were born. They hated New York. They said that it was very unfriendly. They said that all store clerks, salesmen and owners were all are very cold people. No one seemed eager to help you. Tom knew that it was true, but it was understandable with a large city that was so crowded and busy. Tom then went to a clothing store to purchase some shirts. All the shirts that he had were very old. If he was going out of town he wanted to look good. He entered a clothing store and found the area where the shirts were. It happened that at that time there were no other byers there. The Cash register clerk and the sales man were over in the corner of the store talking to each other. Neither of the two was interested in what Tom wanted. Neither came to help Tom find what he wanted. Tom finally found a couple of shirts he liked then he walked to the register. One of the salesmen came to the register and without a word sold the shirts to Tom. Tom realized that this was what he had encounter in New York since he was able to go there. It was the standard life in New York. Tom thought about it because he remembered that this was one of the things his parents complained about. Tom then went to the City Employment office. Tom walked up to the front office where a young lady was siting.

"I would like you to find a job for me," said Tom.

"What is your educational position?"

"I am a college graduate and I graduated as a business manager," said Tom.

"How far would you like to travel on your job?" asked the young lady.

"I would like to stay as close to New York as possible," said Tom. The young lady got on her computer and checked all the companies that were hiring. After about ten minutes she turned to Tom.

"I'm sorry," said the young lady, "the closest place that is hiring is in Akron Ohio. The Company is Goodyear Aerospace. They are looking for a Financial Manager."

"I guess if that is the closet," said Tom, "I have no other choice. Can you contact them and tell them that I am interested." The young lady got on her computer and then makes a telephone call.

"I gave them your name and told them all that you told me. They are very interested. You will have to go there next Monday. If you are hired you could start the next Monday."

"Well thank you so much," said Tom and left for home. Today was Tuesday and Tom decided to go there early and look around to where he might have to live. At home he started to pack a suitcase with what he thought he would need for that first week. If he got the job he could come home on the week end and take care of everything else. The next day Tom got into his car at eight in the morning and was on the road to Ohio.

On the way Tom stopped at a restaurant for lunch. After lunch he returned to the road and reached the Akron area at round six in the afternoon. When he got off the freeway the road he was on was the one that lead to the Fairlawn Mall. He noticed that across from the mall was a Hotel. The first thing he did is go to the hotel for a room. He was very impressed by the way the clerks treated him.

"Good morning sir," said the clerk as Tom walked in. "How can I help you?"

"I would like a room," said Tom.

"Any particular place you would like especially the view from you window."

"I don't know," said Tom being shocked by the question. He had never been asked a question, at all in New York, anywhere especially in a hotel. "Can you give me a room that looks out at the mall?"

"Let's see," said the clerk checking her computer. "We have one on the third floor. Will that be alright?"

"Yes thank you." Tom was surprised with his response. He didn't remember ever saying thank you to anyone. After he signed in and the clerk gave him the key to his room Tom took his suitcase and went to the room. He was also impressed with the room. It was larger than he expected. He sat down and made a list of what he wanted to see if he was hired. After settling in he went back to his car. First he drove down the main street to see what he could find that was written in his list. The first thing he saw not far from the hotel was an Auto rental shop.

"He stopped there and walked in to the front desk.

"How can I help you?" said the man at the desk. Tom had to get used to this service that he never got in New York.

"I need to rent a truck. Can I do that here?"

"What do you need the truck for?" asked the man. "That will determine the size you will need."

"I live in New York," said Tom. "I am in the process of getting a job here and I want to sell my home in New York and move here. So I need a large truck to carry the furniture I want to bring here."

"Well that will mean that you will need a closed haling truck. We can get one for you," said the man. "How soon will you need it?And how long will you need it?"

"I am not sure I will get the job," said Tom. "I will get back to you as soon as I am sure I got the job. I think I will need it for about two or three days. How soon would it take you to get the truck?"

"It will take a few days maybe a week," said the man. "So let me know as soon as you are sure of your job."

"See you soon," said Tom and left. Well, he thought, he had his most important need available. He next needed to have a place to live where he could place his furniture. He remembered seeing a real estate company across from the Mall. He went there next.

"Hi sir," said a young woman as Tom entered the door. Tom found it hard in getting used to the friendly and quick service by the Ohio sales people. For that matter, all the people in Ohio seem to be that way.

"Hi," said Tom. "I would like to know what is available to rent and to buy."

"Tell me about you situation so that I can determent what would be best for you," said the young lady. "By the way my name is Mary. "I will be glad to help you find what you need."

"Well I come from New York. I think I have a job here. I will not know for sure until Monday. I am alone and am single. I need a small apartment to rent or a small ranch house to buy."

"Well I will be available to you any time. After you are sure of your job come back and I will show you all the available small Apartments and small ranch houses," said Mary. "I will search while you are gone. Come back Monday after your meeting and I will have it ready for you."

"I will see you Monday afternoon," said Tom and left. That weekend Tom relaxed and prayed to the lord that he will get the job. He realized that after spending the time he did he didn't want to return to New York. He had become spoiled in Ohio.

Monday morning he arrived at the Good Year plant at a quarter to eight. His meeting was schedule for eight o'clock. As he walked in the door a young woman was walking by who stopped to talk with Tom

"Are you Mr. Ladosi? She asked.

"Yes that is me," answered Tom.

"Well good morning," said the young lady. "You are a little early. However I think that Mrs. Radcliffe is in her office. Follow me please." When they got to the office the young lady stuck her head it the door and spoke.

"Mrs. Radcliffe," said the young lady, "the young man you were meeting with is here."

"Please come in and have a seat," said Mrs. Radcliffe. "Thank you Cathy." She said to the young lady that brought Tom to her office. "Mr. Ladosi, before we talk about your job and your salary I would like to ask you some simple questions."

"Of course," said Tom, "and please call me Tom."

"All right Tom," said Mrs. Radcliffe. "And you can call me Martha. She then started to ask Tom some very technical questions. Tom was surprised that she was so intelligent. He answered all her question. It took about a half hour to answer all her questions. "I am very impressed with your knowledge," said Martha. So let's talk about your job. I need an assistant to help me with the job I have. I need a Financial Manager. I think you will be good at the job. The cost that the president approved is all that I can offer you. She then told Tom what the job would offer him. It was almost fifty present more than he had expected. Not to let her know how well he liked the salary, he said his acceptance like he had to think about it.

"Well I can accept that at least until I prove very valuable to you."

"Good, then you are hired," said Martha. "When can you start? What do you have to do before you can start?"

"First I have to rent a large truck. Next I have to find a place to live here in Ohio. Then I must go to New York to pick up all the furniture I want to keep and then sell my house in New York."

"Sound like you are going to have a very busy week or more," said Martha. "I understand your position. Go and do what it takes to move here. By the way, I would like to make a recommendation to you if you don't mind."

"I will appreciate any recommendation you can give and thank you for considering my problems."

"I recommend that you buy a small ranch house here in Fairlawn instead of renting. The monthly payment for a house if you can afford the down payment is much less than the monthly renting cost and you will get a house, where renting you get nothing. I recommend you buy in Fairlawn; first the taxes and cost are less than anywhere else in Ohio."

"Thank you," said Tom. "I will consider all that you have told me. Anyway I will try to get back as soon as I can."

"Take your time," said Martha. "Your job will be here waiting for you. Don't do a quick job that you will regret later. Do a complete job. I would not want you to have to leave after you have started to work."

"I will do my best," said Tom. "Is it alright if I leave now?"

"Yes," said Martha, "and God be with you."

"Thank you and goodbye for now." Tom then left and went directly to the car rental. He went directly to the fellow he had talked with before.

"Hi," said Tom. "I did get the job, so I need the large truck we talked about."

"Sit down and I will see what I can get right now," said the man. Tom walked across from the front desk and sat at one of the chairs. The man got on the phone. Tom could not hear what was going on but a few minutes later the man hung up and waved to Tom. Tom got up and walked the front desk.

"The truck will be her tomorrow afternoon," said the man. I will call you when it gets here."

"Thank you so much," said Tom and left. He went directly to the Real Estate office. He walked in and walked up to Mary

"Hi Mary," said Tom. "I got the job. I now need a place to put my furniture when I bring it from New York.

"Well said Mary. "I have picked out two rentals and two ranch homes.

"Forget the rentals," said Tom. "I decided to buy and I would like it in Fairlawn."

"So you have made up your mind," said Mary. "I will show you the two that are available in Fairlawn. Although I recommend one, it is larger than you need and a little more expensive but you have to see it. It is fantastic. I love it. I would love to buy it for myself."

Well," said Tom, "let's go see it." Mary got her purse and a few papers and they left in her car. It was only a block away. It was on Bancroft Road. Tom was impressed when he saw the outside of the house. It had an attached garage as Tom preferred but the garage door was in front facing the street. Tom liked it better if the garage door was in the rear of the garage. He didn't like the idea that if he left the garage doors open people could see everything he had in the garage.

"There will be more traffic then you like going down this road, but you don't have kids to worry about," said Mary as the pulled into a driveway. Mary pulled in the driveway and got out of the car. Tom followed her to the front door. They walked into a large entrance way hall. It had a door on the right which he found was a bathroom. It had a doorway on the left which went into the front room, and following the left doorway was the guest closet. At the end of the hallway was a doorway which leads into a large Family room. Mary led Tom into the family room.

"On your left as you can see is the kitchen," said Mary starting to describe the house. The kitchen and the family room were divided by a small railing. On the other side of the railing you could see the kitchen table.

"That is a very large kitchen," said Tom. "I can see a built in grill there across from the table. That is fantastic."

"Look over here," said Mary as they walked up to the kitchen. "You have these cabinets between the eating aria and the cooking aria. On the other side is the refrigerator and across from the refrigerator is the stove, and above the stove is the Microwave. They are all built in." Tom could see that the doorway on the left side of the kitchen was the Living room. On the right of the living room door was a built in closet. As you turn to the right was the door way to the dining room. Mary led Tom into the dining room. There were two short walls that divided the living room from the dining room. On the other side of the short wall in between the living room hidden by the small was the hall way opening to the bed room area it was hidden so that one sitting in the living room would not see the opening that led to the bed rooms.

"This is a very beautiful and livable house," said Tom

"Do you want to go down the hall," said Mary, "to see the three bedrooms and the two bathrooms down there?"

"They have two bathrooms by the bedrooms?" asked Tom looking surprised.

"One of the bathrooms is off of the Main Bedroom. The other is off the hallway for the people in the other two bedrooms. Let's go in and I'll show them to you," said Mary

"No," said Tom, "that will not be necessary. I am sold. I want to buy this house. What is the best price you have for it?"

"Let's go back to my office," said Mary. "I think I can contact the owner. We can then negotiate the price. I think he want to sell as soon as possible. He has to move to another state for his job." They got back to the office and Mary turned to Tom. "The price they are asking is three hundred and fifty thousand. We can offer less and then see how much they are willing settle for. What do you think we should offer first?"

"Think if they refuse to take less I will pay the asking price," said Tom. "The price I will get from selling my New York house will more then cover the asking price. So in the negotiations I don't want to lose the purchase."

"I will remember that," said Mary. She said then that she will ask two hundred seventy five thousand. Let see what he will come back with." She then dialed the number of the owner. It was his Cell Phone and he answered right away seeing who was calling him.

Mary told him that she had a buyer who was interested in buying his house, but he could only come up with two hundred seventy five thousand. They talked back and forth for several minutes. Tom lost their conversation. However, When Mary hanged up she turned to Tom.

"He is willing to go for three hundred thousand cleared. Any other costs, like my charge for my effort, State taxes and any other will be your deal. I told him that you accepted his price. He is come right over and he will bring all the documents we will need." About an hour later, the fellow showed up.

"Hi Jason," said Mary. "I want you to meet Tom Ladosi. He is the one who wants to buy your house. Tom, this is Jason York the owner of the house. She then sat down around Mary's desk and she filled out all the papers required for the sale.

"I hope you understand Jason," said Mary, "that Tom can only give you fifty thousand as a down payment. Then he is going to New York to sell his house there. What I am saying is that after he sell's his house and he comes back here, he will give you the rest of the money. Is that acceptable to you?"

"That is fine," said Jason. "I don't think that it would take more than a month for us to settle the sale."

"It shouldn't take that long," said Tom. After all the papers were signed, they said good bye and Tom left and went to the car rental place. The truck had just gotten there.

"Hi said the sales man. I was just ready to call you to tell you that the truck is ready. You came just in time. He then gave Tom the keys to the truck and Tom drove it to his new home. He left his car there at the rental shop. He slept on the floor with a small blanket he kept in the back seat of his car. Fortunately he took the blanket when he picked up the truck. At six in the morning Tom got up and got into the truck and headed for New York. He didn't eat until he got to New York.

Tom got to New York, to his house, about six in the afternoon. The first place he went was in his kitchen. He quickly took out of the refrigerator whatever food he had there. There was enough for a large dinner. After he ate he settled down in the family room and turned on the TV. He needed some rest.

The next day was Thursday. Tom got up early and started to move some of the smaller things he wanted into the truck. The larger furniture he could not move. He needed help. He did find that he could take apart his bed room furniture. He loved the bed room furniture more the any other thing in the house. It was special furniture that he had found in Long Island. The most important was the men's unit. It was about five feet wide and had three sections with four doors. The door on the left has shelves that Tom kept all his underwear and special shirts. In the center were two doors that covered the place Tom hung all his suits and special sports jackets. It took him about an hour to take it all apart so that he could bring it into the truck. The other unit was the regular dresser with the mirror on top and three large drawers in it. Tom could carry the drawers and place them in the truck. At about eight he called the Real estate Company that was not too far from him.

"How can I help you?" said a woman's voice.

"I am moving to Ohio," said Tom. "I need to sell my house here in New York and I need help in moving my heavy furniture in the truck before you put sales slip on my remaining furniture and sell my house."

"I think you need someone from the unemployment house. You can hire someone to help you move the furniture. Call me when you have moved all the furniture that you want and then I will send someone to evaluate the furniture and house."

"Thank you" said Tom wondering why he said that. He was getting used to Ohio philosophy. "Can you give me the phone number of the unemployment House? The woman gave Tom the phone number and hung up. Tom then called the unemployment house.

Hi," said Tom when a person picked up the phone. "I need to hire a man to help me move some furniture from my house into the truck. I will only need him for about two hours. What will it cost me?"

"We only allow our unemployed to work no less than one day. That will be one hundred dollars."

"That is fifty dollars an hour," said Tom. "See if anyone was willing to work two hours for fifty dollars." Soon there was a young man who offered to work for fifty dollars however as a minimum. If he had to work longer than two hours, he asked for twenty fifty dollars an hour more. Tom quickly agreed. It only took one hour and a half for them to move all the furniture Tom wanted. The man left with both of them happy. Tom then called the real estate Company.

"Hello," said a woman's voice. "This is Tom," said Tom. "I called before about selling my house here in New York."

"Yes I remember," said the lady. "Did you get the furniture that you want into your truck?"

"Yes I'm ready," said Tom. "Come and evaluate my house and furniture."

"I will send someone right away," said the woman. She then checked his address and cell phone number and after Tom said it was right she hung up. About ten minutes later a woman showed up.

"Are you the woman I talked to over the phone?" asked Tom.

"No I'm Dolorous," said the woman. "I am going to evaluate your furniture and house." She then went through each room evaluating each piece of furniture. After evaluating each unit she then placing a price tag on it after she did the evaluation. It took her over an hour to check all the furniture that Tom wasn't taking with him. After she finished checking all the furniture she got out her computer and a tape measure and she checked the size of every room. Finally she got on her computer and came up with a cost.

"What value?" asked Tom, "have you come up with for the house?"

"You can start the sales at any price you want," said Dolorous. "But the minimum should not be less than six hundred and fifty thousand dollars."

"Let's go with it," said Tom. "What do you think we should go with?"

I'm setting it at seven hundred fifty thousand. I can negotiate down to the minimum." I have several people that have asked for a home in your area. I think it shouldn't take long to sell your house. Let me know when you leaving for Ohio. I would like to take care of this while you are still around. We have a lot of paperwork to take care of to sell your house?"

"OK," said Tom. Tom then when home and found several people looking at his furniture. Tom walked around with them to see if he could negotiate with them. Tom didn't really care for the cost he would get. He just wanted to get rid of it all. Tom was surprised how

Angelo Thomas Crapanzano

fast the furniture was selling. Before evening he had lost all the bedroom furniture. He wondered where he was going to sleep tonight. When he asked the head sales lady when she thought that the sale would end she told Tom what he didn't want to hear.

"The next two days, Saturday and Sunday," said the lady, "are the best days to sell because people didn't have to work on weekends." That evening when the sales woman closed down and went home Tom locked the house and walked to the nearest hotel. He was lucky that it only took half an hour for Tom to get to the nearest hotel. He got a room there for the next two days.

The next two days went bye with great success. They sold all the furniture at near asking prizes. The only furniture left were a few old kitchen chairs. On Monday morning Tom called Dolorous.

"Hi dolorous," said Tom when she answered the phone. "How is the house sale going?"

"I have a couple who want to think about it," said Dolorous. "The only one that wants to buy it now offered five hundred seventy five thousand dollars. I declined."

"Did you try to negotiate?" asked Tom.

"Yes but he was too low," said Dolorous.

"Tell him that I will accept six hundred thousand dollars," said Tom. "I would like to get this off my mind."

"Hold on," said Dolorous. "Let me call him and tell him that he has one hour to accept the offer since you are leaving town and will like to get rid of the property while you are in town." She then got on the telephone. She told him all the facts of the offer. She told him that the sale price is now because once he gets to Ohio he was willing to wait to get the maximum price. To the surprise of dolorous and Tom, the buyer accepted the deal. One hour later he showed up with his lawyer. It only took about an hour to get all papers signed and Tom to get his money. Tom stayed one more night at the motel. Happily he was on the way home by seven in the next morning. He arrived home about four in the afternoon. The first thing he did is call Mary at the Real Estate office.

"Hi Mary," said Tom. "I'm home from New York. Can you recommend someone who can help me move my furniture from the truck to the house?"

"Hi Tom," said Mary. "I see that you have taken care of your belongings from New York. Glad you got home safely. As for someone to help you, I think Paul can help you. He is ready to go out to look at a home that will be for sale. It will take you less than a half hour to move everything inside. I'm sure Paul will be happy to help you. Just a minute let me ask him." A few minutes later Mary came back to the phone. "Mike said he will be happy to help you. It is on his way to the house he is going to see. He will be right there.

"How much will it cost me?" asked Tom.

"You are not in new York," said Mary. "There is no charge. He is a friend. When you have a minute, will you come in and tell us about your experience in New York. Talk with you later." She then hung up. A few minutes later, Paul came.

"HI Tom," said Paul. "I don't think you remember me. I have seen you at the office."

"You look familiar, but I don't remember when I saw you. Come help me get the large furniture in the house and place it where it needs to be placed. I don't want to hold you up to long."

"Don't worry," said Paul. "I have all day to do what I have to do." It was less than a half hour when they had every large piece of furniture in place and everything else in the house where Tom could take care of it. After Paul left Tom put everything where he wanted it. Monday morning Tom went to his Goodyear to start his job. When he got there he went to Mrs. Radcliffe's office.

"Good morning Martha," said Tom. "I'm ready to go to work."

"Glad you came," said Martha. "We have a very big problem. I need you to look into it immediately. She then showed Tom the paper documents that showed the problem. Tom recognized the problem He had worked on a similar problem one summer with a job he had between his college years. It was a tough one back then. He decided not to tell Martha. He wanted her to respect his work ability.

"Let me go into my office and work on this," said Tom. "I will get back to you when I find a solution." Tom then went into his office and worked out the solution. It was only one hour later that he went back to Martha's office with his solution to the problem.

"Did you get an idea as to where to start to solve the problem," asked Martha as soon as she saw Tom.

"I think I have everything we need to solve the problem," said Tom. "I think this is the solution to the problem." He then handed her the solution in a document he had written up. She looked at the solution and was amazed that Tom got the answer so soon.

"You are a good worker," said Martha holding back how much she really was shocked at how fast he solved the problem. She didn't want him to get over conceited. She then gave Tom new problems to solve. Two weeks went by and Tom work very hard. He wanted them to appreciate him. Tom was very much appreciated for his work by Martha. She had a very high respect for him. It was on a Wednesday the next week that Tom was surprised. After work that day he drove home and pulled into his drive way. He opened the garage and pulled in his car. He was about to walk to the curb where he saw what looked like a newspaper. As he started to walk down to the curb, a car pulled into his drive way. A woman got out of her car and yelled,

"What are you doing here?" Tom was too shocked by the way he suddenly felt. She was the most beautiful woman he had ever seen. Her voice thrilled him. He felt butterflies in his stomach. He didn't answer her because his mind was out of sync with everything. The woman was also under a shocked moment. Tom didn't notice her expression.

"What," he heard himself say.

"Who, what?" said the woman. They stood there a while just looking at each other. Tom recovered first.

"I don't know what you want so let's sit on the couch on my porch and settle down a little. She didn't answer but followed him to the porch and they both sat on the porch. "I don't remember what you said," said Tom. "Will you repeat what you said?"

"I asked what you were doing in my house," said the woman recovering a little.

"You think that this is your house?" asked Tom. "I've lived here for over a month. I paid cash for the house. I don't owe a Penney.

So how do you think this is your house? Maybe you have the wrong street." The woman opened her purse and pulled out a document. It was an inheritance document. It stated that upon the death of her parents, Joseph and Nicola Costa, that Tina Costa would inherit the house and their bank account.

"Listen Tina," said Tom. "I don't want to take away anything that is yours and I don't think that you want me to lose all the money I paid for this house. Let us be friends and work together on this."

"I agree one hundred percent," said Tina. "I am positive that you can bring out a document showing that you also inherited this house. I agree let's work together."

"Before we start on that lets go eat dinner," said Tom. "The dinner is on me. I would like to know you better."

"Sound good to me," said Tina. "I would like to know you better too." Realizing that she is Italian also he made an Italian Pasta.

"Tell me Tina," asked Tom, "How come you are looking for your home over five years since your parents died? I noticed the date on the document."

"I was going to collage when they both got into an accident and were killed. After I graduated I got a temporary job before my job here in Ohio was to start I got a job in Rome teaching English to a special children's class. I just came home from there. I am an English and Math teacher. So I work here and I thought it was great that I had a home here."

"How about you," said Tina? "What is your story?"

"My story is very short," said Tom. "I grew up in New York. I went to college and got my degree in Management but mostly in Financial Management. I got a job here in Ohio and I moved here about a month ago."

"Listen I have to go," said Tina. "I have to find a place to live. I have all my belongings in my car. I expected to move in here."

"Why don't you sleep here tonight?" said Tom. "There are two empty bedrooms"

"No way," said Tina. "I am a born-again-Christian. I don't even want neighbors to see me stay here. Thanks any way."

"I am a Born-again–Christian also," said Tom, "all my neighbors know this."

"I'm sorry but I don't like the idea," said Tina.

"Well go north on this street and turn right when you get to the main road. Across from the Mall is a nice hotel. Will I see you tomorrow?"

"I will come here after dinner time. We have a lot to talk about."

"Well why don't you come here around four o'clock," said Tom. "I want to go and see a friend in the Real Estate office to see if she will help us." After Tina left, Tom then called the Real Estate office.

"Hi," said Tom when a male voice answered the phone. "May I speck to Mary please."

"I'm sorry," said the man. "Mary had some special personal problem come up. She will not be back until this Monday."

"Thank you," said Tom and hung up. The next day Tina showed up at four O'clock as she had agreed.

"Good afternoon," said Tina when Tom answered the door.

"Hi Tina," said Tom. "Come on in. We have a little problem. The person I wanted to see will not be there until Monday. We will have to work on it ourselves until then."

"Oh no," said Tina. "I start teaching my first class Monday."

"What time do you get out of the school?" asked Tom. "I have to go to work Monday. I wasn't going to take a day off. I have only worked there about one month. What time do you get out in the evening?"

"I get off about four thirty," said Tina.

"I get off at four thirty too," said Tom, "Why don't we meet here at that time. I will make sure the person I want to talk to will be there. Come here when you get out of school so that we can go to the Real Estate office together. Until then let us try to figure this thing out ourselves."

"All right," said Tina. "Where do we start?"

"First let's try your side of the problem," started Tom. "If I remember right you received the inheritance from your parent right?"

"Yes," said Tina, "They were both killed in an auto accident"

"Do you have any Idea," asked Tom, "where your parent got the house?"

"I think they purchased it," said Tina, "although they may have inherited from my mother or father's parents."

"We will have to see the Ohio real Estate office Monday. If this action was done here in Ohio they should have a record of it," said Tom. "Now let's look at my side. I bought this property from a fellow named Jason York. Let me see if I can locate him. Tom could not locate him even though he tried through many Real estate offices around Ohio. They had no results. He question whether any of the people they were looking for had moved out of Ohio. Tina and Tom searched the rest of the week with no success. Monday Tina went to the school where she was to teach the fifth graders. Tom went back to work. Later in the day Tom called Mary at the real estate office. She answered.

"H Mary," said Tom. "Is everything ok with you? I have been calling you and you have not been there."

"I'm fine," said Mary. "I had a little private mater I had to take care of. What can I do for you?"

"Last week a woman showed up at my house with a document that said that she was the owner of my home. I need your help. Can you stay a little later today? We both get out of our job at four thirty. We would like to come directly to your office."

"Sure," said Mary, "I'll be here."

"See you then," said Tom and hung up. At four thirty both Tina and Tom showed up at the Real Estate office

"Hi Mary," said Tom as he entered the office. "I want you to meet Tina Costa.

Hi Tina," said Mary. "Please come in sit in the chairs that are around my desk. And let's get started. Tina, do you have your inheritance papers with you?"

"Yes," said Tina She then went into her purse and brought out the document and handed it to Mary. Mary looked the document over and looking up she said.

"I see we defiantly have a problem. Somewhere in the past, someone sold the house to two separate people. We have to go back with each of your background to see where the error was made. First let's start with you Tom. I have most of your background in my records. You bought the house from Jason York. He inherited it from his parent's Ron and Cathy York, Five years ago. Before he sold it to you, since we couldn't sell it, he rented it for four years to John and Lisa Mason. After they left Jason sold it to you. So our job is to find out where Jason's parents got the ownership of the house."

"How do we do that?" asked Tom. "We have been trying to contact the old relatives but can't find any."

"Let me check my records," said Mary, This house is in my area and I should have a record of every transaction that happened in the last few years. If it goes past that I have to find another Real Estate business wherever I find the original owner's family lived"

"Where do we go from here?" asked Tom.

"Why don't you guys go home," said Mary. "I will call you when I get more information." It was two days later in the evening that Mary called Tom.

"I got all the information," said Mary so can you come tonight at four thirty as you did before?"

"Yes," said Tom. "We will be there." Tom contacted Tina and the both went to the Real Estate office right from work.

"Hi," they all said when Tom and Tina got there.

"Come in a sit down," said Mary. "As we discussed the last time we met, we found out that Jason Inherited the house from his parent Ron and Cathy York. They bought the house from Sam and Lora Nicori. The house was actually inherited by Lora from Harry and Tammy Picket. So now let's review your background Tina. You inherited the house from your parent Joseph and Nicola Costa. They bought the house from Nick and Gale Stow. Now this is the interesting information. It was Gale that also inherited the house from Harry and Tammy Picket. The house was built by Harry Picket. He and his wife Tammy moved to Canton and went to a Real Estate company in Canton to sell the house Tammy had two baby twin girls the month before. One day the house caught on fire. Harry who was in the garage at the time ran upstairs and grabbed the two baby girls and brought them outside to his neighbor. He then ran in to save his wife. He didn't save his wife or got out himself. The baby girls were taken in by the city's and put out for adoption. They were eventually adopted by different parent. One of the parents that adopted one of the babies moved to Canton. The girls grew up and got married. The girls were not aware that they had a twin sister. When they were twenty they received the document telling them that they inherited the house in Fairlawn Ohio. They both, at different times, sold the house both thinking that they owned the complete house. I don't know how the Real Estate Company or the city didn't catch the error, so technically you both own half the house. Do you want me to see what we can do to fix this problem?"

"No," said Tom. "We have three alternatives. I think I and Tina should discuss them. We will get back to you when we decide what to do. Tina, let's go home we have a lot to talk about."

I agree," said Tina. "Let's go at our house and discuss the options you have."

"See you later," said Tina to Mary. They then left and went directly to the house.

"Let's sit in the back yard and talk," said Tom. "It is such nice weather. In the back yard they sat on the bench that was under the trees.

"Tina," started Tom. "We have three options. One is that I give you half of what I paid for it and the house will be mine. Secondly you give me half of the cost and the house will be yours. And third, my recommendation is that we don't change the house ownership. Tina, I know that we haven't known each other long enough for this third option; however, I don't need more time. I was attracted to you when I first met you. That is why I didn't understand what you said. I had butterflies in my stomach. I think it was love at first sight. So this is my third option." Tom then went down on his knees and pulled out a little box from his pocket He showed her an engagement ring. "Tina will you marry me. Then we could put the house together as one owned by one couple."

"I though you would never ask," said Tina. "I felt the same way when I first met you. The feelings in my stomach were like butterflies. Yes I will marry you." Tom then hugged Tina and kissed her.

Angelo Thomas Craparzano

The hugging and kissing continued until their marriage and continued afterwards without an end in sight.

The End

Story Number Eight

Let's put the New In Place Of the Old

Peter had just entered the building when Martha stopped him.

"Good morning Mr. Alison," said Martha. "I stopped to tell you that Mr. Talver wants to see you as soon as you get here."

"Thank you Martha," said Peter. "Please call me Peter." Peter then went straight to his boss's, Mr. Talver's, office.

"Hi Mr. Talver," said Peter as he walked in his office.

"Come in Peter," said Mr. Talver. "Have a seat. I have a special assignment for you. Are you aware of the show that is going to be shown at the new Play House that was just opened here in Cleveland?"

"Yes," said Peter, "I have never been there. I don't think they have performed yet."

"That's right," said Mr. Talver. "Please call me Mike. Mr. Talver is for new employees and strangers. Anyway, they have purchased a building in Akron and want to change their show into a real restaurant. I don't know what their show is but they want to do the show in real life. That sounds like a real story. Go; find out want that is all about. Let me know anything you find out. However, stay and interview them all and stay for their first opening show if you think you could get a good story out of it."

"I'll go right now," said Peter. "I don't have any other story that I was following. This sounds interesting." Peter then left and headed to the new theater. As he walked in the side door, which was open, a heavy set man stopped him.

"Who are you and what are you doing here? Get out or I will call the police and charge you with breaking in."

"Wait a minute George," said a young man. "This man could be a reporter from the Cleveland Press. Do you want a bad report from the newspaper?"

"Just stay out of my way," said George and left for the back stage.

"I'm sorry about him. He is the director, and thinks he is the boss. I think if he doesn't straighten up I will let him go. I'm Frank Belington. I own the business. Please follow me to my office in the rear of the stage." Peter followed him to his office.

"I see that the hall back here has many offices," said Peter. "Are these the offices of the stars?"

"Yes," said Frank. "After we talk, I will take you to talk to some of the stars." They entered the office and Peter sat down on chair that was on the end of the desk.

"How can I help you?" said Frank.

"I see that the stage has stage settings. What are all the tables for?"

"That is a restaurant set up. The play that we perform is about an old boyfriend of one of the waitresses that won't give her up. He keeps pestering her at her job at the restaurant."

"I'm beginning to see the picture now," said Peter. "But why do you want to start a real Restaurant?"

"This is our first time in Ohio," said Frank. "We have been performing our play in the far west and far south for ten or more years. They have all gotten tired of the play. Also the actors have gotten tired. Two are real chefs. When I hired them they had lost their job. They were glad to take a job as actors. They didn't have to pretend very hard. The waitresses were also in need of a job. Two had been waitresses at some time. Anyway they all would like real jobs. One waitress, Trina is tired of bringing fake food to people who are not really customers."

"Do they all want to be real chefs and waitresses," asked Peter?"

"We may have to hire some after we get started at my new business. You can find out when you talk to them."

"Have any of your present actors told you that they want quit?"

"No not definitely," said Frank.

"Since you have played this show for many years, why is it taking you two weeks to open the show here in Ohio?" said Peter.

"We have made a lot of changes," said Fred. "We are also in a very different building and stage set up. We did not have the chef's area this open."

"I think I have all that I need from you," said Peter. "How do I get to talk to the actors?"

"I will take you to the first," said Frank. "Then I will ask her to take you to the rest."

"Sounds great," said Peter. "Let's go." Fred then led Peter to the first door in the hall. He knocked on the door.

"Hi Tania," said Fred. "Are you in an acceptable shape to let us in?" The woman came to the door and opened it. Peter was shocked. She was the most beautiful girl he had ever seen. He had never felt this way for any one. No wonder she was hired, thought Peter.

"Come on in," said Tania showing a strange emotion. "What, I mean, what do you want. She was emotionally moved also.

"Are you all right," said Fred seeing how strangely she was acting. He did not realize that she was surprised by seeing Peter. Of all the men that had come to see her no one affected her like Peter did.

"What" said Tania to Fred's statement?

"You seem like you are having some kind of problem," said Fred. "Can I help your?" Tania got control of herself.

"I'm alright," said Tania. "I can't figure why you want to see me."

"This is Peter, a news reporter," said Fred. "He wants to talk to you about your job as an actress here with this company."

"That's fine," said Tania. "Come in and have a seat." Peter went in and sat down in chair that was at the end of the room. Fred stayed in the door way.

"Listen Tania," said Fred. "I have to go. Will you take Peter to see the other actors please?"

"I will be glad to," said Tania." Then turning to Peter she asked,

"What would you like to know?" asked Tania.

"I would like to know how you feel about your job here," started Peter. "Are you happy? Do you love the job as an actress? Is there another job you would rather have?"

"I'm afraid to answer you," said Tania. "I don't want to damage the shows future. Frank gave me a job when I was out in the street without a job or home."

"Well let me tell you why I'm here," said Peter. "I was asked to write articles to promote your show. I promise that I will not write anything bad about the show or what you tell me about your feelings. I would like to know for my own information. I think you are a very beautiful woman and deserve a better job than a fake waitress."

"I don't know if I can trust you," said Tania.

"I am a Born-again-Christian," said Peter. "I promise in God's name."

"Wow," said Tania. "I am also a Born-Again-Christian. There are not many left that I know of. I trust you one hundred percent. What do you want to know?"

"Tell me how you like your job and why?" said Peter.

"I hate my job. First it takes up the most important time of the day. I don't get home until ten in the evening. I eat a very late dinner if I wait until I get home. Most of the time, I eat at a restaurant closest to the theater. I would like to meet the love of my life and have some children. With this job it seems impossible."

"Start from the beginning," said Peter. "How did you get here and why?"

"I went to college to become a store manager," said Tania. "I got a job at a restaurant as a manager. I was the financial Manager. It was my job to see that they were always earning the required amount to stay in business. Unfortunately they sold the restaurant and the new owner was going to take care of their own finances. They let me go. I went over five months without income. I couldn't find ever a simple job. The day I lost my apartment is when Fred found me begging for food. He hired me on the spot. I became the waitress for his show. I had no choice, but to go with him."

"I understand completely," said Peter. "Have you looked for a better job since then?" "I feel like I am way below my capability, however Fred is a wonderful man," said Tania. "He helped me when I needed him most. He needs me now. I will not leave him unless he finds someone to replace me. I have to help him open the new business. After that, I may find a way to leave."

"That tells me a lot about you," said Peter. "If I come up with another question I will ask you. Until then why don't you take me to another of the actors?"

"Follow me," said Tania. She then led Peter to the next door down the hall. When she got there, she knocked on the door.

"Is it alright for us to come in," said Tania? A young man opened the door.

"Hi Sal," said Tania. "This is Peter. He is from the Cleveland Plain Dealer. He would like to ask you a few questions."

"Come on in and sit down," said Sal. "I hope you will write something nice."

"I promised Fred that I would," said Peter. "I'll have more nice things to say after I see your show."

"What do you want to know?" asked Sal.

"I would like to know what you think of your part in this play," said Peter. How do you like your job?"

"I love it," said Sal. "I will love it more when we change to a real Restaurant. I spent about three years as a chef in a real restaurant. I would like that better. I spent four years studying to be a real chef."

"Do you have any problems with the staff or the other actors?" asked Peter.

"No," said Sal. "They are all like brothers and sisters."

"Would you like to recommend any changes to the program?" asked Peter.

"I recommend that we hurry to the real restaurant. I would like to be back as a real chef."

"I have all I want to know from you Sal," said Peter. "Thank you for your time. It was nice to meet you."

"Nice to meet you too," said Sal as he saw them out of his room. Tina then took Peter to the room next door. It was Ryan's room. Tina knocked on the door. Ryan opened the door.

"Come on in," said Ryan. "I hear a little of what went on next door. So you want to know my background is that right?"

"Yes," said Peter. "Really, I would like to know you. It is hard writing about someone you don't know."

"Well," started Ryan. "I was a Chef for Red Lobster. I loved to cook fish. I came up with several new recipes. Some were from Italy. My boss loved them. I loved working for them. They are the best restaurant for fish dinners. They are also fantastic also for all the other meals they offer."

"If you loved it there why did you leave?" asked Peter.

"I was stupid," said Ryan. "I thought that it was a beginning to being a Hollywood star. Remember, this show started in California."

"So what is your future plan?" asked Peter.

"I will love being a chef for the new restaurant. Everyone here is like family. I love them all. I have a special attraction for one of the waitresses. We have plans for after we move into the new restaurant and settle down."

"Well I feel like one of your friends," said Peter. "I wish you the best happiness with your waitress girlfriend. Take care, I will see you later." They then left and Tania took him to the next room. The door was open and the two waitresses were there together.

"Hi," said Tania. "Peter, the newspaper reporter, would like to talk with you girls. May we come in?"

"Sure," said Adele. "My name is Adele. What would you like to know?" After they entered to room, Peter answered her question.

"I just want to know what you think of your job here."

"We both love it here," said Laura. "We were just discussing that. We are actresses here. That is a great position. We are proud to be actresses. The new position that is coming up we will be just plain waitresses. We feel like we are being demoted. However, we don't see that we have any choice. "We can see if we can be accepted in Hollywood as actresses. We would then move there. But we think it is just a bad dream. We will just become plain waitresses."

"That tells me all I want to know," said Peter. "I think a good waitress is at a high level of achievement. Good luck to you girls." With that said Peter and Tina left.

"Where do we go next," said Peter. "I think I have a good picture of the show actors."

"Let's go see the boyfriend who put pressure on one of the waitresses. We don't know who that is going to be. The new stage set up makes it difficult to do the show as before. And most of all it will be different when we get to the real restaurant." Tania then took Peter to the last room. Tania knocked on the door.

"Come in," said a male voice. They walked in and found the good looking young man.

Hi, Ray," said Tania. "This is Peter. He is a reporter. He would like to ask you how you like your job."

"How can you ask?" said Ray. "I work about thirty minutes and am respected as an actor. I also get paid for a full day. How can you ask?" The only trouble I have is that I'm not sure I will have a job in the real restaurant. They won't have a lover chasing after a waitress. I may soon be out of a job."

"I think I hear Frank say that he would find a job for you," said Tania. "Trust him. He is a very wonderful boss. I think Frank may want a young man at the door receiving gests."

"That would be great," said Ray. "I know that you are a great Christian. Will you pray for me?"

"We both will," said Peter. "I am a Born-Again-Christian. I will pray for you."

"I think that covers all the actors," said Tania. "Let's go back to my office." When they got back to her office Tania turned to Peter.

"I think I have to say goodbye for now," said Tania. "I have a new role in the real restaurant. I have to study it and the current role both. So please excuse me. I would like it if you will attend the first practice show this Wednesday. The first show with the real audience will be this Friday. Please pray for our success."

"All right Tania," said Peter. "I enjoy being with you. I would like to spend more time with you."

"I'm glad to hear that," said Tania. "Please have patience. Let's get over the real restaurant effort. I owe Fred a lot for giving an inexperienced girl an acting job. Let's get his real restaurant going. After that I would like to leave this kind of business. Let's see what I will do after that."

"I fully understand," said Peter. "That is one thing I like about you. You are not selfish, thinking only about yourself. I will be around to see you whenever I can." Peter then left to write his page on the great show that is coming to the area.

On Wednesday Peter went to the rehearsal of the show. He sat in a seat in the front row. Two other people he did not know sat several rows behind him. The story began with Tania walking up to the table in the far right area of the stage with a great smile on her face.

"Good afternoon," she said. Peter could hardly hear her. Then the show showed two other waitresses coming out with jolly looks on their face and did the same thing as Tania had done. One at a time the waitresses walked up to the back wall where there were four opening where you can see the cooking area and the chefs doing the cooking. The waitresses went there and ordered the meal that their customer ordered. This went on for about a half hour. Then suddenly Ray walked in and approached Tania. He started yelling that he loved her and wanted a second chance. He was very emotional and loud. He would not take no for an answer. He even got a little rough with her. Tania backed away and told him that she was no longer interested in him and that she had another boyfriend. He then took her by the shoulder and told her that she was his. She fought her way out of his hand and went into cooking area, where no one was allowed to go. When he tried, Chef Ryan came up to him with a great knife. Ray left with a very angry look on his face. Five minutes later everything got back to normal. It was about an hour later that Ray returned and forced Tania against the wall. He told her that she was his and that he would never let her go. This time Frank came out with a pistol. Ray then did disappear. Ray apparently waited outside until he saw frank leave. He then went back in and began slapping Tania on the face. Suddenly Frank came back with a police officer. Ray was arrested on the spot. After the police took Ray out, Frank grabbed Tania by the hand and led her to the end of the cooking area telling her how much he loved her. There he hugged her and tried to kiss her. Tania turned her head so that his kiss landed on her cheek instead of her mouth. The stage screen then closed. The show was over. Peter then walked back to Tania's room.

"Tania, said Peter, "you did a marvelous job. I didn't know that you would be the bad guy's girlfriend. When did that change?"

"Peter," said Tania. "I'm glad you came back here. I didn't know if you were in the audience.

"I wouldn't miss it," said Peter. "I noticed that frank wanted to kiss you, and when he tried to kiss you, you turn your head. Is there anything about you two?"

"No, said Tania. "The kiss was in the script. I didn't want you to see me kiss someone else. I explained to Frank. He understood."

"I see that you have realized that I have feeling for you," said Peter.

"And I'm sure that you know that I have feelings for you," said Tania. "But we must not take it any further for now. There are too many things in the air for now. Please have patience."

"I understand completely," said Peter. "I have feelings for you that I have never had before. In plain language, I have fallen in love with you. I will never let you go even if it takes a year. We can at least tell each other how we feel."

"We have already done that," said Tania. "That is, you have. Now it is my turn. As if you didn't know, I am madly in love with you. Let just find out everything about each other. Let's wait until I finish the acting job." After Fred starts the real Restaurant, I want to leave that job as soon as I can. However I owe Fred for helping me off the street."

"We will just be lovers for now," said Peter. "I will have great plans about a year from now. For now however, you better go home. It's nine thirty. I'm sure you are very tired."

"You are right," said Tania. "Please try to see me as often as you can." Peter then just hugged her. He felt that she wasn't ready yet for more. After the hug, they each went to their own home.

It was Friday that the show was provided to the public. Peter went and had a hard time finding a seat. The theater was full. Peter thanked the lord that he found a seat in the front row. Most people don't like sitting in the front row. The play started at eight and ended in nine thirty. After it ended Peter went to the private room for Tina. Just as he got to her door he saw the young boy who had originally played the part of the angry boyfriend. Peter had noticed that in the play tonight an older man took his place. The young boy had a suit case in his hands and was leaving the theater. He looked very sad and disturbed.

"Hi Ray," said Peter. "I see that you were replaced as the lover of a waitress."

"The dirty rats," said Ray. "Why did they do that? I did a good job."

"Ray," said Peter, "you are not thinking strait. You are too young for Tina. When they decided to use Tina as the waitress being your old girlfriend, they had no choice. Anyway why does it make a difference? You will not be the bad boyfriend at the real restaurant. You would have lost you job in a month or so. I don't believe that this stage action would be done in the real restaurant."

"Wow," said Ray. "I was so disturbed that I never thought of that. I would have been out of a job anyway. Thank you for reminding me of it."

"Anyway you didn't necessary lose your job. They may need a man to do a lot of work around the restaurant. They will need someone to keep the food trays full. Pray to God or Jesus. Have faith. Trust the Lord. He will not let you down."

"I don't believe in a God and his son," said Ray. "That is all a scam to control the people."

"Ray," said Peter. "Let's go back to your room. I need to talk with you." Ray didn't hesitate. He wanted to hear what Peter had to say. When they got there they sat down.

"Have you heard about your great, great, great parents?" started Peter. They all came from the same place. Did they each design their children in some one's stomach? Do you also think that years ago the strong wind blew some sand so strongly that it formed a baby? If so where did the other babies come from? Ray, there is a power that designed the first human, and also each of us. Don't try to understand all of God's functions. You are not smart enough. Let me explain it to you in this way. When I was home with my parents, we had a very smart cat. It seemed to understand all the things we asked it. One day I put it on my lap and asked it to tell me what the mathematical sum of two and three were? The cat had absolutely no understanding of math. I understood math very well. I was only about ten percent smarted than the cat. Then I thought that God was infinitely smarter than me. So I realized that I had no way of understanding what God was doing. That was when I decided just to trust God."

"I never thought of that," said Ray. "I never considered the fact that we had to come from somewhere. Thank you so much. Do I just tell Jesus that I believe in him?"

"Remember that Jesus died for all our sins. So tell him with all of you heart that you accept his paying for your sins and be his servant."

"I have a lot to think about," said, Ray. "First I have to start reading the bible. Next I have to start going to church. I will pray that God will see that I get a job at the real restaurant. I hope to see you there some day." With that he grabbed his suitcase and left. Peter then went next door. Tania had already left. Peter then went home. Friday Peter went back to the theater. The play was pretty much the same as the last time he saw it. After the show was over Peter went to Tania's room.

"Hi sweet heart," said Peter as he went through the open door to her room. "You get better every time I see the show. You are a great actress."

"Hi Peter," said Tania. "I was hoping that the current experience would make me a Hollywood Star. If you remember, I started in California."

"I think you will make a better wife and mother, said Peter. Tania just smiled.

"I see that your article in the paper brought a house full of customers. Keep up the good work."

"You had better go now," said Peter. "I understand that your show will not be open on Mondays and Tuesdays. Can I see you then?"

"I'm sorry," said Tania. "I will be in Akron working on the real restaurant. I will only see you after the shows are over here in Cleveland."

"I guess I could live with that," said Peter. After a half hour they parted. Peter then went home as usual. This went on for four weeks. On Friday the fourth week Peter went to the show as usual. He was surprised that there were only about twelve customers there. He had noticed that each week they had decreased but not as bad as this week. After the show he went to Tania's room as usual.

"Hi Tania," said Peter. Before he could say anything else she spoke.

"I'm surprised that you had the nerve of coming here today," said Tania showing anger in her voice.

"What are you talking about?" said Peter surprised at Tania's reaction.

"You promised that you would always write positive columns in the paper," said Tania. "Today you wrote that the show was over and that it was not good enough to keep on operating."

"Dear Lord," said Peter. "Someone must have changed my article. I said great things about the actors. I didn't even mention that you were soon going to close. Tomorrow morning I'm going in to see my boss. If he changed it without telling me, I will resign."

"I'm sorry that I got angry," said Tania. "I should have known better."

"Don't be sorry," said Peter. "I know that if you had thought for a while you would have figured out that I would never have written something like that."

"If I would have stopped to think I would have known better, said Tania. "I think I heard Frank say that the results of today's audience will make us close sooner. I think I am glad for that. Let's get the Restaurant open and working. Then I can plan my future."

"Well, go and rest," said Peter. "I will call you after I talk with my boss. Have a good night's rest."

"Aren't you going to have dinner?" said Tania. "I had a sandwich as I left the stage just after the show ended.

"I'm not hungry," said Peter. "I had a large lunch." Peter then left. He went home and before he went to bed he spent time writing notes on what he wanted to say and if he resigned what he would do. After that he went to bed.

The next morning he got up early, ate breakfast and was at his boss's office at eight.

"Hi Mister Mr. Talver," said Peter. "I need to speak to you for a few minutes."

"Come on in," said Mr. Talver. "I only have about one minute. What's your problem?"

"I wrote an article about the stage show at the Play House Theater. It was revised by something different and far from the truth."

"IT was a lousy show. It was about to shut down. They were leaving Cleveland and going someplace else to open a new show. Obvious the show was a failure. I will not back up a failure."

"You got the whole story wrong," said peter. "They are all great actors. I interviewed each one as you requested. Before they started the show the chefs were real chefs and the women were actual Waitresses. The problem is that they were all getting old and would like a new job that didn't require pretending they were someone they were not. They decided to open a real Restaurant. They have been a very successful show for over ten years. "They started in California and have traveled to many states. I checked their background."

"I found out enough to make my decision, said Mr. Talver. "That was the last article of that show. We have more important things to write about."

"The real problem I have," said Peter, "is that you did not follow the ruled that most newspapers have with their reporters."

"And what rule is that?" asked Mr. Talver.

"It is the rule that when the Manager questions the reporters write up. He called him in his office they discuss the actual facts."

"I don't agree with that" said Mr. Talver. "I'm boss and I make all the decisions."

"I don't think you will have your job for very long," said Peter and left. He had planned on resigning but now he thought he could do that any time. First he wanted to follow the plan he had made. The first on his list was to see if he could find another job nearby. The first place he went was to Akron Beacon Journal. When he walked in he went to the desk he saw.

"Hi" he said. I would like to see the head of the reporters," said Peter. "I'm looking for a job. Is he available?"

"Let me see," said the young woman at the desk as she picked up the phone. Peter couldn't hear what she said, however, she hung up the phone and turned to Peter.

"He only has a few minutes," said the woman. "Go down the hall on my right. It is the last office on your left. Peter followed her direction and soon got to the last door. He knocked on the door.

"Come on in," said a male voice. Have a seat. What can I do for you? Before Peter could answer the fellow continued. "My name is Jim Bison. I'm the head of the Akron Beacon Journal Reporters. I think I know you. I've seen you before. What is your job?"

"I am a reporter for a Cleveland newspaper." said Peter."

"Of course," said Jim. "You are Peter Alison. You are a reporter for the Cleveland plain Dealer. I thought I recognized you. I am so jealous of your newspaper column. I always get the Cleveland paper and read your column. You do such a wonderful job. So I can't imagine why you are here. Do you want to write up something about the Akron News Paper?"

tell me a Story

"I am having a difficult time with my boss at the Cleveland Plain dealer," said Peter. "He rewrote one of my columns without telling me or discussing the differences in our opinions. I wrote a nice report on a show that is in Cleveland which is closing down. They had a wonderful show. However, they were all tired of performing and are in the process of stating a new business. I went there and spoke to each of the actors and came out very impressed with their history and why they want to change. My boss changed it and wrote that they were closing because they were a failure and out of money. His article did cause them to close down sooner then they wanted to. What I am saying is that I am not happy with my job."

"If I disagree with one of my reporters write up," said Jim. "I call him in and we discuss the different information we had. Most of the time we compromise, and he rewrites a column we both agree on. Most of the time, I hate to admit, that the reported had the most accurate information. After all he was out there getting the facts."

"That is the right thing to do," said Peter. "You have to give the reporter the chance to explain what he has written."

"So do you want us to write a column showing how your News Paper is incorrect?" said Jim.

"No," said Peter. "I am looking for a job here. I got the job in Cleveland because I graduated from a collage in Cleveland. My parents live here in Fairlawn. I would love to move back here."

"You are hired," said Jim. "How soon can you start?"

"I have to go and resign from the Cleveland paper and then move back to Fairlawn. I will need at least one and maybe two weeks. I am renting an apartment and I did purchase some furniture that I want to keep and no place to move it into yet."

"Well," said Jim, "let us know when you will be able to come and work here. Here are the employment papers. Fill them out and bring then in the next time you are in Ohio." Peter got the papers, said good bye, and left. He headed for his parents' house. When he got there his mother opened the door.

"Sweet heart," said his mother. "Come on in. It is so great to see you. What are you doing here? Did you lose your job in Cleveland?"

"Hi mom," said Peter. "No I resigned. I want to come and live in Fairlawn. However, I need your help. Let's sit and settle down and I will tell you everything."

"Whatever you say," said his mother. "Can I get you a cup of coffee?"

"Sounds good," said Peter. His mother then went and got a cup of coffee for both of them.

"Well what is your problem?" asked his mother.

"I quit my job in Cleveland and got a job here at Akron Beacon Journal," started Peter. "I now need to move from Cleveland to Akron. So I need to rent a truck and need to rent or buy a home here in the Akron area."

"That is a fantastic coincidence," said Peters mother. "Mary, a good friend of ours, works for the Fairlawn Real Estate Company. She is having a big problem.

"What kind of a problem is she having?" asked Peter.

"A customer, that has a beautiful ranch house has been transferred to South Carolina and has to start tomorrow. They are willing to sell the house at a very low price. Let me call my friend Mary and see if they still have the house." She then got on the phone. Two minutes later she called Peter who had gone to the bathroom.

"What did you find out?" said Peter.

"Here is the address," said Peter's mother more excited than Peter expected. "They will meet you there now." She then gave him the address. "It is walking distance from here. That is what I like about it. Just drive down Bancroft road past the stop sign on Elgin and go to the next road on your left called Asbury Road." Peter left immediately. When he got there he met Mary in front of the house waiting for him.

"Hi Peter," said Mary. "The owners are going to leave the area. If they go they are going to leave the house to a relative that lives outside of the city. If that happened then the price will go up to what the real estate estimate is. Right now they are ready to accept two hundred and fifty thousand which is less than fifty thousand that it is worth. It is a great buy."

"Let's see it," said Peter. Mary showed Peter the house from top to bottom. Peter loved it and the price was well within his ability to pay for it. I like it. I want to buy it," said Peter. "Where do we go from here?"

"Let me call them," said Mary. "Perhaps I can get a better price for you. She got her phone and called the owner. "I am Mary from the Real Estate office. I have a young man who likes you house, but he needs a better price. He offered two hundred thousand. Can you lower you price?" She then turned to Peter. "He is willing the go half way with you. "He wants Two hundred twenty five thousand.

"Tell him I agree," said Peter. "I have my checkbook with me and I can give him a down payment of fifty thousand dollars. I then could pay the rest with in a few months. Mary told the owner what Peter offered.

"He said to meet him at the PNC bank," said Mary. "He said that there you can close the deal and you can get a mortgage there."

"That's OK said Peter. "I guess he wants his money right away. I can then pay off the bank whenever I want. Let's do it." Mary stopped at her office to get all the paper she need and they all met at the bank. It took about one and a half hour to get all the papers sign and the money given to the owner. Mary promised Peter that she would have the ownership document the next day. Peter, after all was done, wrote Mary a check for her help and he then went home.

"Well mom," said Peter. "I now have a house to live in. Do you know where I can rent a truck to go and get all the furniture that I own in Cleveland? The house I just bought has only a complete kitchen. It has a great refrigerator and a Micro Wave above the stove. It even has some silver ware and a toaster. I need all the other furniture."

"Did you buy the furniture that you want to bring here," asked his mother?

"I bought the Bedroom furniture," said Peter, "and the Family room couch and chairs."

"I hope you have the sales slips," said his mother. "The owner of the house could give you a problem."

"Thanks mom," said Peter. "I have them all in my bedroom drawer. I better get them and take them with me."

"I think you make be able to rent a car at the Auto Rental Shop," said Peter's mother. "I think they will have a truck for rent there also." Peter got the address and went directly to the Auto Rental Shop.

"Hi," said Peter to the first man he encountered when he walked in. "Do you handle the rental Job," asked Peter.

"Yes said the man, "I'm Nick, what do you need?"

"I need a truck to move furniture from Cleveland to Fairlawn," said Peter.

"How much furniture will be moving?" asked Nick? "We have three different sizes."

"I'm moving a complete Bedroom set and five pieces of Family room furniture. The largest is a couch."

"You will need the large closed in truck. I have one available tomorrow morning at eight o'clock."

"That would be perfect," said Peter. He then went to the grocery store and bought some food. He bought some for breakfast and enough for a couple of sandwiches. That night he went and slept at his mother's house. His dad was till out of town on business. The next morning after Peter ate breakfast he rented the truck. He left from there and arrived in Cleveland at about nine thirty. He was surprised to see that a woman was in the house.

"What are you doing here," said Peter, "and who are you?" I'm Martha from the house rental agency. I have a customer that wants to rent a house. I was checking it to see if it fits their requirements."

"Well Martha," said Peter, "I am Peter the one who is still renting the house. After today you can have the house. But first I need your help. I have a truck outside to take all the furniture I own and move to my new house in Akron."

"I don't think you can take any of the furniture," said Martha. "It all belongs to the house owner."

"All the furniture in the kitchen and, some in the living room were in the house when I moved in. I had to buy the rest. I have all the receipts here." Peter then took them out of the brief case he had, showed them to her. She took out a pad she had with her, and wrote down the name of each of the furniture that Peter owned. She then got on the phone.

"One of our employees, Jeff, will be here in a minute," said Martha. "He will help you move the furniture."

"That will be fine," said Peter wondering if they were going to charge him for his help. A few minutes later a young man showed up.

"Jeff," said Martha. "We have to move Peter's furniture to the truck. I have a list here of his furniture. Let's start in the bed room. Martha call out each piece of furniture from the list just in case there was a piece of furniture that wasn't Peters. Peter and Jeff moved the furniture one at a time as Martha calls it out. After the finished the bedroom they move to the rest of the house removing only the furniture that was on her list. About an hour later Martha turned to Peter.

"I think we are all finished," said Martha. "You are free to leave. Nothing in this house now is yours. Good bye." Peter was so depressed at her attitude that he left and didn't even say goodbye. He was happy that she didn't charge him for the help Jeff gave him. Peter got to Fairlawn around noon. He went directly to his house. He was too tired to do anything that day. Home he parked the truck next to the house and brought in only the bed mattress and a blanket. He had enough food for a sandwich for lunch and one for supper. In between he took a rest and watched TV. The next morning he called Mary of the Real Estate agency's rental office.

"Hi Mary," said Peter when she answered the phone and peter recognized her. "This is Peter."

"Hi Peter, said Mary, "did you clear up everything in Cleveland?"

"I cleared up everything in Cleveland but now I need help here."

"You need someone to help you move your furniture into your house, right," said Mary.

"You hit the nail on the head," said Peter. "Can you help me?"

"Let me see," said Mary. "I think Mark is available." Peter could hear Mary calling Mark. A view minutes later, Mark grab the phone.

"Hi Peter," said Mark. "I don't know if you remember me, but I remember you. You have been here many times. I even helped clean the house while you were gone. I am going to look at a new house that is going to be available. I will pass your house area on the way. Can you go right now?"

"That would be great," said Peter. "Follow me in my truck."

"I know where it is," said Mark. "Go right now, and I will meet you there. Go and get everything ready inside." Peter said thank you and goodbye to Mary and left. At the house he turned on all the lights and made sure all the area that the furniture went was clear. Two minutes later, Mark got there. It took them less than an hour to get all the furniture in place.

"Thank you Mark," said Peter when all was finished. "What do I owe you?"

"Mary tells me that you are a strong Christian," said Mark. "If so, say a good prayer for my health and safety."."

"You will have more than one great prayer," promised Peter. After Mark left he called the Akron Beacon Journal. A woman's voice answered.

"This is the Akron Beacon Journal. Who do you want to talk to?"

"I would like to talk to Jim, the head of the reporters."

"Just a moment," said the woman. Soon Jim answered the phone.

"Hi Jim," said Peter "This is Peter Alison. I have solved all my problems. When do you want me to come in?"

"Peter, Thank God," said Jim. "I need you right now. Come on in and bring all your papers."

"I'll be there before you can hang up," said Peter. He then hung up grabbed his papers and left for the newspaper company, Peter was sent on a special assignment. A woman had been shot to death in her own home. Peter was given a hard time by the police. Peter finally convinced the police officer to let him come in and help them investigate. He told them that he had a lot of experience solving problems when he was in college and the Cleveland Plain Dealer. The police investigating the crime were surprised and pleased with the evidence Peter found on the floor and behind the desk. That was a place they had not considered to look. That evidence found by Peter solved the case. It led to the murderer. The police sent a very grateful message to Peter's boss. They explained how it was his effort that helped them solve the case. When peter got back to the office he wrote a very good report on the murder. After he finished his column he went to the restaurant that he though Tania was working at. He decided that she would be the dinner waitress and he would have dinner there. Peter was very surprised when he got there, to find out that Tania was not working there that night. When the waitress that Peter had never seen brought his food he asked her where Tania was. The waitress didn't know and with all the clients they had that night, she didn't want to delay to talk to Peter. After all she never saw Peter and didn't know who he was.

The next morning two of the other press reporters that both had heard of Peter and had read his Cleveland reports, that their boss had shown them as a good example. Now they read his report on the woman's murder. Peter decided to have breakfast at the restaurant two buildings away from the paper company's office. He decided to eat breakfast at the restaurant instead of his house, because at home he had to make the breakfast and afterwards do all the cleaning required. When he walked into the restaurant he saw two of the reporters that worked at the newspaper office with him.

"Good morning Peter," said one of the reporters. "Come sit with us. I see that you don't like to cook breakfast either. If you don't remember, I am Jason and this is Bill. Peter joined them. After a small conversation Bill told Peter what he was reporting. The story was about a husband coming home early and seeing his wife kiss a fellow on their front porch. He left and disappeared. The fellow she kissed was her brother who was from a distant city that was just driving by. I'm not sure how to handle this news."

"If I were you, I would find out all about the wife. I would write a very nice story about her. How sweet, and lovely she is and how honest and trustworthy she is. Tell how lucky the husband is. He should trust his wife and always let her explain anything she does that he doesn't understand. Tell how broken hearted she is."

"What do you think about my assignment," said Jason. He then explained what he was reporting. Peter gave him a similar story.

"Always say good things about the person who is in trouble," finished Peter. We had better go to work. It is very nice to be able to talk with you guys. I hope we can do this often. They paid their bills and left for their assignments. Later that day, Peter came back to his office and wrote his newspaper column. Since it was near dinner time Peter decided to go and have dinner at Tina's restaurant. He hoped that she would be the one that served him. When he got there he was seated by a waitress that he didn't recognize. When she brought him the dinner he ordered he asked her about Tina. She didn't know her and told Peter that she just started to work there. After he ate he looked into Frank's office. He also was gone. Peter wondered if he was in the wrong restaurant.

The next morning Peter went to the restaurant that he had gone before. Bill and Jason were there.

"Good morning Peter," said Jason. "Did you talk to Frank?"

"No," said Peter. "How do you know he wants to talk to me?"

"Don't you stop at the office before you come here?" said Bill. "You should do so also so that you can get some late instruction. Jason and I stop in the office before we come here. Our jobs begin at nine because we can't go and see people too early in the morning. Frank however sometimes starts as early as seven depending on how much work he has."

"I didn't know that," said Peter. "I thought we all started at eight. Thank you for telling me. I will stop at the office before I go on my assignment." Peter did just that. When he finished breakfast he went into his office. There he found a note from Frank asking Peter to see him before he left for his assignment. Peter walked to Frank's office.

"Good morning," said Peter.

"Good morning," said Frank. "Come in and sit down.

"Is there a problem?" asked Peter.

"No it is just the opposite. I just wanted to tell you how pleased I am with your work. You not only wrote a wonderful piece on your assignment but the other two reporters wrote very good write up, but told me that you were responsible by helping them. That is great. I want you to continue your good work and to continue to help your buddies."

"They are exaggerating," said Peter. "I just told them what I would have written. I just think that the newspaper should say nice things when they could and especial about the one that got hurt and his or her relatives."

"So keep up the good works," said Frank. "See you later." Peter went to his assignment. His write up and the write up of his co-workers were again very good in Frank's eyes. The next day Peter stopped at the office and was surprised to see another memo asking him to see Fred.

"Hi Fred," said Peter using Fred's first name. He was not used to calling his boss buy his first name. "What do you need now?"

"I need you to travel to Columbus. They are having a political fight and I think you are the only one we have that could handle it."

"When do I leave?" asked Peter.

"I would like you to leave right now if you could. I don't think you will have to stay more than two or three days."

"I will go home, pack a small suitcase, and be on my way," said Peter and left. It was fifteen minutes later that Peter was on the way to Columbus.

In Columbus Peter found himself a room in a hotel and then went to the city hall where the argument had taken place. He met the city medical doctor Dr. Ross. Peter had no trouble getting him to talk.

"I think he is out of his mind," said Dr. Ross. "He wants to eliminate a drug, I don't want to name it, but it is a drug that I need to save people's lives. It is the only drug that can cure a disease that can end up in death."

"Can't you come up with a compromise?" asked Peter. "Make the drug illegal except when used to save people that come up with that disease?"

"I never thought of that," said Dr. Ross. "Mr. Downer, the city's councilman was so strong and harsh that he was impossible to talk to. His whole argument started when he found that one of his family got cancer from the drug. He didn't even want to discuss it. I am fighting it because I have two patients that will die if I can't eliminate the disease from their bodies.

I think I understand," said Peter. "He is one of the cocky know it all councilman. Let me talk to him. Don't let him know that you have talked with me. Let me let him think that the compromise was his Idea. That kind of man needs to think that is the smart one."

"All right," said Dr. Ross. "You are right. I will give you a couple of days. Peter then went looking for the councilman, Mr. Downer. It took him two days to get to talk with him.

"Please your honor my I have two words with you?" said Peter. "I am a reporter and have one question."

"Well, quickly ask it," said the councilman. "I only have one minute."

"Can't you come up with a compromise? Make the drug illegal except when used to cure the deadly disease that Dr. Ross is fighting. That way you will save two persons one that cannot and doesn't use the drug, and one that uses it to cure its disease."

"I will think about it," said Councilman Downer, and left. Peter never saw either one of them again. In the morning when he got the Columbus paper he noticed an article that talked about how Councilman Downer came up with a compromise. Peter just packed his suitcase and headed for home.

The next morning peter went to his newspaper reporter's office at seven. Frank met him there in Peter's office.

"Hi peter," said Frank, "I see that you succeeded in ending the quarrel."

"I just talked to the Councilman Downer," Peter said. "I set it up so that he got all the credit. He bought it."

"You did a fine job," said Frank. "I am very proud of you."

"What is my next assignment," said Peter. "It is usually in on my desk. What's up?"

"Listen," said Frank. "The write ups of your co-workers were not as good as the one's they wrote after you talked with them. I am promoting you as the reporters Manager. I have hired another reporter. His name is Alex Belanto. I would like each to report to you. You give them their assignments and direct them in what to look for. At the end of their assignment you check their write up before it is entered into the system. Do you accept the assignment?"

"Wow, that is a big job," said Peter. "Will Alex, Jason, and Bill accept this?"

"As a matter of fact, said Frank, "it was Jason and Bill that suggested it after I talked to them while you were in Columbus. They liked your help. They said that you had a special attitude about people's action. They would like your input. It will make them look better."

"I accept with one condition," said Peter. "I would like one day off, like tomorrow."

"You can take off tomorrow after you help the reporters," said Frank. "That will give you noon and the rest of the day. Can you do what you have to do in the afternoon?"

"I accept that," said Peter, "except I will take this afternoon off instead of tomorrow. I will be back full time tomorrow?" He had hardly finished talking when Jason walked in to Peter's office.

"Am I too early," said Jason. "I have to get used to this new system."

"You are just in time," said Peter.

"I will talk to you guys later," said Frank. "You however, Peter, can take off this afternoon." Frank then left them.

"I think we will probably make changes as we get along," said Peter. "For example, you and the other two are to come a half hour apart. However I think that hearing what I have to say to each of you may help you think of your assignment."

"I agree with that," said Jason. "Let's see what the others think of it." That said they went into Jason's assignment. It took more than half an hour each to finish the task with all three reporters. It was about eleven when they finished and Peter left for the Restaurant hoping to see Tania. He arrived there about a quarter to twelve and he went directly to Tina's office. To Peters delight Tania was there. When Tania saw Peter she threw herself into his arms.

"I thought that I lost you," said Tania.

"You are the one that had disappeared," said Peter. "I have come here evening believing that you were working late. The waitress I asked about you didn't even know you. I thought you left town."

"I have gone back and forth," said Tania. "But let me bring you up to date. First I was promoted to assistant director. My main job is financial managing. Yesterday I moved into an apartment. Up to that time I have been living in the hotel across from Summit Mall. I admit that I have been going back and forth to Cleveland moving all my possessions here and now am completely moved here. Now tell me where you have been."

"I admit that I have also been very busy. First I had to go to Columbus. Then I got promoted to reporter manager. All the reporters report to me. Next I took off and bought a house here in Fairlawn. Then I moved everything I had in Cleveland and now am a full Fairlawn resident."

"Then you don't have do a lot of traveling," said Tania. "That is great. We both will have evenings off."

"Yes and how about this evening," said Peter. "Can I pick you up here tonight at about four thirty when you get off? We have to spend a lot of time to get to know each other. I love you with a very strong feeling, which I never even dreamt of before, but I think we have to get to know each other's character, to insure that this feeling will last forever."

"I would love that," said Tania. "I however, think I know enough about you that my love is a permanent one already. I have learned all about you from you write ups in the paper. You have a very loving heart. But I would still love to spend the time with you, however please pick me up at six o'clock at my apartment. I want to dress up so that you will find that you love me as much as I love you."

"I will let you go then," said Peter. "I will see you at six, but only if you give me your address." Tania then got a piece of paper and wrote down her address and gave it to him. He then gave her a soft and quick kiss and left. That night at six Peter was at her door at six, Tina was ready. They spent that night at the Red lobster Restaurant. She wanted some fish. They spent all night getting to know each other. First Tina told Peter everything about her past life. Peter followed and told her all that he could remember about his whole life. Then they started to discuss everything they liked and didn't like. That night they covered about ten percent of their lives. When Peter took Tania home he kissed her at her front door. The kiss was like an electrical shock. They couldn't part for the night. Finally Peter separated himself with a great effort and left. They repeated the same discussion and action of that evening, every night all week. Although Peter had originally wondered if they could get tired of each other, he found that his love grew and that the results was that he wanted to spend more time with her. The next week was excitably the same. They could not finish telling each other what they liked and disliked. On Friday Peter arrived at Tina's apartment forty minutes late.

"I was worried about you," said Tina. "Are you all right?"

"Yes," said Peter. "I'm so sorry. I had a very important thing to do. I also have cooked a special dinner that will show you that I could cook when you cannot cook." He then took Tina to his house. Before they sat down to eat he showed her around the house. She loved it. After they sat down and waited until the food was ready about ten minutes later. It was Covatelli, peter's mother's famous Italian food. They sat down and ate. Tina loved it. She wanted the receipt.

"Well where do you think we should go from here?" asked Peter.

"I don't know," said Tina. "You are the driver. Where do you want to go? I will go where ever you take me."

"That is what I wanted to hear," said Peter. Peter then got down on his knee and took a little box out of his pocket. "This is why I was late. Tina, I love you with all of my heart. Will you marry me?"

Tina got tears in her eyes. For a while she could not answer. Finally she said yes.

"I thought you would never ask," said Tina, after she recovered." She then got down on her knees and kissed Peter. The kiss last longer than they expected.

"I think this fall is too soon to get married. We have to find when your family is available to come up from California. We also need to know when my family is available. I am thinking of May tenth. It is the first Saturday in May. That gives us a little over six months to make all the wedding arrangements."

"I have two things to say," said Tania. "First let's set the date on May tenth. May tenth gives them plenty of time to make arrangement. Then I think that this fall we have to visit my family. I think it should be Christmas. We will be with your family on Christmas the rest of their lives."

"Well we can discuss it with my family. They have invited us this Sunday after Church. You will have to transfer to my church. It is closer to my house."

"I will go with you this Sunday. I have not registered with any church. I hate to omit it that I missed church a couple of times before I was promoted. I had to work on Sunday."

"Sunday Tania joined Peter at Peter's church. There Peter introduced her to his parents.

"Mom and dad," said Peter. "I'm sorry that I haven't introduced Tania earlier, but we both have been very busy, mostly both have changing jobs and both have moving from Cleveland to the Akron aria.

"Hi Tania," said Peters mother. "Peter has told us about you but hasn't had the time to introduce you. We will get to know you today at lunch Time."

After the service Peter went into the pastor's office. He made arraignment for his wedding. Then he went to his parent's house for lunch. They had a very sweet time. Peter's parents loved Tania. Tania felt much better. She felt like she was home. Peter's parent's had a million questions to ask Tina. After they ate Peter started to discuss the coming Christmas holiday. Peter wanted to discuss their plans for the holiday.

"Mom and dad," started Peter. "Tina and I would like you and dad to agree that we spend this Christmas at Tina's parent's house in California. We will be spending most Christmases with you here in Ohio most of our lives.

"We will miss you very much," said Peter's father. "However we understand, unless there is a chance that you guys will move to California."

"Not in a million years," said Tania. "I hate California. It is a too liberal of a State. They are trying to take Christ out of everything. "I even hate to visit California. By the way, I am a Born-again Christian. I'm sure Peter has told you. That was one reason we got together."

"Great," said Peter's mother. "We are related that way. There are not too many of us. You think California is bad. I think the whole country is declining in the beliefs of God."

"You are right," said Peter. "There are not too many of us anywhere in this country. That evening went by too fast. Soon it was time for Peter and Tania to go to their homes in Ohio.

The next months went by quickly. Soon Tania and Peter went to California to Tania's parent's house. They spent Christmas there. Tania's parents accepted Peter like he was a son. Peter also respected them like parents. They enjoyed the holidays like they had never before. After New Year's, celebration, Peter and Tania left for their homes in Ohio. The month of May came up faster than they expected. They were surprised at all the work and effort that was required to set up a wedding. They were very thankful for all the help Peter's parents did for them in setting up the wedding. They had to set up the wedding hall, the food that they had to serve and all the chairs that were required for the number of friends and family that would come to the wedding. Some things that had to be taken care of never entered Peter or Tania's mind. The wedding was fantastic. Tania's little sister was the Maid of Honor and Peters best friend at the new paper was his Best Man. All the reporters and their wives attended the wedding. Peter and Tania were at a daze threw the whole affair. Soon they found themselves on their Honey Moon. After the Honey Moon they moved into Peter's house. Everything soon became common. Peter and Tania went back to work. They were the happiest couple in Fairlawn. It was around the first week in august that Peter got up to go to work and found that Tania was still in bed when he came out of the Bath Room. Peter went up to Tania and shook her.

"Get up honey. It's time to go to work."

"I'm not going today," said Tania and turned around to go back to sleep.

"Are you alright?" asked Peter worrying about her actions.

"I'm fine," said Tania. "I resigned from my job yesterday. I decide that it was time to stay home take care of you, keep the house clean, cook supper meals and take care of your son." It suddenly dawned on Peter the game Tania was playing.

"Sweet heart," said Peter," are you pregnant?"

"I'm going to give you a son," said Tania. "It is a present for being such a loving husband." Peter never said a word. He jump into bed and started to kiss Tania. That day was the first day that Peter was late for work.

The end

Story Number Nine

Looking For the Beginning

Larry was driving home from school. He was so happy that his students all past the final test of that semester. He felt like he had done a fine job in teaching. He was now going home to enjoy the summer vacation. Usually he found a job during the summer. He usually worked as a carpenter. He was very good in woodworking. He learned some from his father who was an Industrial builder. The thought of the word father got him to thinking. Many summers he had considered spending the time finding out who he really was. He remembered living in an orphanage called Boy's Town. It was a woman called Sally that kind of raised Larry. She saw that he went to school when he was five. He was twelve when Sal and Jeanette Kozar came to Boys Town and reviewed all the boys there. Larry did not understand why but Mrs. Kozar chose Larry and they adopted him. He remembered that he was unhappy to leave Boys Town. It was home to him. However after a full summer with them he started to enjoy what they did for him and where they took him. He enjoyed the time they spent at the park. After a couple of years he accepted them as his parents. They have been so good and loving that he couldn't help but to love them back. They send him to college to study science which he showed them that he was interested in. When he graduated they talked him to continue and get a master's degree. He went back and studied Electrical and mechanical Engineering. He then was hired by the Akron University. He has been a professor at Akron University now for four years. He was very well respected at his job. However, he couldn't wonder who his real parents were and why they gave him away to the Orphanage. However he was very happy with his new parents. The only problem he had with his current parents, who, he learned to call Mom and dad, is that they tried to fix him up with a girl. They wanted him to be happily married. He was now twenty three years old. Finally he got home.

"Hi Larry, said his mother, "How did everything go at school?"

"All went fine," said Larry. "All my students passed the final test. I am so proud of them."

"Perhaps you should look for another job here in the Akron area."

"You know mom," said Larry. "I love you and dad very much. You have been excellent parents."

"We love you very much also," said his mom. "What is this all about?"

"I feel that since I have all the summer and I don't need any money, I should work to get a question out of my mind."

"What question do you have?" said his mother "I'm sure I know what it is."

"I know mom," said Larry. "I'm sure you have the same question circulating in your mind. I want to know who I really am."

"You are my only son," said Jeannette his mom. "I would not love you more if I had given you birth."

"I know mom," said Larry. "I also assure you that I could never love my real mom as much as I love you. You have given me everything I have."

"You do what your heart tells you," said his mother. "I will not stop you nor will I help you." Larry then got on his computer to get an address for the Boy's town location. He was shock when he saw that there were twelve Boy's town locations. There was one in West Lake Ohio. After he wrote down the address, he got in his car and drove to West Lake. He found the Boy's Town building and entered the front door. As he entered he ran into a nice looking young lady.

"Can I help you?" she said.

"I would like to find out who set me here. I was adopted when I was twelve. I would like to know who my real mother is. Can we look at your records to see who placed me here?"

"We are only a very small unit. The top unit is in Nebraska. They are the main unit. But let's go see Mrs. Careen. She is the Manager here. We all refer, to her here, as our chief. She has all the records." She let Larry to the main Office

"Mrs. Careen," said the young lady. "There is a gentleman here to see you."

"Let him in," said Mrs. Careen, "Come have a seat. Do you want to adopt a child?" "No," said Larry. "I was placed in a Boy's Town home when I was born. I was adopted when I was twelve. I would like to know who my mother is. The parents that adopted me are the most wonderful parents one could have. I think they are the nicest people you will ever meet. I am not here to change anything. I just want to know my real mother and to help her if she needs help."

"Do you know your real mother's last name," asked Mrs. Careen?

"No," said Larry. "I only know my last name, which is, Kozar.

"How old are you, "asked Mrs. Careen?

"I am twenty three years old," said Larry. Mrs. Careen looked through all her records. She went to her cabinet and looked the records back sixteen years ago.

"I'm sorry," said Mrs. Careen. "Are you sure you're from here?"

"To tell you the truth," said Larry. "I don't recognize this place."

"I recommend you contact our branch at Nebraska."

"Thank you so much for your time and effort. God Bless you." Larry then left and got home in time for dinner.

The next day Larry checked everything he could on the Boy's Town operation. He finally decided he had to go to the Nebraska branch. From everything that he learned, it was the main branch. If they couldn't help he had to find another way to find his real mother. He found the address and then check the flight and time that he had to take to get there. The next day in the afternoon he got to Nebraska. He got a cab and went to the Boy's town building. Inside he found it very similar to the other one in Ohio. However, to his sadness he didn't recognize any of it. Soon a young man came up to him.

"Sir," said the young man "is there someone you would like to see?"

"Yes I would like to see the Manager who has access to all the records here."

"You want to see Mr. Zara" said the young man. Come follow me. Larry was taken to the main office.

"Mr. Zara," said the young man sticking his head in the office door. "There is a gentleman who wants to see you."

"Bring him in" said Mr. Zara. "What can I do for you?" Larry explained to him all that he had said to the other manager in Ohio. Mr. Zara looked through all his files. Is Kozar the only name you have?" he asked.

"Yes," said Larry. "If I had my real mother's name I would have found it through regular channels."

"Well I can't find anything under the name Kozar," said Mr. Zara. I highly recommend you look under the Local Orphanage. We are a private business. We are supported by the gifts given by our lovely American public. I'm sure you got gift request letters from us. However, most orphanages are locally supported by the government or the local residents. They will have more information then we have. If I were you I would check one nearest to where you live."

"Thank you," said Larry and left. "The next day he found that the nicest orphanage was in Wooster Ohio. After breakfast, he headed for Wooster. He found the Orphanage and entered the front door. As he entered he was surprised to see the most beautiful girl he had ever seen, He was very shook up by her presents there. In that shock position he spoke.

"Can I help you?" Larry said in his confused state.

"What?" said the woman in a confused state also?

"I'm sorry," said Larry recovering a little, "What I meant was, can you help me?"

"No," said the woman. "I don't work here. I am waiting to see the Orphanage Manager. She is in her office talking with another woman who needs help."

"My name is Larry Kozar," said Larry. "I need help also."

"My name is Tanya Nestor," said the woman. "What is your problem? Are you here to adopt a child?"

"No," said Larry. "I was raised by the Boy's Town agency. I was adopted by a family when I was twelve years old. I'm here to see if they could find my real mother. Why are you here?"

"I was raised here," said Tanya. "I'm looking to find my mother also."

"Were you adopted and at what age?" asked Larry.

"No I was never adopted," said Tanya. "I was raised right here. I was given permission to leave when I graduated from High school. I got a job and saved enough money to go to college."

"Did the family that adopted you treat you badly?" asked Tanya.

"No," said Larry. "They are the most wonderful parents any one can have."

"So If you are happy, why are you looking for your real mother?" asked Tanya.

"I am happy," said Larry. "My present Parents got me through high school and seeing that I had high grades, they got me through college and even got me to go back for a master's degree."

"So what do you do, and why are you not there?" asked Tanya.

"I am a science instructor at Akron University. I teach electrical and mechanical engineering. I am off for the summer and since I didn't want to get a summer job, I decided to find my real mother."

"So you are a teacher," said Tanya. "That's funny, I am a teacher too. I teach science at a high school. "Do you believe in God?"

"I believe in God," said Larry. "I am a Born-Again-Christian."

"That is fantastic," said Tanya. "I am a Born-again-Christian also. There are very few of us left. I have only known two Christian in my life. I think God has brought us together."

"I agree with you," said Larry. "I am very attracted to you. But let us not get ahead of ourselves. Let's finish our first goal. Then we can look at the road that is ahead of us after we find our real mothers. Until then I would like to call you my girlfriend. But we can ask question for now. I am very curious on how you got to be a Christian being brought up in an Orphanage."

"One day, dear boyfriend," said Tanya agreeing with the relationship, "I was in the library and I found a Christian book. It explained how there had to be a God. We could not have been created by a sand storm. After getting a lot of information, it caused me to look for a bible. After studying the bible I was convinced that there was a God and that he offered his only son to save us. I was convinced, so I accepted Jesus as my savior. That made God my heavenly father. From then on God helped me become the teacher I am. God has guided me since then. I believe he is guiding me now." Before Larry could answer the woman came out who had been speaking with the manager.

"He is all yours," said the woman as she left.

"You go first," said Tanya to Larry.

"But you got here first," said Larry. "It is your turn."

"I'm too nervous," said Tanya. "I don't know if I can wait for you after I am done."

"Let's go together," said Larry. "We have the same question. But before we go in what is your last name?""

"My last name is Nestor," said Tanya. "Let's try it. Let's see if he will accept us both at the same time."

"I will tell him," said Larry, "that you are my girlfriend and I will not let you go alone." That said they walked into the manager's office together.

"Hi," said Larry. "I am Larry Kozar and this is my girlfriend Tanya Nestor. We are two that came out of an Orphanage. We would like to know who our real mothers are."

"Well, come in and sit down," said the manager. "My name is Tom Alison. We will see what we can do." He then turned on his computer and started to type. "Miss," asked Tom, "what is your current name?"

"I don't have any Idea where the name came from. I think the people at the Orphanage make it up. However they called me Tanya Nestor."

"Whatever they call you, or name you, it has to go down on the records," said Tom. "And I did find it. Your real mother was Ashley

Harris." Larry took out his notepad and wrote down the name. "And you sir," continued Tom, "what is your name?"

"My name is Larry Kozar." A few minutes later Tom spoke up.

"Your mother's name is Victoria Zara," said Tom. "Is there anything else you would want to know?"

"You wouldn't have their address would you?" asked Larry.

"I'm sorry," said Tom. "We don't have that information." Larry and Tania both said thank you and goodbye and left. Outside Larry asked Tanya what she have planned for the rest of the day.

"I don't have any plans," said Tanya. "It is late afternoon. If you don't have any plans let's go and have lunch and talk about our next move."

"Sounds like a smart move," said Larry. They left for the parking lot. Larry drove. They stopped at the nearest restaurant and got their very late lunch there. While sitting at the restaurant table they talked about what they would do next.

"I think we should find your mother first," said Tanya. "We can work from your house. We will do it together."

"I don't have a house," said Larry. "I live with my parents. I do have an office there. We can work from there. It would be very private."

"Will your parent's mind?" asked Tanya.

"That's a good point," said Larry. "Why do you want to do mine first?"

"I need time with you and time to give me courage and hope," said Tanya.

"Alright said Larry. "First we will go to my house and introduce you to them. I am one hundred present sure about how I feel for you. I will tell them that you are my girlfriend and we can see their reaction."

"That's a good plan," said Tanya. "It will answer my first concern. Will your family accept me as your girlfriend?" They finished their lunch and then went back to the Orphanage for Tanya's car. Tanya then followed Larry to his home. When they got there Larry's mom opened the door.

"Larry," said his mom. "I'm glad you got home. Your dad is on his way home. He finished early today. Who is this pretty girl that is with you?" Larry didn't answer until they got inside.

"Mom," said Larry. "This is my girlfriend. I have kept her from you until I got to know her better and was sure she was the one for me."

"Well I'm so glad to meet you," said Larry's mom. "Come on in and let's get acquainted."

"Hi Mrs. Kozar," said Tanya. "Larry has talked a lot about you. He loves you and his father so much.

"So why would you talk about us?" asked Jeannette, Larry's mother.

"We probably should tell you how we met," said Tanya. She then looked at Larry to see if he approved or he wanted to tell her.

"You can tell her," said Larry. "But let's wait until dad gets home. We don't want to go into our romance twice."

"I hope you will stay here and have dinner with us," said Larry's mother.

"I don't want to impose on you," said Tanya.

"You will not be imposing," said Larry's mother. "We would love to have you." Just then Larry's father walked in.

"Who is this beautiful girl?" said Sal, Larry's father when he saw Tanya. "How did we get so lucky to have her here?"

"Hi Dad," said Larry. "This is my girlfriend. Let's sit and have dinner and I will explain everything."

"It is too early for dinner," said Larry's mother. "It's only five o'clock. Dinner will be ready at six. It is in the oven. Let's sit and talk about your romance."

"Well to start," said Tania, "Larry and I were both raised in an orphanage. I was there until I was seventeen and then got a good job. I saved enough money to go to college. I became, and still am a high school science teacher. So Larry and I have the same kind of work and more important at this time is that we are both off in the summer. We met at one of the Orphanages. We were both shocked at the great attraction we had for each other. We both had butterflies in our stomach. We both are interested in finding who our real mother was." We got together and decided to work together. We also, from working together and talking with each other, found we have the same religion. We are both born-Again-Christians. We are both thinking very similar about everything. We feel we are like mental twins."

"You are lucky you found each other," said Larry's father. "What are your plans from here on?"

"First we are going to spend time together." said Larry. "Secondly, since we are both interested in finding the woman that gave us birth, we will work together to do this. Looking for the answers this summer will give us the time together that we would like to have to get to know each other better."

"Sounds like a good plan," said Sal, Larry's father. "Where are you going to start?"

"We have already done half of the job," said Larry. "I have visited several Boys' Town places to see if I came from there. I could not get an answer from there. I then went to our local Orphanage. There we got Tanya's and my mother's names. I hope you don't mind," said Larry, "if when we finish eating we go into my office and try to reach these people."

"No it's your office," said Larry's father. "Good luck." At six Larry's mother brought in the food. When they finish eating Tanya thanked Larry's mother for the fantastic dinner and they went into Larry's office. Larry started his search. He found several Zara families in the country. He wrote down the names and phone numbers of all the Zara families he found.

"Honey," said Larry to Tanya. "Let me start calling some of these numbers. In the mean while when I am calling you get behind to computer and see if you could find all the Harris families. Larry started to call the numbers he had. Several he called he decided was not the one he was looking for. Three didn't want to answer his questions. He decided to see the one that gave him the hardest time. All three were in the Ohio area. Before the day was over he had three addresses and Tanya had two that sounded like they could be the ones. The next morning they visited the first family that Larry picked. When they visited them they realized that it was not possible for them to be who they were looking for. They were oriental. They then went to the second family that Larry suspected. That one told them that they had heard of the name but they are not in the area anymore. Larry decided to see the police station or the city hall to see if they had any information. At the police station one of the officers told him that the name was familiar. He looked through all the police records. He was about to give up when he decided to look at the record of all the problems. He soon found the answer he was looking for.

"Here I found a possible answer to your question," said the officer. The family of Zara had a very bad accident. The woman, I see here, was called Victoria. She lived for a little while and died after a few months."

"Did they have any children with them," asked Larry?"

"There is a very strange marking here," said the officer. "It has the name boy but there is a question mark next to his name. The woman was taken to Akron General Hospital. Maybe there was a boy involved. I don't have any answers here." Larry and Tanya left and went directly to Akron General Hospital. After talking to a few nurses, they were directed to the main office.

"Hello," said the person on the desk. How can I help you?"

"There was an auto accident about twenty three years ago," said Larry. "A woman named Victoria Zara was brought here and there is no record of what happened to her. We want to know if she survived her accident."

"I don't know how to answer you but there is a nurse who was here twenty years ago. She knows of many strange things that happen here in the hospital. Let me call her." She called and a few minutes later an older nurse came in.

"How can I help you?" said the nurse.

"About twenty three years ago," said Larry, "there was an accident and a woman named Victoria Zara was brought in here and then vanished."

"I remember an incident that was very strange. A woman was brought in here and she was dead. But the doctor brought her back to life but her head and brain seen dead. Her body was giving strange results. After much checking they found that she was pregnant. They removed the child and as soon as the little boy was removed the lady passed away. It was like she waited for her son to be born."

"Do you know where the body was buried?" asked Larry.

"No," said the nurse. "I think they got her will and she asked to be cremated.

"Well thank you very much," said Larry. "You have answered all my questions. Thank you. Come Tanya, we have finished this task." When they got to the car Larry turned to Tanya.

"I think it is early enough that we could go to your first family."

"I think that we should go to the Harris family first," said Tanya. "First it is the closest to where we are. Secondly, I have a very strange feeling that this is the one. The woman's voice on the phone had a strange effect on me."

"Give me the address," said Larry. Tanya gave him the address and Larry headed there. A few minutes later they arrived at the house. They got out of the car and headed to the front door. Larry knocked on the door. An older woman opened the door.

"What can I do for you?" asked the woman.

"Are you related to the Harris family?" asked Larry.

"Yes," said the woman. "I am Helen Harris. What do you want?"

"We would like to talk to you about your daughter, "said Larry. "Is she home?"

"No," said Helen. "She is working. She will be home about four thirty. What is this all about?"

"Is your daughter's name Ashley," asked Larry

"Yes," said Helen. "What does this have to do with her? Is she in trouble?"

"We think that she had a daughter called Tanya," said Larry.

"Oh dear Lord," said Helen. "How did you know? I tried to keep it a secret from every one. How did you find out?"

"Why did you try to keep it a secret?" asked Tanya.

"I keep it a secret because it happened very suddenly," said Helen. "Ashley doesn't ever know.""

"Why don't you start from the beginning," said Larry, "and tell us the whole story."

"First, who are you?" asked Helen. "Why do I have to tell it to you?"

"You are right," said Larry. "Let me introduce each of us. First I am Professor Larry Kozar. I teach at the Akron University. This is my fiancée, Tanya Nestor. Her real last name is Harris." They thought that Helen was going to pass out.

"Are you my granddaughter," said Helen. "I thought that there was something in your eyes," said Helen as she threw herself into Tanya's Arms. "Come inside and tell me what is going on."

"First start from the beginning," said Larry. "Tell us the whole story."

"Well Ashley was sixteen," started Helen. "She was engaged to a fellow named Ben. Ben was from a town in the Ukraine area. When they started to be attack by their enemy, I don't know who they were, but Ben went to help his family. During one of the battles he was killed. I don't know if this started Ashley's problem, but she loved him very much. She was very depressed with the loss. About a week after ben's death, she passed out at her job and went into a coma. They couldn't wake her so they sent her to the hospital. There they called me. I rushed to the hospital. The doctor there told me that she had a stroke. The doctor said that he could not tell if her brain was affected and how badly it was damaged from the loss of blood to the brain, He told me that he was surprised by all body tests that she was still alive. It was about six months later, that a specialist came to see Ashley. The doctor and every one were surprised that she was still alive. She was unconscious and her body was just barely keeping alive. Later the doctor told me that he found a problem that could affect her life. He told me that she was pregnant. He said that the baby was nearly born so they decided to help it out of her womb. The baby was born alive. But Ashley remained in a deep unconsciousness. The doctor said that all her vital sign were getting lower and he expected her to pass away any day. I was worried that after she passes away what I am going to do with the baby girl. I couldn't care of her so I gave her to the Orphanage. It was a fantastic surprise to all, that two months later, Ashley started to get better. About a month later she came to. They kept her for two months later and then released her. That is my story."

"Well you never know what God will do," said Larry. "How is she mentally?"

"She is just fine," said Helen. "For a while she had bad memory, but today she is as well as she was before she went to the hospital." After that story they all went into the kitchen and had some coffee.

"I wonder how Ashley will take the fact that she has a twenty two year old daughter," said Tanya. "Will she believe it and accept me?"

"We will see in a few hours," said Helen. "Will you stay for dinner? I can make some Italian Covatelli. You have to stay a while to get acquainted with Ashley."

"I don't know," said Larry. "My parents expect us to come home for dinner."

"Why don't you call them and tell them what you have found," said Helen. Larry calls his mother. He found that his mother was all for it. They spent the next few hours, each telling of their past. Tanya told them how she spent her years in the Orphanage. They all seemed very interested. Soon it was time for Ashley to come home. Helen took Tanya and Larry to the Living room. Ashley usually came in the back door which led to the family room. "Stay here," said Helen. "I think I will have to talk with Ashley alone first." Five minutes later, Ashley came through the rear door as usual.

"Hi mom," said Ashley as she walked into the family room.

"Hi sweet heart," said Helen. "Listen, we have to talk. It is very important that we discuss our family."

"What family," said Ashley? "The last I heard it is only you and me."

"Well there is the possibility of our family to grow to six."

"What are you talking about," said Ashley. "Are you, at your age, planning on getting married?"

"No of course not," said Helen her mother. "Let's sit here and let me tell you what I need to tell you." They sat down on the couch.

"All right," said Ashley. "What have you been up to?"

"Remember when you were in a coma for around eight months?" said Helen.

"Yes I remember," said Ashley. "How can I forget?"

"Well you were trying to get over Ben's death, "said Helen. "You and Ben were not very good Christians because you had sexual relationships with him. I don't know how many times but you did at least once."

"How in the world did you know that," asked Ashley. "I think it was only twice. After the second I refused to go with him to his apartment. We were just so much in Love. Did you see that I was not a virgin when I was in the coma?"

"I don't know how to tell you this, said Helen. "I think I had better take a deep breath. And get it out. During the examination the doctor found that you were three months, pregnant."

"What" said Ashley almost falling out of the couch? She sat there with her mouth open and looking like she was about to pass out. She just sat there for about ten minutes before she gained mental control.

"Are you all right honey?" said her mother

"What did they do about it?" asked Ashley finally.

"It was born alive, but the doctor told me that after the birth your body was showing signs of decline. The doctor said that he though you would not make it more than another day. So here I was with a pretty little baby girl. I was alone in this world without you. How could I take care of it? I named it Tanya after your grandmother and gave her to the nearest orphanage. I never thought that you would survive. You were almost dead for two more months before you began to recover. It took two more months before you were released and came home."

"So why do you bring this up now?" said Ashley. "That was over twenty years ago."

"This afternoon a gentleman and his fiancé came looking for you. They have information about you daughter."

"What," said Ashley where are they? How can I find them?"

"They are upstairs in the Living room," said Helen. Ashley jumped out of her seat and rushed to the Living Room. Helen had a hard time keeping up with her.

"Are you really my mom," yelled Tanya as soon as she saw Ashley coming into the room. Ashley ran up to Tanya and hugged her kissing her on the checks.

"I was not sure until I saw you," said Ashley as she pulled away. "Your face is a little like my grandmother. I can tell by your face that you are a family member.

"I agree with Ashley," said Helen. "I don't know why but I feel like I have seen the face before."

"And you are my grandmother," said Tanya to Helen. "I feel like I'm home after a long trip that took me away from home for a long time." She then hugged Helen again.

"And you are going to be my grandson," said Helen. She then hugged Larry. Ashley then walked over to Larry.

"And you are going to be my son, said Ashley. "That seems so great. I hope I'm not dreaming. If I am please don't wake me up."

"Me too," said Tanya. "If this is a dream let it last for a life time" After they finished talking, they all hugged each other again. Helen decided to make some coffee. They all sat around the Living Room table and had coffee.

"Where do we go from here?" said Helen.

"We will have to go home," said Larry. "I promise that we will keep in touch. We have to see what my family wants to do. You are both part of our family. Don't forget that. You are both very important to us. We will start planning our future with you in it.

"Will you stay and have dinner with us?" asked Helen.

"My mother told me that if you asked us to stay for dinner to say yes. She said that we will have to know each other. So yes we will stay for dinner." At dinner they all talked about their past. Larry told about his time in the Orphanage. He told them all that he could remember. The other three followed Larry with their stories. They all got to know each other so great that they felt like they were all already old family members. At about ten Larry decided to go home.

"Honey," said Larry to Tanya. "I'm sure my mother is still up waiting to hear about our time with the Harris family. Then, turning to Helen and Ashley, he said. We are so delighted to have met you. I promise that we will keep in touch. He then hugged Helen and after Ashley and Tanya finished hugging Larry hugged Ashley. They then left, and when they go to Larry's house he was right. His mother was waiting for them.

"Hi kids," said Larry's mom. "Come on in and tell me about Tanya's family," she said to Larry after he came in. She was surprised to see Tanya came in after Larry. Hi sweet Tanya. I'm so happy to see you. I am surprised that you came here tonight it being so late."

"I wanted to see you, and say good night," said Tanya. "Don't forget that in a few months you will be my mother. I already love you like one. It does feel strange that soon I will have two mothers."

"Of course," said Larry's mom. "You are always welcome here. And I want you to know that I love you like a daughter already. So how did you make out today?"

"Mom we found Tanya's mother and Grandmother," said Larry. "Mom, I could never have a mother better then you, but I feel like Tanya's mother, Ashley Harris is already my mother. Both Tanya's mother and grandmother, Helen Harris are fantastic woman. I fell in love with both after talking with them for a while."

"What do you think of your family?" said Vickie, turning to Tanya. "You never knew them did you?"

"They were so loving I felt like I was home. They were both happy that I found them. My mother never knew that I existed. My grandma gave me to the Orphanage thinking that I would not survive"

"Well," said Vickie. "I can't wait to meet them both. They sound like they will make a loving part of our family. I will call them tomorrow and make some party arrangement. For now, you guys go to bed. We will talk about future plans tomorrow. I am so excited."

"Good night mom," said Tanya. I'm looking forward to the future. Have a good night."

"Thank you stopping here before you went home. That should tell us how much we love each other. Good night, Favorite daughter."

Tanya smiled as she left. On the way home, she though that she was not yet a daughter in law. And she realized that if she was a daughter, she would be the only one.

The next week went by quickly Vickie called Helen the morning after Tanya and Larry had met them. They made an arrangement for them all to get together Sunday after lunch for a "Get together Party." Sunday came quickly. It was the first time that every person who was invited felt a period of joy. They felt that they were a part of a family. Up to that time they all had the feeling of loneliness. The party was a great success. They decided that they would do it often. The next Sunday they were all invited to Helen's house for what Helen call the "Reunion day." The dinner was fantastic and the joy of the get together was over whelming. The happiness that filled all their hearts was enjoyed by all. At the end of the party Tanya asked Larry to remain behind so that they could talk. After every one left Tanya and Larry went out on the porch to talk.

"What do you have on your mind?" asked Larry. "I'm all ears."

"I would like your opinion on something, "said Tanya. "I will not do anything without your approval."

"Go ahead," said Larry. "I'm listening."

"My mother," said Tanya "has asked me to move in with her until the wedding. She would want us to be mother and daughter for at least a few months. What do you think?"

"I think it is a wonderful Idea. That shows how much she loves you. I am so glad she asked you that. I wondered how much she loved a young lady she had never met or knew she existed. Go, next week school starts. We are going to have a very busy year. Can you imagine what Thanksgiving and Christmas are going to be like as out two families become one?" Tanya did move in with her mother and grandmother.

The next week Helen invited all of Larry's family. It was as enjoyable as the one they had at Larry's family's house. This went on a least once a month at Helen's house and once a month at Jeannette's house. Larry and Tanya spent every day together until the first week of September. That was when school started. Tanya and Larry were tied up most of the week even in the evening when they had to prepare for the next day's session. Their evenings off were never on the same day. They only saw each other on the weekends. One day on Wednesday which was the busiest day for Tanya, Larry went out for lunch. He seldom did this but his school had the afternoon off for a special school cleaning. At the restaurant he went to, he met a special friend he had gone to high school with. His name was Nick. He also was adapted from an Orphanage. They had a lot to talk about. They had not seen each other since they were around twelve years old.

"So what are you doing now," asked Nick?"

"I'm a Professor at the Akron University," said Larry. "I teach electrical and Mechanical Engineering. How about you what are you up to?" asked Larry.

"I'm a Real Estate sales man," said Nick. "I own and run a very lucrative business"

"I can tell that it must be a great business by the suit you are wearing," said Larry. "It sounds like a great enjoyable business. Do you travel to all the houses you deal with?"

"I love my job," said Nick, "however, I have a problem right now. I have a small ranch house that a single fellow owns. He was offered a fantastic job in Arizona. The job is a higher position that he has now at double the salary. But he has to be there by this coming Monday. He madly wants to get rid of the house. It is a very beautiful house. I would by it if I wasn't married. It is great for a single man. He is willing to sell it at a price that is much lower than it's worth. I can't find anyone who is interested."

"Well you found someone now," said Larry. "I am getting married in May. We have no place to live in. My fiancé' lives with her parents and I live with mine. Can you take me, after we eat, to see it?"

"I would love to," said Nick. They both ate as fast as they could. They left there and Larry was surprised that the house was on Bancroft road about a half mile from where his parent's house was. Inside, Larry was thrilled. He loved it. He could not understand why he had a problem selling it.

"I love it said Larry. "It would be a great place for me and my wife to spend the first years of our lives. I see that it has three bedrooms. We could have two children with their own bedrooms. How much is he asking?" Nick told him the price the owner was will to sell it for. Larry was shocked. It was much lower than he imagined.

"We can offer lower and see how low he is willing to go," said Nick

"Let's go for it," said Larry. "I see that it has a lot of furniture. Does all the furniture go with it at that price?"

"Yes "said Nick.

"Can we meet here about five this evening? We can settle the deal here. But I want my future wife to see it. I know she will love it, but I don't want to buy a house without her seeing it."

"Sounds reasonable, said Nick. "Let me call Rick, the owner, and get him here tonight. He called and after hanging up he told Larry that everything was set. Larry went home and told his mom everything that had happened. That evening Larry drove to the school, and finding Tanya's car he sat on her bumper and waited for Tanya. It was about four thirty that Tanya showed up. Larry explained everything and then they went to the house. Nick was already there. Larry took Tanya around the house and even the basement. She loved it. About five thirty all showed up. Larry offered ten percent lower than he asked. Rick agreed to split the difference. Larry accepted the final price. Nick had all the required papers and by seven thirty the deal was closed. Larry wrote a check for the amount that was required and they left with Larry having the ownership papers and the keys to the house. Larry and Tanya couldn't wait to move into the house.

The next week things went back to normal. Soon it was Thanksgiving Day. They all got together again. It all took place at Larry's parents, Sal and Jeannette's house. Jeannette felt and treated Helen like she was her mother. Love in the family was spread and felt like it had always been there. That day was as enjoyable as all their past parties. They were all sad when it was over. Before they realized it Christmas was there. Larry and his father Sal decorated the house, inside and outside, like their lives depended on it. Of course Helen and Ashley were invited. When Helen and Ashley arrived at the house they were surprised at all the Christmas trimming that was on the outside of the house. There were stings of colored light everywhere. The outside of the house had lights. Each window had lights. The entrance way had light. The door way had light and of course the Santa and the dears had lights. They were just as surprised in all that they saw inside. The most beautiful was the heavily lighted up Christmas tree with packages surround it. They all hugged each other and Helen put three packages she brought, under the tree. That day was the best day they ever had as a whole family. They all felt like an old member of the family. They even knew each other so well that they gave each other gifs that fit perfectly into what they each wanted. That day was the most joyful day they ever had. Though they all wanted the day to last longer it soon was over. They all went home with loving hearts. For the New Year each family had plans of their own. Larry and Tanya went to a restaurant that had New Year celebration. After Larry and Tanya got a few drinks they spent the rest of the evening dancing. They loved having their arms around each other. Larry and Tanya never realized how much work is needed to plan a wedding. They were so happy to have their mothers and fathers to help. Finding a place to celebrate their wedding took a lot of church checking. Most places were not available until late in the year. Larry and Tanya didn't want to wait that long. They eventually found one for May tenth. Getting these was the big things that had to be taken care of. There were more than a dozen smaller things that had to be taken care of. Soon it was May ninth. That evening they had the Rehearsal Dinner. Larry and Tanya went earlier to the church where the pastor showed them what to expect and what they had to do. They went to the rehearsal dinner before it started. Larry's father Sal gave the rehearsal speech. He told how the great love the two had for each other, spread to both families. How the two families are now one family. He went on telling them how their joyfulness makes them a joy to have around. He continued telling of all the good things the two lovers were involved with. He told how they met. Them the food came and he thanked God for everything, including the two children and the food. Every one enjoyed the dinner. The next day the wedding started after lunch at two o'clock. Sal, Larry's father led Tanya down the aisle. Larry felt like he was in another world. He gave his speech and Tanya gave hers and Larry suddenly found Tanya kissing him. The next thing he knew they were at the dinner hall where Sal's father gave the speech. It was almost the same as he gave at the rehearsal dinner. Helen, Tanya's grandmother gave the next speech. The next thing Larry knew he had finished eating dinner and was dancing with Tanya. After dancing with several other women, including his mother, Helen and Tanya's mother Ashley, the party was over. Larry still in a stunned condition didn't remember the drive to his house. That night was very enjoyable when he made love with Tanya. The next thing he remembered was that they here in his car driving to their honey moon. His heart was full of joy and happiness; however a part of his tired body was glad that it was over.

The End

Story Number Ten

It was Long Ago and Far Away

"Hi little brother," said Stella. "I was wondering when you would come home."

"If I would have known you were coming I would have come home earlier. So what is going on?"

"I come to see if you want to come with us," said Stella. "My husband is in Rome getting approval for us to go to America."

"Why do you want to leave this country," said Joey?

"Haven't you heard? Germany and England are at war. They think that Italy will join Joey decided to go home after a full day at his farm. He dismissed the hired workers and walked to his small shed where he kept his farming tool. There also he had his horse tied to a post that was there for that reason. It was a fifteen minutes horseback ride to his home. That was the thing in that part of the country that was mostly farming country. Every farmer in that area lived in the city of Barrafranca. All the farms were away from the city. That was that way to protect each farmer's house. It was that way as far back as joey had ever heard it was. Joey was eighteen years old. Joey's real name was Giuseppe Crazano. When he was a little boy his parents bought the house from an American family who built it and were moving back to America. After Joey's parents moved in the Americans were delayed and stayed with the Crazano family until their problem was solved. The American woman treated Joey with great affection.

tell me a Story

"You know Giuseppe that in America the name Giuseppe is translated to Joseph. The short name for Joseph is Joey. I think I will call you Joey." She called him that until she left. Joey liked it so much that he told everyone from that day on that his name was Joey. Joy's mother died when he was a little boy and his father died last year. In Sicily the law was that if the parents died the oldest son inherited everything the family owned. It was the son's duty then to take care of all the other members of the family. Joey divided the farm between himself and his three sisters. Maria was Joey's favorite sister. She was his oldest sister. She was like a mother to him. Her husband had died and her son Filippo took over the farming. His next sister was Lucia. She was married to Stefano Didio. His third sister was Stellina. Stellina was married to Giuseppe. Joey had never met Giuseppe. Before Dad died Stellina had moved to Mazzarino. There she helped design cloths. Joey divided the farm in four equal sections. He then gave each family a piece of the land. Stellina hired a farmer boy, to take care of her land. She met Giuseppe Belanto in Mazzarino and they got married with only two friends who were Best man and Maid of honor for them. When Joey got home he saw a strange horse in front of his house. When he looked around he saw a woman talking to his neighbor Rosetta. He recognized her as his sister Stella,

Stella," he yelled out. "What are you doing here? I'm so glad to see you." Stella said goodbye to Rosetta and walked up to Joey.

"The war will come soon. I think we will be saver in America."

"You came all the way here to talk me into going with you?" asked Joey. "How can I leave? I have this large house that used to be our parents and I have a double farm thanks to you. I can never leave. Also I don't think Italy will get involved in the war."

"Actually I came to get rid of all that I have here in Barrafranca. I also have to sign a paper relieving all my ownership of the farm land. It is all yours." They then went inside. Joey made a good dinner that his mother had taught him and they both ate.

"I wish I could have met your husband," said Joey.

"Sell the land and come to America. I understand they need a lot of workers in their factories."

"I don't think do," said Joey. "I'm happy here. I would not know any one there. When I get to the age when I want to get married, who would I find there?"

"They have a lot of Italians who are going there to get away from the war," said Stella. "There you could find a good Italian wife."

"I understand you cannot just go to America. You need a special document."

"Giuseppe got a document that fills the required," said Stella. "He searched and found a company in America that needs worker. He has a job in a place called New Jersey."

"Well you have a good life," said Joey. "I'm staying here." Stella stayed in Barrafranca for about three days. She took care of all to be free of anything in Barrafranca. Then before she left, she stopped at Joey's house to say goodbye. Joey missed her greatly after she left.

Stella arrived in Palermo at noon. She then she took a small boat to Rome. There she met her husband.

"Hi Stella," said her husband. "Did you take care of everything in Barrafranca?"

"Yes," said Stella. "We can never go back. I signed over even the farm. We have nothing there."

"I have a document approving our going to America," said Giuseppe. "I also have a cabin on the boat to America."

"When do we leave?" asked Stella.

"We leave Wednesday. That is two days from now, said Giuseppe, "however, we can get on the boat this afternoon." They did get on the boat as soon as they were allowed. Stella loved the room. It had a very large bed, and an attached bathroom.

"We have a whole day," said Giuseppe. "Let's walk around the ship and get used to all the rooms. I especially would like to know where the cafeteria is. I think we will have to wait until tomorrow morning to get some food." Giuseppe was wrong, as they walked into the dining room they saw people getting served at several tables. It was dinner time and the passengers were served dinner,

"Are you hungry?" asked Giuseppe.

tell me a Story

"I am a little," said Stella. "Let's eat while we can. We don't know what the schedule is after the ship leaves port." They ate their dinner and then went back touring the ship. The ship left on Wednesday as planned. It took eight days for the ship to reach America. After the ship docked they got a cab to take them to New Jersey and to a motel nearest to the company Giuseppe had the job offer. The next two weeks were very hard on them. Not too many people there understood Italian. Stella and Giuseppe went to a night school that there to train foreigners that didn't know English. There were three classes, a German class, a French class, and an Italian class there. After Giuseppe got his paycheck he rented a car. He had to try twice to get a driver's license. After a few months they rented an apartment walking distance from Giuseppe's job. Soon life became livable.

In Sicily Joey was working hard trying to run his now large farm. He had no thought of the future. One day five months later he heard that Italy had joined England and America in the war against Germany. About a month later he got a notice. He had been drafted. He was to report to Palermo the next Monday. When he got to Palermo he and eleven other draftees were taken to a military post just west of Palermo. There they were trained as young soldiers. After three months of training they were shipped to Africa. In Africa they joined the American and English armies fighting the German army. Slowly they were pushing the German fighters to northern Africa. It took several months before Germany withdrew its army and they disappeared in the northern mountain area. The American army followed them over the mountain. Joey and his company were asked to stay behind and keep any Rear Attack from happening. Joey and his fellow soldiers went up the first mountain they found. Near the top of the mountain they found a cave. They all got into the cave when they heard rifle shots and a noise on the east side of the mountain. Since it was near midnight, they decided to stay there till morning however they drew lots as to who would walk out on the mountain as to guard against any enemy attract. They took turns. Each was to stand guard for two hours. This was to take place all night long. In the morning they would move north to Sicily behind the American and English armies. It was two in the morning when it was Joey's turn. He was out there for only ten minutes when he heard a great explosion. He ran back to the cave and found that the explosion was at the cave. The entrance was fully covered with dirt. Joey dug into it to see if his bodies were alive. They were all covered with dirt and stones. Joey tried to revive them with no success. He couldn't understand where the bomb came from. He was fully awake wile on guard. He saw no one come near the cave. Was it perhaps one of his mate's bombs that went off accidently? He then went down the mountain and heard some noise from the left side of the mountain. Joey hid himself behind a rock. Soon he saw them and recognized that it was the English army with some of the American army approaching the mountain. Joey ran up to the American Army and found the leading officer.

"Hi Sir," said Joey. "I would like to join your people."

"Why," said the captain. "Where is your company?" Joey told him the full story.

"Alright," said the captain. "Please join Corporal Alison's Company. It lost two of its members." Joe found Corporal Alison and approached him.

"Sir," said Joey. "Your Captain told me to join you."

"Good," said, Corporal Alison. "We can use more men. Just walk and fight with us. Whenever we stop for a rest, I will introduce you to the others in you company."

They spent over a year chasing and fighting the German Army which tried to hold on to the parts of Africa they had. Joey wondered why they were spending so much time in Africa. He wanted to save Sicily. The German Army suddenly retreated behind a mountain and disappeared from them. They soon caught up with the German Army. They were crossing the Mediterranean Sea on to Sicily. There they set up a post to resist the enemy to come on to Sicily. However, an army from England crossed over from Grease. The Germans, when they were told about it from one of their guards, they disassembled their post and headed down the western side of Sicily headed for Rome where they had their larger Army. That was the main Army and it which had taken over most of Italy. The American and English army assembled all their separated Companies and they became a solid Army ready to fight the final fight. Joey found himself standing next to the English Army Commander.

"Sir," he said in his best English, "how long will it be before we get a boat to pick us up, and where will it take us?""

"It will take a couple of hours," responded the Commander. We will invade Sicily. Why do you ask?"

"Sir," said Joey. "I think that the Germans are headed for Rome where they have all of their Army together by now. We should head directly to Italy and land a little south of Rome so that we can then approach their main Army on the ground."

"You are a smart kid," said the Commander. He then got on the phone and called several people. One was the security guard the he had in Sicily. The guard told him that German army was not on Sicily land.

"You are right," said the commander. "We will head directly to Rome." He notified all the Army personnel, that where not with them, of the plan. It took two days before they received a ship to take them across the Mediterranean Sea. They were shipped directly to the southern tip of Italy. They landed in the port of Reggio di Calabria. They traveled up Italy about five miles and were met by the German army. They fought their way up to Salerno and were held when the German Army received reinforcement by a part of their army that had stayed near Rome to fight off a small Italian Army that had retreated from the fighting to straitening its Amy with new Italians who had earlier resisted joining the army. It took several months when the American and English Army began to overtake the German Army. They slowly started to move north. It took several months for them to reach south of Rome. The German army surrendered just south of Rome. Joey had no information as to what took place after that. He suspected that they send people to take over the German government. He and the four Companies that make up the part of the Army he was in, was a month later, shipped back to Palermo. Their Joey and the others were discharged and released. Joey started walking his way back to Barrafranca. A man driving a car, seeing Joey dressed in his army uniform, stopped to see if he could help him.

"If you are going my way could I give you a lift?" said the young man.

"I am heading to Barrafranca," said Joey. "Are you going in that direction?"

"I am going at least three quarter of the way," said the young man. "I am going to Caltanissetta. Come in. I can at least take you most of the way." Joey jumped into the car so happy to be able to get a ride most of the way home.

"Thank you so much," said Joey.

"I should thank you," said the young man. "It is because of you soldiers that Italy and Sicily was saved from the Germans who wanted to kill all of us."

"You have to thank the Lord. He is control of everything." Joey then told him all that he had gone through.

"I see that the Lord saved you twice," said the young man, "by the way my name is Salvatore. My families all call me Toto."

"My name is Giuseppe, but everyone calls me Joey." Thy drove for about two and a half hours, when Toto stopped the car at a place where the road was divided with the one they were on that was running south and one heading east. Most of the trip from Palermo was running south.

"I see that you are going to take the road on the left," said Joey, "that will take you to Caltanissetta," said Joey. Joey then got out of the car and closing the car door he said thank you and goodbye. It took Joey over an hour for him to reach Barrafranca. As he walks into the city he was shocked at the damaged done to the city. It looked like it had been bombed several times. Most of the damage was done in the center of the city. Fortunately Joey's house was not damaged. After going through his house he went to his sister Maria's house. He found that she was not there. He then went to his sister Lucia. She was home.

"Giuseppe," yelled Lucia. "It's so good to see that you are alive and home. How are you?"

"I'm alright and happy to be home," said Joey. "I am worried about what has happened to all. I see that the city was badly damaged. How are you all and how did you escape the murdering Germans?"

"Well first let me tell you about my husband Stefano," said Lucia. "About two years after you left Stefano got sick. I think he got a heart attack. We took him to the hospital but they couldn't save him. He is buried near were you dad is buried."

"I am so sorry," said Joey with slight tears in his eyes. "I will miss him so much. Also I miss Sister Maria. What happened to her?"

"She is in the back bedroom sleeping," said Lucia. "She has had a hard time with this war. Let me tell you all that happened here. First the German airplanes bomb the center of the city. Then as the people ran out into the farm field the airplanes swapped down and with their machine guns shot all the people that where running in the field to get away from the airplanes."

"They shot the people that were out in the field?" asked Joey not believing that the Germans could be so cruel.

"We then went to our farm that had a lot of hills. We found the hills that were more the eight feet high and we dug a cave in each. So did a lot of people. We then spent the rest of the war in the caves. We came out only to get food and other things we had to do and when we hear the sound of the planes we rushed and hid in the caves. That is how most of us survived the Germans.

"By the way," said Joey. Do you know what happened to my horses?"

"Yes," said Lucia. "One of you horses died during one of the attacks. The other two we took them in to feed and protect them for you. You can have them whenever you want and need one."

"It is late now," said Joey. "I don't want to wake up Maria. What time would be a good time for me to return to see Maria?"

"She will be up for breakfast about nine o'clock, "said Lucia. "Come here tomorrow morning and have breakfast with us."

"Sounds like a good plan. See you then," said Joey and left. The next morning Joey was there on time.

"Good morning," said Lucia. "Maria will be here in a little while. She is dressing up now knowing that you will be here." It was a few minutes later that Maria showed up dressed like she was going to church.

"Giuseppe, dear brother, it is so good to see you. I was so worried about you" she then threw herself into his arms kissing his cheek.

"Hi Maria," said Joey. "It is so good to be home and to see all of you. Where are your children? Where are Pepino, Nino and Pietro?"

"The all got together and went to the place the Germans were trying to enter Sicily. They joined the Italian Army. They are all fine. We have heard from them. They're presently working for the government. I'm not sure of what they are doing." After much time together Joey went home. The next few weeks he saw his sisters often but spent most of his time checked his farm. He was not happy with what he saw.

In America Stellina got very sick. Giuseppe, now called Joseph or Joe, took her to the hospital there in New Jersey. They found that she had a large tumor in her body that was cancerous. The next day she had a surgery to remove it. After Stella recovered from the surgery, the doctor came in to see her.

"Hi Doctor," said Stella. "How am I doing?"

"Good morning," said the doctor. "How do you feel?"

"I feel very tired but other than that I'm ok."

"Well I have good news and bad news," said the doctor. "Which do you want to hear first?"

"How about the good news," said Stella? "I have had too many bad news. I want at least have some good news."

"The good news is that we got the whole tumor and that all the cancerous cells have been removed. You will soon be back to normal.

"I hate to ask," said Stella. "But I guess it is better if I know."

"One of the cells that had the tumor was the one needed to become pregnant. You can never give birth to a child." It was later that day that Joseph came in to be with his wife. He found her crying.

"Honey," said Joseph. "What is the matter? Will you be alright?"

"I will be back to normal," said Stella. The problem is that the because of the surgery I will never be able to have a child."

"But if you find it that you have to have a child we can adopt one. Let's leave that for a future decision. Write now I have some news for you. The reason I wasn't here earlier was that I was asked to go to my boss's office."

"Oh no," said Stella. "Did they fire you? Did you lose your job?"

"No," said Joseph. "It was just the opposite. I got promoted. I will get almost twice the money and a private office."

"At least we go some good news," said Stella.

"There is one problem," said Joseph. The new job is in Cleveland Ohio. It took about a month for them to get everything settle. They then moved to Ohio.

In Barrafranca, Joey was unconvertible. He didn't have enough help and the ground had grown massive amount of weeds and other unusable plants. He remembered that the officer in Palermo told him that since he had fought on the side of America and England that if he had a family that would accept him there; that he could get a document that will allow him to enter America. Joey then went to see his sister Lucia.

"Hi Lucia," said Joey when she let him in her house. "How are you doing?"

"I'm doing fine," said Lucia. "I miss my husband and my son. My son is trying to get our farm back to good operation. The stores in town are all slowly opening and are requesting some vegetables. They mostly want wheat to make bread. How are you doing?"

"I'm not doing too well," said joey. I can't get enough help. I don't have the money or anything that I can use to hire help. I was thinking of getting a job outside of Sicily to earn enough money to hire helpers."

"I'm sorry that we can't help. Pepino is home but is helping his mother's farm. Nino and Pietro are also helping our farms. So there is no one here that could help you."

"If I could earn some money," said Joey, "I could hire someone outside of Barrafranca." The next day after dinner Joey went back to Lucia house. There he met Pepino who came home first.

"Hi Pepino," said Joey So good to see you."

"Hi Giuseppe," said Pepino "How are you?"

"I'm fine," said Joey. "First call me Joey. Ever one calls me that. Then, I would like your help."

"What do you need Joey?" said Pepino.

"I need to go to Palermo tomorrow. I need to use my horse to get there. I would like you to come with me and then come back here bring both horses back."

"That is a long ride," said Pepino. "I will have to take all day off my farming job."

"Do you want me to pay you for doing this?" asked Joey.

"No you have done enough for us all," said Pepino. "What time do you want to start?"

"Let's go as early as we can," said Joey. "Let us go after breakfast, about eight o'clock. Will that be ok with you?"

"I will meet you at your house at eight tomorrow morning. Pepino did exactly as he said. At eight he was at Joey's house. They soon were on their way to Palermo. They got to Palermo at about eleven thirty. Near the port that Joey was going to leave from was a nice restaurant.

"Let us have a nice lunch here before you leave to go back home," said Joey. "The meal is on me."

"That is a good Idea," said Pepino, "but you don't have to. I could go home and have a big dinner."

"I owe you a lot more," said Joey, "besides I would like the company."

"Let's get it over with," said Pepino. "I would like to get home for dinner." They ate a nice lunch and as soon as it was over Joey hugged Pepino they said goodbye and Pepino left with both horses. Joey left for the boat port to take a boat to Rome where he would get a boat to America. On the way he saw a sign that said it was a language school. Joey stopped at the building that had the sign and went in and asked the woman at the desk what languages were they teaching.

"We are teaching three different classes. We are teaching German, French and English languages."

"How much does the English class cost and when does it start," asked Joey.

"Well the English class will start tomorrow morning. The cost is a daily cost. People stay as long as they want. They can leave any time they feel they had enough," said the woman. The woman then told Joey what the daily cost was. Joey was thrilled to find out that it was very low. He then signed up to start the next day. Joey then found a motel nearby and after he had dinner he went in to his room to rest. The next morning he went into the school, paid his daily cost and went into the English class. There only six other student there. Joey stayed five days and then felt he knew enough and left for boat port. He took the boat to Rome. He waited only two days before he got a ship to America. Before he got on the ship he found a phone in one of the nearby restaurants and called his sister in Ohio. He left a message and got on the ship. It took eight days for the ship to reach America. When he got off the ship in New York a man called out to him.

"Giuseppe," said the man, "I came to pick you up. Come over here."

"Hello," said Joey, "How are you? What are you doing here?" Joey had never met Stella's husband but he recognized him through a photo that his sister had sent him.

"I came to pick you up," said Joseph. "I was afraid that you would get lost trying to find us. By the way herein America the name Giuseppe is translated as Joseph. However the people call the short of the name, Joe. So call me Joe. And I understand from your sister that you like the name joey. So therefore, we know how to call each other,

"Well Joe," said Joey. "It is nice to meet you. Since we never met how did you recognize me?"

"You sister has pictures of you all over our house," said Joe. "Come on follow me. We have a long way to go."

"How did you get here?" said Joey wondering if Joe had brought a horse for him. "Did you bring a horse for me?"

"There are a very few horses here in America," said Joe. "I learned how to drive a car and perched one. Come with me and I will drive you to our house in my car." Around the next corner he

Angelo Thomas Crapanzano

walked up a nice blue car. Joe put Joey's suitcase in the trunk of the car and they were soon on the way to somewhere Joey didn't know. At about noon they stopped at a little town and finding a restaurant they stopped for lunch. After they were seated and they looked at the lunch menu, they were approached by a waitress.

"What can I get you?" she asked. Joe was surprised that Joey told her want he wanted in English. After both put in their order, Joe turned to Joey. Where in the world did you learn English?" he asked.

"Just east of Palermo I went to a school that taught English to Italians. I went there before I got on the boat. I was afraid that I could have gotten lost in America trying to find you." A few minutes later they were back on the road. It was about five o'clock when Joe and joey pulled into Joe's drive way. Stella came out when she saw the car pull in. As the two men got out of the car Stella ran up to Joey.

"Joseph, sweet heart," said Stella to her brother. "I have missed you so much. Glad to see you here." She then hugged him. After a few hugs they went inside.

"Why did you call me Joseph?" said Joey to Stella.

"Well," said Stella, "your name is Giuseppe and the American translation is Joseph."

"But everyone calls me Joey. That is what I am used to."

"But Joey is the American version for a teenager," said Stella. "You are over twenty years old and should be called Joseph or just Joe."

"I will have to get used to one of these names," said joey. "What is your husband called? I would want each to have something different so that we do not get mist up."

"I call my husband Joseph. You can then be called just Joe." That was accepted by both but strange as it seemed many people he met called Joe, Joey.

After several days together, discussing their past experience, Joey felt like he was imposing on his sister. One day he brought the subject at the breakfast table.

"Joseph," joey started. "I need to find a job. I can't just stay here and live off of you. I need to get a job."

"The only thing I have heard of is that they are working on expanding the track for the Trolley. They are bringing it out to the western suburbs. It is the trolley that takes you down town."

"Can you take there when you have some time off?" asked joey.

"Before we do that," said Joseph. "Are you planning to stay here in America?"

"Yes," said Joey. I don't think I can work on a farm any more. You don't know what the future brings, but as for now I expect to get married here and raise a family here."

"Then the first thing we have to do is teach you how to drive, and after that get you a car so that you can do whatever you want. I have a two week vacation coming, perhaps I can help you."

"That would be great," said Joey. "When can we start?"

"Let me check with my boss and see what work we have a head of us," said Joseph. "Anyway I could start to teach you how to drive using my car."

"I can hardly wait," said Joey. The next day when Joseph can home from work he approached Joey.

"We can start next Monday to get you a car and a job." said Joseph. However I can start teaching you how to drive after dinner." After dinner Joseph took Joey out to a side road and after explaining all the functions and what he needed to do, he placed Joey behind the driver's wheel. Joseph was surprised on how quickly Joey was learning. There were three days until Monday. Those three evening Joey was taught how to drive a car. On Monday Joey was ready to get a job and a car. Monday morning Joseph took Joey to get a job first. Joseph thought that he would need the job to buy or rent a car. At the Trolley Corporation office they asked him who he was and what experience he had.

"My name is Joseph Belanto. I was a farmer most of my life," said Joey. When they learn of his experience as a farmer they realized that he had a lot of experience outdoors digging into the earth. They immediately offered him a job. He was to start next Monday. After they got the papers they need to prove he had a job they went to the Auto Company. There they had a car that was equivalent to the Ford. At that time in history there were only two auto manufactures.

One was Ford in America and the other was one made by Germany. They were all very small, and each manufacturer only built one type of car. The company had only one available to Joey. Joey brought it and after paying a down payment he promised to pay an amount, acceptable by the company, every month. Then Joseph and Joey both drove their own cars home.

The next Monday joey drove to work in his own car. This went on for three years. Sometimes he spent weekends with Stella and Joseph and sometimes he spend weekend with friends he met at work. With his friends, most of the time, they travel around the country visiting highly respected parks and cities. When he started his fourth year the times changed. The country went into a deep depression. Joey's job went down to two days. This went on for several months. Finally they stopped all the work they were doing and laid off all the workers. Joey looked for a new job but the depression hit every business. No one was hiring and most released some of their workers. Being out of work Joey couldn't pay off the mortgage on his house. Finally he made a deal with the owner that Joey would return the ownership of the house and the money he paid would go as rent. Joey took the deal and moved back in with his sister Stella. Joseph's job was reduced to two days a week. Joey realized that he was going to be a burden to his sister. After several week, and it looked like things were not getting better he decided to go back to Barrafranca Sicily. There he had a home and the farm. Stella and Joseph decided to lend Joe enough to get to his home in Barrafranca. Joey left his car to Joseph telling him to sell in when thing got better and use what he got for the car as part payment loan Joey owed him. Two days later, Joey had taken care of every he had to do to leave Cleveland, and was ready to leave. Joseph got ready to drive Joey to New York. Before they left Joseph pulled Joey away from Stella. He gave Joey a package and an envelope with money.

"I would like you to take this package and the money to my family in Barrafranca. Give it to Nino and Anna Belanto." He then gave him a piece of paper. "This is their address." Just as they were getting into the car, Stella ran up to Joey with large tears and hugged him. Her action got some tears in Joey's eyes.

"Goodbye," said Joey. "I love you." Stella couldn't talk but she gave Joey a tighter hug. Soon Joseph and Joey were on the road to New York. They got to New York in the late afternoon.

"What do you want me to do?" said Joseph. "Do you want me to drop you off at the port?"

"Drop me off at the port," said joey, "but I want you to wait. I want to see how soon I could get on board. Then if it is not too soon or if I have trouble getting a ticket, I may have to decide what to do with those conditions."

"Yes, I could wait," said Joseph. "It is probably is too late for me to drive home." He then drove Joey to the port. Joey got out and went inside. It was about ten minutes before Joey came out. Joey then walked over to the car.

"I have very good news," said Joey. "The ship is leaving tomorrow morning. It was glad to see me. They are low on passengers. I got a room on the ship and I could on right now.

"So this is goodbye," said Joseph. "I think I will start to travel home right now. I could stop at a small town on the way home. The hotel room will be much cheaper in a little town."

"Dear Joseph," said Joey. "Thank you so much for all that you have done for me. God Bless you. Good bye.

"Good bye," said Joseph as he drove away. Joey went directly to his room on the ship. He was so tired that he fell asleep right away. It took eight days for the ship to reach the Strait Of Gibraltar. It was the next day that they pulled into the Roman port. Joey then got a boat to Palermo. He was very happy that Pepino was there to pick him up. Three hours later they pulled into Barrafranca. As Pepino pulled into the garage they were met by a crowd of relatives. First his sister Mary grabbed and hugged joey. Next Lucia hugged him. Since Joseph pulled into his garage by Mary's house. They and all their children had a party there. It was a very jolly night. The next night they had a party at Lucia's house. That night was also a fantast night. Joey need the next day to rest all day. The next morning Pepino asked Joey to come with him to the farm.

"I need you," said," Pepino "there is so much work to do that I need help.

"I will gladly come to help you," said Joey, "However I need to be home for dinner. After dinner I have to go your Aunt Stella's husband's family. I have a package that I have to give them and money that Stella's husband is sending to his family."

"Any time you can spend to help will be greatly appreciated," said Pepino. Joey then got on one of the horses and they both went to the farm. At six in the evening Joey said good bye to Pepino and left for Maria's home. After dinner he went to the Belanto home. He was accepted with great joy.

"This is my wife Anna," said Michele her husband. "And I am Michele. Everyone calls me Michel."

"So nice to meet you," said Joey. My name is Joey. Your son Giuseppe is a wonderful Man. He is like a brother to me. Just then, a young woman entered the room. Joey was sock at how beautiful she was. She showed shyness that was unusual for her. However Joey did not know this.

"This is my niece Marianna," said Michel. "She is my brother's daughter. My brother and his wife were killed in the world war two bombing of Barrafranca. I have raised her like my own daughter.

"Hi Marianna," said Joey. "It is so nice to meet you." Joey found himself being very nervous.

"Nice to meet you too," said Mariana. "I would like to hear all you can tell me about my cousin Giuseppe. I miss him so much." Michel noticed that both were very nervous. He decided that there could make a very nice couple. He decided to do whatever he could to keep them together.

"Joey," said Michel, "We are very grateful for your bring us the gift and the money. We would like to show you our gratitude. Can you come here tomorrow and have lunch and dinner with us. We would like you to spend all day with us."

"I would love that," said Joey," but I promised Pepino, my nephew, that I would help him on his farm. He needs help so badly. There is no one around he could hire. I could possible come for dinner."

"Please come as soon as you can," said Michel. Annie then called them to the kitchen. She made some cookies and coffee. They all came in and sat at the table. Joey became aware of Marianna's shyness. So did the others at the table.

"Marianna," said Joey. "What have you been doing in your adult years?"

"Nothing" said Marianna. "I don't like to go anywhere alone. There are too many mad boys out there."

"Were would you like to go?" asked Joey.

"Not too far from here is a shopping area," said Mariana. It is wonderful area. There are two streets that are separated by a green strip that is about six feet wide. It has benches and a lot of different things. At one end is a stature of the solders that fought in the world war. At the other end is a water fountain. I'm sure you have been there."

"Yes, I have been there, usually during a holiday," said Joey. "But I haven't been there for a long time."

"I also long to go to the theater, witch is there on the other side of the stature," said Marianna. They are currently showing a wonderful romantic picture."

"I'll see when I can take off my farm work."

"When you can't take off from work," said Michel. "Please come here for dinner." Joey took off the next days from work. That day joey took Marianna to the theater. They spent most of the day together. Joey spent the next two days working. He always went to Michel's house after work. Sometimes he was later then Michel could hold off his family from eating at the regular time. Joey and Marianna ate together when Joey got there with reheated food. Three days later, Joey took a day off. That day he took Marianna to the shopping aria. They went early in the morning. At lunch time they ate at one of the restaurant in the area. At dinner time they made it home in time to eat with Michel and Annie. The next few days Joey worked all day. Some of the days Joey worked to late and got to Michel's home late. He then ate heated food. After Joey and Marianna finished eating, Michel called Joey and Marianna together in the living room.

"Listen you two," started Michel. "There is no doubt that you two are madly in love. Why don't you two get married and then you can live together and this eating problem will be your solution." Joey shook his head like saying he understood.

"Let me think about it," said Joey. "I will see what I can do." Joey then left. Several days went by and Michel did not hear from Joey. Hey were worried that they may not see Joe again.

"I guess he didn't want to marry me," said Marianna. "He just needed company." Marianna and Michel were just getting over their hurt feeling when Joey showed up for dinner.

"I hope you have enough food for me."

"Dear Joey," said Michel. "Where have you been?"

"I have been doing a lot of effort to meet you suggestion. First I had to find someone to take my place. Pepino couldn't take care of all the planting he has to do by himself. Secondly I had to find the church who would take us soon. And last of all I had to write cards to invite all my and your family to the wedding. The third thing I had to do I will do now." Joey then went down on his knee in front of Marianna, "Marianna, I love you, will you marry me?"

"Marianna with tears in her eyes responded

"Yes I will marry you," she said. "I love you too." That day went by with great joy. The wedding was schedule for Saturday two weeks from that engagement day. It went by very quickly. It was Saturday after lunch that the wedding took place. Michel walked Marianna down the church isle. Joey was already at the church altar. The priest gave a small sermon on the marriage. Soon he asked for the three vows to be given by Joey and Marianna. Joey promised that he will always love her and to do all that he could to make Marianna happy. Marianna said that she loved Joey and would obey him and follow him anywhere. Soon they all assembled in the church's large entertainment room. There they had supper. Michel gave a speech how he felt that the two of them were meant for each other. Soon the orchestra started to play dance music. Joey love to have Marianna in his arms. The evening went by too quickly. Soon it was time for Joey and Marianna to leave for their first night together. The next morning Joey and Marianna left for their honeymoon. They drove a

tell me a Story

car borrow from his sister's son. They left at eight in the morning an after stopping at a small town for lunch they proceeded to Catania. It was about six the evening. They got a hotel room and got a dinner at a restaurant nearby. The next morning after a quick breakfast they drove to the city of Santa Venerina at the east side of Mount Etna. From there they could see the smock coming out of the volcano on the top of the mountain. They rented a room there and had a dinner at the diner in the nearby restaurant. The next day they ate breakfast and drove to the city of Adrano. It was at the base of the volcano. The next morning joey asked Mariana.

"Let's go up the trail to the top of the volcano "Joey recommended to Marianna. "I have been there. It is so thrilling to look down the volcano and see the melting rocks.

"How do you get there from here?" asked Marianna.

"We drive up the road to a Restaurant that is about one third of the way up. From there we take a box car that is hanging on a heavy set of wires. On the top they give you a coat because it is cold. It is a very exciting."

"Well," said Marianna. "You can take me to the restaurant and then you can go up to the top of the volcano yourself. I will not go any farther."

"You will not go up with me," asked Joey.

"No I will not go up," said Marianna

"I will not let you alone," said Joey. "We are on our honeymoon. I will not leave you. Do you want to leave this area?" asked Joey.

"This is a nice motel," said Marianna. "I love to see the volcano from here. Let's stay here for a few days. We can see and enjoy the volcano from here." They stayed there a full week. During that week they never left the hotel room except for meals. After they go tired of wanting the volcano they decided to go home. They will be gone for almost two weeks. It took them two days to get home. The next day, they celebrated their home coming with Michel and Annie. The next day they visited Joey's sisters. They were asked to stay for dinner but said they had too much to do. The next day Joey went with Pepino to the farm. There wasn't much left to do. It was October. They were busy picking all the wheat to sell. That task was as hard as the other work that is done on a farm. It was the first day of November when all the wheat was Picked and sold. When it was over they both went home. The next day Pepino asked Joey to come to his house where he had a kind of office room.

"I need to go over all the costs and income of the wheat harvest with you," said Pepino. "Sit here and I will go over it with you. I went over it all yesterday." Then he took out a piece of paper and pointed to the top of the sheet. "This is the total amount that we received for the wheat." He then pointed to the next set of figures "This is the cost the seeds and all that other cost that came up. This next item is my salary. It is the total hours I spent on the farm times the hourly income that we all agreed on. I have already taken mine. This next one is your hours times the same hourly income." He then gave Joey his income. Joey was surprised that his hours were less than a third of the hours Pepino had. "Subtracting all the cost, this is the yearly profit me make this year. If you agree, we will split it in half. I will take half and the other half you will take."

"That is ok," said Joey. "However I have a question. If I had worked every day with you we would not have make a profit? Instead it looks like we would have lost money."

"No the number of hours it required was correct," said Pepino. "If you would have come with me every day, I would not have work as hard as I worked this year, If you add the number of hours I spent on the farm with the number of hour you spent there is the total we would have to work there .It would be that if you work more I work less."

"That makes sense," said Joey. "I guess that is all we need to do this year." Joey then went home. He called Marianna to the living room where he sat.

"Honey," he started. "We have a problem. The amount of money Pepino and I make this year is about one third of what I made in America. Not only that, I have to split it with Pepino. So I want you start thinking about us going to America. We could get a smaller house which would mean you didn't have as much cleaning work. Also I would come home from work by four thirty in the evening. I also will not have to work as hard and I will not have to spend all day in the sun. The last time I worked in America I sat by a work bench."

"When do you want to go," asked Marianna?

"I think we should spend the holiday here with our relatives. You may never see them again. I think we could go around March of next year."

"I don't know if I will be happy away from the home where I have grown up in," said Marianna. "However, I will go where ever you want me to go. You are the head of this household."

"Thank you sweet heart," responded Joey. "That is so sweet."

The days went by so quickly. Joey and Marianna spent Christmas with her family and Joey's family all together at the church hall. It was almost like the party they had at Joey' and Marianna's wedding. New Year's eve they spent by themselves. New Year's Day they spent with Marianna's family. The months in the New Year went by slowly. Finally March came. They had told every one of their plan to go to America in March. Pepino offered to take them to Palermo. They visited every member of Marianna's family and all of Joey's family before they left. They said good bye and the morning of March fifteen, Pepino took they to Palermo. They all took a horse. After Pepino said goodbye he took the horses and left. Joey and Marianna took the Fairy boat to Rome. At Rome Joey found where the American office was. He took Marianna there. After much signing of papers, the American consular gave Marianna a passport. They then when to the Roman main port and got a room in the next boat leaving for America. The next boat for America was to leave in two days. They found that they could get aboard tomorrow. They stayed that day and night in the nearest hotel. The next morning, after breakfast, they boarded the ship. The next day the ship left for America. It took eight days for the ship to arrive to New the York Harbor. Joey had sent a message to Joseph to meet them in the Cleveland train station. Joey didn't want Joseph to have to travel all the way to New York. However when the ship docked and joey and Marianna got off they were surprised to see Joseph waiting for them there in New York.

"Joseph," said Joey. "What are you doing here?"

"I came to pick you guys up," said Joseph.

"We planned on taking a train to Cleveland," said Joey. Joseph ignored Joey, and walked up to Marianna.

"Hello Marianna. It is so good to see you," said Joseph. He then hugged her.

"I'm glad to see you," said Marianna. "Except for my husband, you are the only person I have seen that I know. You make me feel a little like home. For the last week I have felt like I was in another world."

"Let's stop the small talk and let get going home," said Joseph. They all walked to the parking lot and got into Joseph's car. Soon they were on the way to Cleveland Ohio. On the way they stopped at a restaurant and had a quick lunch. They got to Cleveland about six in the afternoon.

"Where do you want to go," asked Joseph. "Where do you plan on living?"

"Drop us of at a hotel that is nearest to your house," said Joey.

"First let's go to my house to see what my wife has planned," said Joseph. "I think the people that are renting our upper apartment are leaving. Perhaps that apartment will be available."

"Yes, let's go to your house first." said Joey. "I would like to see my sister." They got to Joseph house a few minutes later. Stella ran out to meet them. When Joey stepped out of the car Stella jumped into his arms.

"Brother dear, said Stella. "I am so glad that you are here. I need to have part of my family nearby"

"What have you planned," sweetheart," said Joseph to Stella. "Joey wants to rent a room in a hotel till he could get a place of his own."

"Nonsense," said Stella. "I have worked all day, clearing the upstairs apartment and moved what I could up stairs. We will give the lower apartment to Joey and his wife. They may need to go in and out more than we do. We will move upstairs."

"I don't want to put a problem on you two," said Joey.

"It's too late now," said Stella with a smile on her face. I just need some strong arms to bring up the heavy things I could bring up. Some of the important things are already up there as part of the apartment." Stella had a fantastic dinner set for them. After dinner the two men took up the furniture Stella wanted upstairs. They also they brought down some furniture that was needed to replace the furniture they took upstairs. When everything was taken care of they sat and had some small talk. At about eleven they all went to bed. Joey and Marianna settled in the lower apartment and Joseph and Stella settled up stairs. The next morning Stella gave Joey the newspaper and showed him all the jobs that were available. Joey called a few that looked nice. He visited two. One was the US Steel and wire Company. He liked that one the best. Joey went there for an interview. After hearing of his background they offered him a job. Joey accepted the job. He was to start the next Monday. About a week later Marianna pulled Joey to the living room.

"There is something I have to tell you," said Marianna. Before we left Barrafranca I was have a little soreness in my stomach. I didn't tell you because I didn't want to worry you. It got worse every day. Yesterday I told Stella and she brought me to her doctor. The problem I have is that I am pregnant."

"Wow," said joey, who up to her last statement looked very worried, now he couldn't be happier. "How soon will we be parents," asked joey.

"I think it will be born about four months from now." She was right it was four months later that she gave birth to a little boy.

"What should we call him," asked Joey

"Well," said Marianna," the old custom of Sicily is to name a daughter after the wife's grandma, and name a son after the husband's grandpa."

"My grandfather's name was Antonio," said Joey. "I think the American people will call him Toney. I don't like that name.

"I don't like it either," said Marianna. "Let's call him Andy. That is our short for Antonio.

"Sound great to me," said Joey. They then wrote his name on the birth certificate as Andy.

Joey loved his job at the US Steel And Wire Company. It was his job to enter steel rods into the machine that heats it, and squeezes it into wire. At the other end is a worker who sends the wire though another device that covers the wire with a plastic covering. It then comes out as electric wire that is used in buildings and houses. Joey went to work at eight O'clock in the morning and got home at about four thirty. About an hour later his wife made dinner. Everything was fine. Joseph and Stella decided to move closer to where Joseph worked.

"Joey dear," said Joseph one day. I am going to move. I hate to do this but I have to sell this house. Please come with us or try to find a new place to live."

O'K, said Joey. "I understand, but I am close to my job here. I know a woman who runs a business selling and renting houses. Let me call her." Joey did that the next morning

"Martha," said Joey. How are you? This is Joey Crazano. I need to find an apartment or a house to live in."

"You called at just the right time. I have a couple who got a greater job and have to move down south right away. They are in a panic to sell before they left. It is located on 143d street in eastern Cleveland.

"Can I see it today?" said Joey. "I am in a hurry also.

Yes," said Martha. "Come to my office right now and I will take you there." Joey called his boss at the US Steel And Wire Company and asked for time off. He described his urgency. Joey then went to Martha's office immediately. She took him to a house she described. Joey loved it. The owners were willing to negotiate a price Joey could pay for. It took three day for everything to go through. The next day they moved. It was a nice place and more important was the fact that it was closer to Joey's job and closer for his kids to go to school. It all turned out for the best. While out Joey bought a new Ford model T Ford. Everything worked out fine. They loved their new location.

When Andy was seven, Marianna gave birth to a daughter. They named it after Marianna's mother who was named Maria. When Andy was twelve years old and Mary was five, something Joey hated, happened at the US steel And Wire Company. For reasons unknown by the workers the company changed the working hours. Perhaps it was because the second shift and the third shift workers complained. They changed each work into working a three shift job. The first week Joey would work the first shift, eight in the morning until four in the afternoon. The next week Joey would work the second shift with was from four in the afternoon till midnight. The third week Joey then would work from Midnight to eight in the morning. This would repeat in the next three weeks. This went on for several weeks. Joey was very unhappy. He could hardly spend time with his wife and children. He then decided to do something about it.

"Marianna," said Joey to his wife one morning when he was home. "We have to do something about this new work condition. I'm very unhappy. I think I would rather do farmer's work in Barrafranca, What would say if we move back to Sicily?"

"I will go wherever you go," said Marianna. "I don't like your job here eider. I never get to see you and the kids don't have a dad." Joey then went to the travel agency not too far from their home. He made plans for Marianna and the kids to go first.

"When are we going?" asked Marianna.

"You are going Monday," said Joey. "I will send you and the kids first. I need to stay behind. We have to see how the kids get along in the different temperature zone. I also will come later after I have sold the house and taken care of the other things that need to be settled." Monday came faster than Marianna wanted. Joey drove them to the New York harbor. After he saw his family get on the ship, he returned home. He found that he had trouble selling his house. He had enough money which he withdrew from the bank. Everything else was taken care of. It was nine months later when the newspaper told about the break out of World War Two. What interested Joey the most was that Italy joined with Germany which made Italy in high danger. He then decided that they were all better off in America. Sicily was going to be in the middle of the action. He quickly sent a telegram to Marianna. He said that he paid for the American ship to bring them home. Marianna found that there was a young man with a car who provided business men the way travel to other part of

Sicily. That was the only car available and she hired him. Before she left another man came up to the car.

My name is Joseph Urbo. I need to leave here and go to America. However, I find that you have hired the only car available. Can I please share it with you?"

"Are all Sicilian men called Joseph?" asked Marianna. "Of course, Get in." Little did she know what a delightful man he would be, to her and her family in the future? In the eight days it took to get to New York Joseph got off at every stop the ship make. He asked permission of Marianna to let him take her kids. He took only Andy. Joseph treated Andy like he was his son. He bought him Ice cream and candy at every place the ship stopped. Andy would never forget him. Eight days later they arrived at the New York harbor. Joey was there. Marianna introduced Joseph to Joey. She told Joey all that Joseph had done during the trip. Soon Joey and his family were on the way home.

"What happened at home," asked Marianna? "Why couldn't you sell the house?"

"The war in Europe has done a lot of changes in America. They are drafting most young men into the US army." That night they got home about eight. They did not stop for lunch. They were all pretty hungry. Marianna quickly made a dinner for all of them. The next two week went by too quickly. Joey was running out of money. He was looking for a job, but things were very quiet due to the possibility of a war starting. After a week went by Joey got a call from US steel and wire company.

"Hi" said the voice on the other end of the phone. "Is this Joey Crazano?"

"Yes this is he," said Joey. "Who is this and what can I do for you?"

"This is Nick from the US steel and wire Company. I am calling to offer you a job."

"I'm sorry," said Joey, "I can't work with your work hours."

"The work hours on the job that I am offering you is eight am to four pm."

"What is the job," asked Joey. "Is it the job I had before?"

"No," said Nick. "It is at the other end where the wire is coated with the plastic shielding. The salary is ten percent greater than you got before."

"I accept," said Joey. "When do I start?"

"I would like you to start this coming Monday," said Nick.

"I accept the job," said Joey. "I will see you Monday. That said they hung up. Joey told Marianna that he got a job back at US steel and wire Company. She was as glad as he was. Several years went by. When Andy turn 21 he went to college. Mary was fourteen when Marianna told them she was pregnant. She finally had another girl. They named her Catherine. That birth made it a final decision. There was no thought in any one's mind to ever go back to Sicily. They were all fixed Americans.

The End

Story Number Eleven

Was it A True Occurrence or An Interesting dream?

Andrew had medical problem as long as he could remember. When he was six he had surgery that removed a small growth in his belly. Fortunately it was not cancerous. When he was eight he began having constipation problems. The doctor gave him an enema, which clear the blockage. After that he had to watch what he ate. Sometimes his stool output turned to diarrhea. He had to take stool softener most of the time. Andrew was now twenty one. He was on his way to the doctor's office because of chest soreness.

"Hi Andy," said the nurse when he came to the doctor's office waiting room. Please sit down. The doctor will be with you in a little while."

"Good morning Sally,' said Andrew. "How are you today?"

"I'm fine," said Sally. "Thank you for asking." Andrew sat down. It was few mutes later a nurse came through the door and asked for Mr. Avola.

"That is me," said Andrew. He was very shook up by the nurse. She was the most beautiful girl he had ever met. He then got up and followed her to the doctor's office.

"Hello Andy," said doctor Ryan. "Come and sit down on this chair. Tell me what your problem is."

"I have this soreness on my chest. It seems to be on the right side of my chest."

"That could be very dangerous," said Doctor Ryan. He then checked him with his equipment. He found that his blood pressure was very low, his heart rate was low, and his temperature was very low.

"What did you find Doctor," asked Andy.

"You do having a problem," said the doctor. "We need to have an x-ray of your body. One of your organs is giving you trouble." He then turned to his nurse. "Annie, please take Mr. Avola to the x-ray room." He then handed a sheet of paper to Annie which named all the test he wanted performed.

"Come with me Mr. Avola," said Annie.

"Please call me Andy," said Andy. "My first name is Andrew. Everyone calls me Andy"

"Follow me Andy," said Annie. She then took Andy to the x-ray room. They had to wait in the waiting room. The x-ray operator was giving another patient the tests ordered by another Doctor.

"What do you do for a living," asked Annie.

"I am in collage," said Andy. "I am studying, Corporate Management. My most important subject is Financial Management."

"How far have you gone?" asked Annie.

"I am in my last year," said Andy.

"Have you found a place to work yet," asked Annie?

"Yes," said Andy. "My father owns an Industrial Parts Manufacturing Company. He is thinking of retiring and I will take over the job of running the Company."

"What kind of parts does he manufacture?" asked Annie.

"The biggest department is the automobile parts department. Than he has a department that manufacture home parts for kitchen appliances." Then the x-ray nurse came out and took Andy into the x-ray room, it took about twenty minutes before Andy came out. He was surprised to see Annie in the waiting room waiting for him.

"That took longer than I thought," said Annie.

"What are you doing here?" said Andy being surprised that she was out there waiting for him.

I am assigned to you," said Annie. "You are my responsibility."

"Don't you have other patient?" said Andy being surprised at what she said.

"Yes I have a couple that I am taking care of," said Annie "You are the one that currently needs the most attention. Anyway, let's go back to the doctor's office." She then led Andy back to the office waiting room. The doctor had another patient. It was about an hour before they saw a nurse walk into the doctor's office.

"That looks like the x-ray nurse," said Andy.

"Yes," said Annie. "I hope she is bringing the x-ray result to him." The nurse then came out and went over to Andy.

"The doctor has to take a good look at the x-ray results," said the nurse. "He will call you when he has reviewed the x-ray results" She then left. It was about ten minutes later that the doctor called for them to come into his office.

"Sit down here I have a lot to tell you," said the doctor. "I have reviewed the x-rays and found that most of your body organs are affected by the infection. We are not sure what caused the infections. I want you to register into the hospital. We have a lot of work to do to bring you back to a healthy life." He then turned to Annie.

"Annie, will you see that Andy gets accepted into the hospital and get a bed room for him to stay in."

"How long do you think I will have to stay here" asked Andy?

"It's hard to say," said the doctor. "In the past, the results of our work on any patient, that we had that was infected like you, I found that it varied on two things, first, the cause of the infection and secondly if we had a drug that would fix the infection." Annie then took Andy to the waiting room.

"Please wait here," said Annie. "I will go and get you registered in the hospital. When I get a room I will come and get you. Relax it won't be long. She said that because she saw how restless and nervous Andy was. Half of his problem was because he felt such strong feeling for Annie. They were feeling he never had before and never expected that they would happen. It only took a few minutes and Annie came back.

"Follow me," said Annie as soon as she got there. She then led him to the second floor to room 212. She handed him a set of pajamas. "Please put on these pajamas. I will be back in about fifteen minutes," She then left. Andy put on the pajamas and got himself into the bed. About fifteen minutes as Annie said she came back. "I think I need to give you a shoot to relax you." She then gave Andy a shot in his right arm. It only took a few minutes when Andy fell asleep. Annie then went to the doctor's office. She wanted to know what the doctor found out.

"Hi doc," said Annie. "What have you found out? Have you had time to review the tests?"

"Come on in and sit down," said the doctor. "I have to talk with you about a couple of things."

"It's time for me to go home," said Annie worried that he would take an hour.

"It will only take five minutes," said the doctor. Annie then sat sown across from the doctor's desk.

"What is the problem?" asked Annie.

"I have notice that you have a very fondness for the patient Andy. You know that it is against the rule to have a relationship with a patient. You could get fired.

"What difference does it make," said Annie. "I don't think he has any feeling for me."

"I think he had more feeling for you then you have for him," said the doctor. "I could see that he is a normal human being when you are not around. However when you come in he becomes very excited and can't stand still."

"I have never in my life felt like I feel for Andy," said Annie. "I never even dreamed I could feel this way. This is a very important part of life. I will try to keep our feeling to our self. However, if I can't take care of him here and now, I will quit my job and come and see him as a friend."

"Please don't leave us," said the doctor. "I will not tell anyone if you hide your feeling when someone else is around."

"Thank you doc," said Annie. "Now what did you find in the tests?"

"Andy has three problems," said the doctor. "Number one, he has a hole on the wall on the right side of the heart. That lets water in which impairs the movement of the heart. Secondly, he has problem with the little flap in his throat that keeps liquids and food from going down the wrong side, the lungs. Sometime in the past he must have had an infection on it which keeps it from working correctly some times. Thirdly he has a blockage in his colon It blocks the movement of his stool. It makes him have constipation. We have to have a surgery on the wall of his heart so that water will not enter and impeach the operation of the heart. We have to do that first because it is the most dangerous. It could stop the heart."

"So what is our next move?" asked Annie.

"The first thing in the morning say at eight O'clock we have to operate."

"I'll be there," said Annie as she left. As she said, she was at the hospital at seven thirty.

"Good morning sweet Andy." said Annie as she walking into Andy's hospital room. "How do you feel this morning?"

"What are you doing here this early?" asked Andy.

"You are my responsibility," said Annie. "Now answer my question."

"I feel a little week," said Andy. "I get these dizzy spells ever so often." "Well to answer your question, I am here to help the doctor give you a simple surgery to relieve you heart of all the water that keeps it from operating normal. After the surgery you will feel stronger and will not have dizzy spells any longer." About ten to eight Annie brought Andy to the operating room. She did all that was necessary to prepare Andy for the doctor to do the surgery. At eight the doctor walked into the operating room. It took the doctor about thirty minutes to do the operation. Annie was right. It was a simple operation. The doctor after opening up Andy's in the heart area found that the area on the right side of the heart had a hole in it. That let some of the water in that traveled on that side of the heart. The heart had a hard time beating with water filling the heart area. The doctor sewed the opening closed and then closed the area where he had opened to get to the heart area.

"I wonder how that hole got there," said Annie, who saw the complete event.

"Who knows," said the doctor. "I have seen a lot like that. It apparently is a weak spot in his body. Anyway let's see if it helps one of his other problems." After Annie cleared all that was required to release Andy. She then brought him to his hospital room to recover. She checked on him about every hour. The next morning she went directly to Andy's room.

"You again," said Andy when he saw her come into the room. "Why are you here? Don't you have other patients?"

"You are the patient that I have that needs me the most," said Annie. "When you get better I will leave you alone." The next day she came only once a week to check to see how much he recovered. She checked all his function and then left. She stayed away from him for the next several days to keep him from getting too excited. At the beginning of the next week, the doctor called Annie to his office.

Annie," started the doctor. "Sit down I want to talk to you about a surgery I would like to do."

"I am ready to do whatever you want," said Annie, as she sat down. "What do you have in your mind?"

"I see that a new product has been released," said the doctor. "It is a flapper and its attachment parts that can replace one that has been infected and doesn't work properly."

"Do you want me to bring him up to the surgical room?" asked Annie.

"Yes let's do it," said the doctor. "It will help him a lot. We have to wait anyhow for the medicine that we gave him for the colon infection." Annie then went into Andy's room.

"How are you doing?" said Annie. "Are you ready for you next health improvement function?"

"Are you back again?" said Andy. "We need to have a good talk," said Andy."

"Fine," said Annie. "We will have a nice talk when we get back from your next function." Annie then gave Andy a needle shot in his left arm. Andy stared to ask what that was for, but he fell asleep. Annie then took him to the surgical room. The doctor came in and performed the work he had to do to replace Andy's bad flapper. After he got done he gave Annie directions.

"Take him to his room and keep him asleep until later today. Feed him through the arm for the next two days. Also keep check of his colon. See if the drugs we gave him are working."

"Will do doc," said Annie and then took Andy to his hospital room. She also kept him asleep until eight in the evening. The next day Annie went into Andy's room at eight in the morning. Andy was still asleep. Annie sat on a chair and waited for Andy to wake up. She didn't want to disturb him. He did wake up at about nine. He saw Annie siting there.

"Annie," he said as he woke up. "What are you doing here?"

"I'm your nurse," said Annie. Don't you remember?"

"How long," asked Annie, "am I going to have to stay in the hospital?"

"That depends on you," said Annie. "You just had a surgery in your throat. It will be about a week before you will be able to eat. We also have to wait for the infection you have in your colon. We have given you two different drugs to cure that. I have no idea how long that will take. So you had better make yourself at home."

"Well then today is a good time to talk," said Andy getting ready to get his problem off his mind.

"I'm listening," said Annie.

"I was attracted to you the minute I saw you," started Andy. "I have never felt that way before. I have loved my parent, my brother and a few friends but the kind of love I feel now I never imagined how it would be. I also think that you have a little feeling for me. The reason I am bring this up is that my feelings for you increase every time I see you. That is why I want you to stay away from here."

"So what is wrong with all that?" asked Annie.

"Don't you understand? I have a poor body," said Andy. "I have had a problem since I was five. I have been going in and out of a hospital most of my life. I am not good enough for you. You are very intelligent, very sweet, and very good looking. You deserve a better fellow. I am not good enough for you. Any relationship we could develop will never last. I don't want a broken heart as another problem."

"If you are finished let me tell you what I think," started Annie. "First you are the nicest guy I ever met. Most of the fellows I have dated were very arrogant and bossy. I believe you were thinking more of me than you were of yourself. You are kind and gentle and loving. I have the same feeling for you that you said you had for me. I get a great joy and feelings I never had before, just by seeing you. I get butterflies in my stomach every time I am with you. As for you being sick all the time, I will keep you healthy. I am a good nurse. I would love to spend the rest of my live with you. As far as you're being sick all the time, we are going to cure you of that. That is why we are here. So love of my life, let us enjoy our feelings for each other. I think we are perfect for each other. Trust me."

"I am shocked at what is happening," said Andy. "First I trust you. I also believe you. You are too intelligent to make all that up. Just the thought at what you said makes me feel better. I have a lot to think about. However from now on let us be boyfriend and girlfriend. Even if you break my heart it will be worth it."

"I promise you that I will never break your heart," said Annie. "Please promise me that you will never break my heart."

"I promise you with all my heart," said Andy. "Is it alright if I call you sweetheart?" asked Andy.

"I would love that," said Annie. "You can call me anything you want.

"I love the name Annie. It is such a loving a name. Where do we go from here," asked Andy

"We continue as we have been doing," said Annie. "I will do my best to get you well and out of here. Then we will date like other lovers do."

"How long before I can eat like other people do," asked Andy now being hungry.

"I will feed you through you vein for about two days. Then we will feed you first with soup and then with thicker and harder food little by little. Annie then fed Andy with a needle through his left arm. Andy was so relieved of what was bothering him that after he was fed, he fell asleep. Annie went to visit other patients. This went on for two weeks. Annie went in to see Andy about twice in the morning and twice in the afternoon. She stayed about two hours at each meeting. The last meeting was late in August.

"Hi Sweet heart," said Annie as she walked into the hospital room. How are you today?"

"I'm fine," said Andy, "except for the pain I have in my left lower side of my stomach." Doctor Ryan said that he gave me the last drug he knew to solve my colon infection. He said he would come and talk with me this after noon."

"I know," said Annie. "He has tried to solve the infection with drugs, however so far none have worked."

"I suspect," said Andy, "that what the doctor is going to tell me is that I need another surgery"

"Andy honey," said Annie. "You are in the best health that you have ever been. This last surgery will make you as healthy as I am."

"I guess that means I will be here about another three week," said Andy. "There is one problem that disturbs me. You have been staying with me about four hours a day. Wont the hospital management feels that you should spend more time with other patient?"

"Doctor Ryan told me the same thing," said Annie. "I told him if the management complains, I will quit the job and come to see you as a friend."

"Would you really do that?" asked Andy.

"Don't you know that you are so much more important to me then my job?"

"I think that I understand," said Andy. "I start thinking that if I was in your place I would do the same thing." That afternoon Annie walked into Andy's room with Doctor Ryan.

"Good afternoon," said Andy as they walked into his room. I hope you have good news for me."

"I'm sorry," said the doctor. "We have tried everything we know to cure the infection. However nothing we tried has worked. Now it has spread and it is starting to affect the area of the urinal canal. We cannot have that. So I plan on having surgery tomorrow morning. I promise you that it will be the last you will need." The next morning doctor Ryan performed the surgery as promised. He remover six inched of his colon. It could not be saved. He also cleaned around where the infection was seen. He removed it all. The next morning when Andy woke up he felt the pain in his belly. By eight O'clock Annie showed up.

"Hi sweetheart," said Annie. "How do you feel this morning?"

"I'm aching all over," said Andy. "I also have something attached to my stomach. Tell me what happened yesterday morning."

"Well, the doctor cut six inches of you colon out. It was too infected. In fact a small portion was dead. If any part of a person's flesh dies there is no know procedure that will bring it back to life. You were lucky that it didn't' infect your urinal cannel. The thing that is attached to your stomach is the tube and bag that accepts your bowel output. You cannot have normal bowel movement until the colon heels."

"How long will that be?" asked Andy. "How many days am I going to be locked up in his hospital?"

"Normally it will that two weeks," said Annie. "But I am going to get you out of here in two weeks for sure."

"I would like to get out of here in less than three week. I need one more term in college to graduate. The school starts in the first week of September. I have been sick all summer and have not missed any school yet. If I take this last term I will graduate with a degree in Management."

"We will get you there. This healing will be the last days in the hospital. Annie was right. At the end of two weeks Andy felt so much better. They had remover the tube from his chest and he had a normal bawl movement. He was ready to go home. He had one week to get ready to go back to college. When Annie came in, he spoke out the minute she steps in the room.

"Annie, I want to go home," said Andy. "I have so much to do to get ready to go back to college."

"Wow," said Annie. "You are really ready are you?" "Let me see if I can get you released." She then walked out of the room to do what had to be done to release a patient from the hospital. Annie, with Doctor Ryan's agreement, got the release paper and returned to Andy's room. She went into the room closet and got Andy's cloths.

"Get dressed and I will take out of the hospital. I have your release right here," she said as she showed him the document. I will back in two minutes." She left to give him time to dress. About five minutes later she came with a wheel chair. Get in and I will take you to your car. Andy drove himself home. He was alone since his father worked till nine thirty. He had one week before school started to be ready. He didn't see Annie all week. The next week he started college. He would graduate in the first week of March. It was the Friday the second week of his college day's that Andy hear the doorbell ring. He opened the door and was surprised to see Annie.

"Annie sweetheart," said Andy. "What are you doing here?"

"I missed you so much that I decided to see you. I was hoping you wanted to see me two."

"I have wanted to see you so madly that I am going crazy not seeing you," said Andy. But I'm working so hard to catch up to where I left of last spring. I think that we can go on a date every Friday and some Saturdays depending in what I have to study for Monday."

"Sounds great to me," said Annie. They dated every Friday and some Saturdays but never dated on Sunday. This went on until the middle of December when it was Christmas Eve. Annie was invited to spend Christmas with Andy and his father David. That evening they had a nice meal. Andy's father gave the most impressive prayer before they ate. Andy's father invited Annie to spend Christmas day with them. It turned on fantastically. After they ate lunch they sat around the Christmas tree to give each other presents. Andy's father gave Annie a beautiful bracelet with matching ear rings. He gave Andy a beautiful wrist watch. Annie gave Andy's father a nice shirt and a matching tie. She gave Andy a similar gift. Now, it was Andy's turn. Andy gave his father a beautiful belt. He had munched to Andy that since he had gained a lot of wait, that his belt was too short. Then Andy walked up to Annie. He bent down on one knee and after pulling out a small box from his pocket he asked Annie.

"Annie," he started. "I love you very much. Will you marry me?" Annie got tears in her eyes.

"Yes," said Annie. "I will marry you." They spent the next two months planning their wedding. When Andy felt better he went looking for a place to live after the marriage. After several days and several houses he checked and with Annie's approval he purchased a three bedroom ranch house in Fairlawn Ohio. It was on March tenth that they had their wedding. They had a large group attending their wedding. Her parent came in from California where they lived. Andy had relatives come in from Cleveland Ohio. Annie had two nurses and two doctors who came to the wedding. It was a lovely wedding. They soon went on their honey moon. Their honey moon was in Florida. When they got back, Andy went to work with his father. His knowledge of Financial Management helped the business very much. The next two years doubled their income. Annie went back to being a nurse at the hospital. It was a little over two years that one day Annie pulled her husband aside.

"I have dinner ready," said Annie, "but before we eat, I have to tell you something and want to discuss it with you."

"Not now," said Andy looking very ill. "I don't feel well. I barely make it home. I feel dizzy and I have a terrible pain on my right side." He barely finished his words when he passed out. Annie checked his heart. It hardly beat. She checked his blood pressure. She could not feel any. With that information she called 911. She had they rush her to the hospital emergence door. On the way she called Doctor Ryan. Doctor Ryan met them in the operation room.

"I know what it is," said the doctor. "I was afraid of that when I healed the wall. While he was talking he had opened Andy's belly. I was right Thank God. I have the repair item. I got it when I first healed him. The doctor then suctioned all the water out of his heart area. He then took out the repair wall.

"That looks like a slice of baloney," said Annie. "Is that real flesh?"

"Now it is a special material that is soft like the real flesh. He soon attached it and sowed Andy's stomach back. "That is the best I can do. Please stay with him here in the surgery room. I don't think he should me moved. Stay here and keep checking his heart and blood pressure. Keep his blood flowing device on him. He could not recover without the moving of his blood. Keep the air flow in his mouth. His body needs oxygen now more than ever. I will be back in an hour." Annie just stayed there with her head on his chest. She started to wonder what she should pray. She remember one day when she was criticized by her mother for the lack of her Christian action.

"I believe in God and his son Jesus," Annie had said. And her mother answered,

"Believing is not enough. The devil believes in them. Annie sat there and wondered what she had to do.

Andy woke up and was surprised that he was moving up and was about a foot from the ceiling. He wandered what he was on that held him up and was moving him up. He looked down and only saw Annie leaning over a body. Andy was shock. It was his body. Suddenly he reached the ceiling. He closed his eyes thinking that he was going to hit the ceiling. But to his surprise he went right through the ceiling like it wasn't there. Soon he was up in the air. The sky was so lovingly blue. The clouds were set like a tunnel. Andy started to walk down the tunnel. At the other end he saw several people waving at him. One in front looked like his mother who had died four years ago. But this one he saw was much younger. She looked like a twenty year old. He walked faster when he was interrupted by an angel with large wings.

At the mean time down below, Annie was thinking on how to pray. However she remembered what her mother had told her. She said that you had to accept Jesus as you savior and accepted him with all of your heart, and love the heavily father also with all of your heart. Annie then folded her hands and closed her eyes.

"Dear Jesus," she started. "I accept you as my savior. I give you my soul and my heart. I am your servant. Guide me so that I could follow your path to heaven. I know that my husband is a born-again-Christian. I want to join him. You are my king and my master. Please help me be adopted by your father in heaven. She put her head down on Andy's body. She was surprised that she felt a slight heartbeat. She stayed awake all night listening to Andy's heartbeat. It became better as time went by.

tell me a Story

Up in heaven the angel pushed Andy back to the building he came from.

"Why are you doing this?" asked Andy. "I was going up to heaven where I though God wanted me. Did God make a mistake?"

"No, the heavenly father never makes a mistake. However he allows human actions to change some of the rules. Andy was ready to answer when he passed out.

"It was around noon the next day when Andy woke up. He was in the surgery room. He was surprised to see Annie leaning over with her head on his lap. She was fast asleep. Andy felt very tired and lacked energy. He closed his eyes and soon was asleep. Annie didn't wake up until six in the evening. She made up for being up all night. At six she checked Andy's heart and his blood pressure. They were both near normal. Annie in a loud prayer thanked God. Andy heard her and woke up.

"Hi sweet heart," said Andy, "have you been here all night?"

"Yes and I'll stay all day if necessary," said Annie. "I want to spend every minute of my live with you."

"That is very sweet," said Andy. "Don't we have to go to work?"

"Maybe you do, but I don't," said Annie. They both broke into a laughter. From that day the days went by quickly. It was four days later that Andy was released from the hospital. Annie went in to take him home.

"By the way," said Andy. "Before I pasted out when I got sick you said you wanted to discuss something and you had something you wanted to tell me. What was that all about?"

"I wanted to know if it would bother you if I quit work and stayed home to take care of everything."

"Why would you want to stay home?" asked Andy, "wouldn't you be lonely?"

"I wouldn't be lonely," said Annie. "I would have company."

"I don't understand," said Andy.

"That is what I wanted to tell you," said Annie. "I am pregnant." Andy stood with his mouth opened. It was the answer he didn't expect though it was the greatest new he had hear in years. He then grab Annie and gave her the biggest hug she ever had.

"So you see," said Annie. "I want to stay home and take care of the house and my children, and have time to make you fantastic dinners."

"Let's go home and get our fantastic lives going," said Andy. "With the news you gave me I feel better than I ever felt before. You can do whatever you want. If you miss being a nurse at the hospital you can go back when your child goes to school."

"We will see what the future will bring us," said Annie. Annie then drove Andy home. Andy stayed home for the full week. The next Monday he decided to go work. Before he left he turned to Annie.

"Annie honey," said Andy. "I wish you will quit your job and stay at home. I see by the size of you tummy that it will not be long before you will give birth to our first child."

"When I feel I have to stay home I will," said Annie. "Right now I feel great. You go to work. I can take care of myself." It was four months later when Annie gave birth to a cute little boy. As soon as Andy heard he went to the hospital where Annie was.

"Congratulations," said Andy, when he walked into the room Annie was in.

"What are you doing here," said Annie. "I am going right home."

"Don't they want to know the name of the child?" asked Andy. "What are we going to name him?"

"Well in Italy," said Annie, "they have a custom to name the first son after the father's grandfather's name and the first daughter after the mother's grandmother's name. What was your grandfather name?"

"My grandfather's name was Angelo," said Andy. "Do you want to name him Angelo?"

"That sound like a romantic name, let's do it." That afternoon they were at home. Andy was surprised that Annie had gotten all that was needed for the child. She had a crib and a children's stand ready be used.

"For this one day let me make the dinner. You rest. Tomorrow I will go to work and the whole house will be yours." Andy did make a fine dinner.

The years went by with lots of happiness for the Avola family. It was three years later that Annie gave birth to a daughter. They named her after Annie's grandmother. Her name was Mary. So they named her Mary. They were the happiest family in Ohio. Their house was full of love. Andy did a great job helping his father. His education in Financial Management helps a lot in the success of the company. Andy and Annie's were the happiest couple in America. Every once in a while when Andy went bed he wondered. Was his trip to heaven real or was it just a happy dream.

The End

Milton Keynes UK
Ingram Content Group UK Ltd.
UKHW022131291124
451915UK00010B/633